Wolftamer

W. E. Smith

Also by W. E. Smith

Novels
Tanaki on the Shore
Ver Sacrum
Bal Harbour
I've Got a Right to Sing the Blues

Stories
I Wanna Hear It Again
He on Honeydew Hath Fed

ISBN 978-0-9984847-9-2

This book is dedicated to my father

Henry Albert Smith

Wolftamer

Chapter 1

America

ONCE there was only the land, broad and vast. It teemed with animals of all kinds: bear and moose, squirrels and foxes, woolly mammoths and saber-toothed tigers.

Then the First Peoples came. Generation after generation they migrated through the American continents, until they inhabited even those lands at the far ends of the earth: Tierra del Fuego at the southernmost tip of South America.

They hunted the animals of the plains and forests; they fished the rivers, streams and lakes; they gathered the edible plants that grew on the land. They cultivated gardens of corn and beans and built up villages and towns, great cities of stone like Teotihuacan and Chichen Itza, and sprawling pueblos of mud brick in the wide deserts of the American Southwest. In time, the First Peoples separated into many different tribes and nations, each with its own language, its own name. Aztec and Inca, Dakota and Sioux, Cherokee and Iroquois, Hopi and Ojibway: these are the ways in which the First Peoples spoke of themselves.

In 1492 Christopher Columbus and his shipmates on the Niña, Pinta, and Santa Maria sailed from Spain to the island of Hispaniola in the Caribbean Sea. Because he mistakenly thought he was in India, Columbus called the First People he found there Indians. The Spanish king and queen sent conquistadors to invade the cities of the Aztecs and Incas with armies, horses, and guns. They made the First Peoples work as slaves in cornfields and mines. The conquistadors carried great lodes of silver and gold that the First Peoples dug from the earth across the ocean in their sailing ships, and soon Spain was Europe's richest nation.

Envious of Spain's wealth, the kings and queens of Europe's other nations sent their own ships to America. English settlers started colonies around the Chesapeake Bay and in New England, and later in Pennsylvania, the Carolinas, and Georgia. Dutch colonists came to New York, and the French founded a colony far to the north in Canada. Everywhere the Europeans came, they found the tribes and nations of the First Peoples already on the land.

Sometimes the Europeans and First Peoples helped one another. The First Peoples taught the Europeans about the plants and animals of their new homes and shared food with them when they were hungry. The settlers carried manufactured goods the First Peoples didn't know how to produce, metal pots and axes, woolen blankets, and good hunting rifles. These things they traded to the First Peoples in exchange for animal furs. The First Peoples knew the land and its creatures and were skilled trappers of beaver, otter, muskrat, and mink. The furs they sold to the colonists were sent across the Atlantic to make warm coats and hats for the people of Europe.

All too often, the First Peoples and the colonists fought with one another. The people of Europe were very numerous, and the colonies they founded in America grew at a rapid pace. The First Peoples depended upon the forests to hunt for their food, and bitter disputes erupted when the colonists settled on the First Peoples' hunting territories and cleared the land for farming. In time the First Peoples were pushed away from the Atlantic coast where the Europeans were building up their towns and cities. They tried to fight back, but the Europeans, with their superior weapons and greater numbers, defeated the First Peoples. When some of the First Peoples crossed over the Appalachian Mountains to the Ohio Country in the Old Northwest, the British king declared that the colonists could not cross the Appalachians and interfere with the First Peoples there. This way he hoped to preserve peace in America.

In 1776 the American colonists rebelled. They no longer wished to be ruled by the King of England. The king sent his armies across the Atlantic to make the colonists obey his commands, but the Americans defeated the king's soldiers and created a new nation, the United States of America. Now the Americans no longer had to obey the king's command against crossing the Appalachians, and settlers began to come into the Ohio Country, where the First Peoples had taken refuge.

Chapter 2

The Struggle for The Ohio Country

CAPTAIN John Armstrong stood outside his tent. He watched smoke rise from campfires around which huddled tired, shivering soldiers. It was shortly before dawn on November 4, 1791. A light snow fell across the United States Army's encampment, two rows of tents stretching for three hundred and fifty yards along the east bank of the Wabash River in the Ohio Country.

Captain Armstrong felt uneasy. The villages of the Miami Nation were not far away; scouting parties had reported sightings and skirmishes. The soldiers of the First and Second United States Regiments were cold, hungry, and exhausted

Their campaign had been a difficult one.

The troops had assembled in August at Fort Washington on the Ohio River, where the city of Cincinnati sits today. In those days there were no cities in the Old Northwest, only forests dotted here and there with the First Peoples' villages. Captain Armstrong had not been happy with the quality of the recruits. It was said that many of the men who enlisted had been in prison, or were drunkards and gamblers. They had not enlisted from honor but because they needed the two dollars a month offered for their pay. Even worse, Captain Armstrong thought, were the poorly disciplined Kentucky militiamen. They had not even bothered to join the army until well into October.

Secretary of War Knox had ordered General Arthur St. Clair to lead an expedition against the Miami, Shawnee, Wyandott, Delaware, Potawatomi, Ottawa and Ojibway tribes.

4

These First Peoples were attacking American settlers who had moved into their hunting territories. The First Peoples were determined to force the Americans to leave the Ohio Country and go back across the Appalachian Mountains to their towns, cities, and farms on the Atlantic coast.

The First Peoples were encouraged to fight the Americans by the British. Although the British lost the Revolutionary War, they would not give up their forts and fur trading posts in the lands of the Ohio Country. They supplied guns to the First Peoples' warriors and egged them on in their raids against the American settlers. Captain Armstrong had heard tales of these attacks, how the settlers were tortured, tomahawked and scalped, and the women and children taken back to the First Peoples' villages as captives. To his mind, the First Peoples were not civilized and did not deserve to keep their lands. Secretary of War Knox wanted General St. Clair to build strong forts where United States soldiers could guard American settlers and make the First Peoples give up their territories. He especially wanted to punish the Miami nation. They had inflicted a sore defeat on American troops the year before.

Captain Armstrong thought back to September. After marching twenty miles from Fort Washington, it had taken three thousand men more than a month of hard labor with ax and saw to build a second fort. This fort was named Fort Hamilton after the Secretary of the Treasury. The soldiers cut four thousand trees from the forests for the palisades and cleared a wide area outside the walls for a clear line of fire against potential attackers. Captain Armstrong questioned the wisdom of spending so much time building the fort, with winter fast approaching and so much distance to cover to the Miami villages. But he had not voiced his doubts.

After building Fort Hamilton the army continued its march to the north. The going was slow. Since there were no roads in the wilderness, General St. Clair's troops had to cut a trace through the woods. The weather soon turned cold and rainy, and the men who were hired to supply the army with necessities like food, clothing, and tents did not do their jobs well. As a result, the soldiers were often hungry and without proper clothing, good boots, or shelter. To make matters worse, the horses that pulled the army's supply wagons were sometimes stolen by the First Peoples' warriors, who secretly raided the camps at night. This meant that such supplies as the army had often lagged behind the troops. When the hard frosts of October killed the wild grasses that grew along the army's route, it was hard to find pasture to keep the horses fed, and so they too suffered hunger.

Soldiers began to desert. Those who were caught were ordered executed by General St. Clair. No doubt many more would have fled had they not feared to travel through the First Peoples' territories alone.

Near the end of October St. Clair's army approached the Miami villages, and he ordered the soldiers to build a third fort—Fort Jefferson. The work was slow, as the soldiers were hindered by snow and sleet and a shortage of axes; when Fort Jefferson was finally completed, General St. Clair ordered his men to march on the Miamis. But no sooner had they set out than they had to stop and wait for their supply wagons to catch up. General St. Clair ordered the troops to make camp on the banks of the Wabash River while they waited.

It was here that Captain John Armstrong now stood reflecting before dawn. He was not happy with the placement of the camp. It was surrounded by higher, thickly forested ground. If the First Peoples attacked they would have every advantage. Since the men were exhausted from their fort-building labors and marching, General St. Clair had not ordered them to dig trenches as he might otherwise have done, or to make strong breastworks for their defense.

Captain Armstrong wondered where the First Peoples' warriors might be. Tired, hungry, and poorly supplied, his troops were in no condition to face an enemy. He worried also about the women who accompanied the army, laundresses and nurses and cooks, wives and girlfriends, many of them with infants and children. How could they be protected?

He hoped the Miami warriors would not attack.

Little Turtle could not see the soldiers of the United States First and Second Regiments huddled around their fires, or Captain John Armstrong standing outside his tent in the first dim light of dawn. But he saw the smoke that rose through the trees across the Wabash River, smoke which mixed with a lightly falling snow. He was the war chief of the Miami people. He and Blue Jacket, a chief of the Shawnee tribe, led the warriors of the First Peoples of the Old Northwest. Silently waiting in the woods with the Miami warriors were warriors of the Shawnee, Wyandot and Mingo, Delaware, Ottawa, Potawatomi, and Ojibway tribes. In all they were nearly two thousand men, and they had come to attack General St. Clair's troops.

The First Peoples had met in council. They agreed to "eat from one dish," that is, to stand together against the settlers and soldiers who had trespassed onto their territories. Little Turtle had been there. He reminded the other chiefs of the promises that had been made to the First Peoples. The "Great Father"—the King of England—had agreed that the Old Northwest belonged to them. The King had promised that his "children"—the American colonists—would not cross the Appalachian mountains. But the colonists had come anyway. When the colonists rebelled against Britain, the First Peoples remained loyal to the Great Father and helped the English armies against the rebels. But the colonists' armies were victorious, and now the Americans claimed all of the Old Northwest for their own.

The chiefs of the First Peoples met the American General Butler at Fort McIntosh. General Butler persuaded some of these chiefs to accept payment for their lands in the Ohio Country. But Little Turtle had not attended that council, and he refused to agree to the bargain. He said that the other chiefs had no right to speak for all of the First Peoples, nor to sell their land to the Americans. He called those chiefs who had agreed to sell out cowards and said that they were afraid to fight for the lands of their fathers and grandfathers. He set about to collect a band of warriors who would fight back.

These men were now gathered around him in the woods

on the banks of the Wabash River.

Little Turtle had arrayed his warriors in the shape of a crescent moon, with the Wyandots and Mingos on the left, Shawnees, Miamis, and Delawares in the center, and Ottawas, Potawatomis, and Ojibways on the right. The men had slipped into the forest near the American camp in the dark of night. Little Turtle knew much about General St. Clair's army, for his scouts had been following the American troops since they left Fort Washington in September. He knew that the American soldiers were tired and hungry. He also knew that they were encamped across the Wabash River in two rows of tents.

A young brave, Tecumseh by name, approached. He told Little Turtle that General St. Clair had sent his Kentucky militiamen across the river to guard the encampment. These would be the first American soldiers that Little Turtle's warriors would encounter. Tecumseh told Little Turtle that the Kentuckians were not great in number, perhaps three hundred strong. Little Turtle agreed with Tecumseh that his braves could quickly overcome them, rush across the river shallows and attack the American camp. He hoped that his men would be victorious. His eyes scanned up and down the crescent line of warriors. He waved his arms to gain the attention of his war captains. The time had come.

He gave the signal to attack.

Captain Armstrong moved to one of the campfires. He crouched among the soldiers there and chewed a piece of stale bread that was all the breakfast he would receive that day. He looked at the other men. Their clothes were ragged, the looks on their faces worn and worried. A couple of the men gripped their ribs against their hunger. Captain Armstrong began to tell them that they were near the end of their journey—the Miami villages where they would confront the First Peoples—when he was startled by a great racket of gunfire from across the river. He quickly rose to his feet. Soldiers rushed about the camp while officers barked out orders.

Captain Armstrong ordered his company to their posts.

Before they were in position, the Kentucky militiamen, their britches dripping water from the shallow river, charged through the camp. Close behind them came a terrible noise, the combined war whoops of Little Turtle and Blue Jacket's warriors. Captain Armstrong watched General Sargent try to bring the militiamen under control and form a line of musket fire against the attackers, while he himself set about organizing his own men. The artillery positioned at the rear of the camp fired canister rounds towards the onrushing warriors of the First Peoples, but their aim was too high, and the bombardment only managed to create a cloud of smoke that engulfed the camp in confusion. Through this haze, Blue Jacket's warriors fell upon the soldiers of the First and Second United States Regiments. Captain Armstrong led his men toward the center of the camp, where other soldiers of the United States Army were concentrating. Along the way he saw women resolutely clutching children to their breasts, crying and shrieking, or kneeling on the ground in prayer.

General St. Clair tried to mount his horse but it was shot out from under him. The warriors of the First Peoples could spot the United States officers by the symbols on their uniforms, and it was against these especially that they trained their musket fire. Another horse was brought to the general but it too was shot. It did not help that it took so long for the general to mount, as he suffered from a painful case of gout and could move his legs only with difficulty. On the third attempt St. Clair got into the saddle and rushed toward the attackers. They were nearing the center of the camp. He ordered his men to charge with bayonets, but they could not stand in the face of the First Peoples' musket fire.

Within minutes the camp was a helter-skelter of hand-to-hand combat, a thousand different battles with knives and tomahawks and sabers and bayonets. Captain Armstrong fought hard, deafened by a continuous roar of yells and shrieks, the clashing of steel, the groans of the wounded, and the cracking reports of firearms. The soldiers of the United States Army could not hold their own against the braves of the First Peoples. All around him Captain Armstrong glimpsed his comrades dying, tortured, and scalped by the First Peoples' warriors. The First Peoples did not spare the women and children, but put them to death as well. Though he was surrounded and fighting for his life, Captain Armstrong felt an overpowering need to protect them. He strove with all his might to break through. He did not see the tomahawk crashing down from behind at lightning speed.

Captain John Armstrong fell to the ground. It was nearly nine in the morning. The soldiers of the United States First and Second Regiments had battled the warriors of the First Peoples for almost three hours. The ground was covered with the dead.

Captain Armstrong was among them.

Chapter 3

Fallen Timbers, the Prophet, Tippecanoe, and War

SHORTLY after Captain Armstrong fell to the ground, Colonel Darke commanded a bayonet charge against the surrounding warriors of the First Peoples. He and his men were able to break through, and the remaining United States soldiers fled for their lives. They ran toward the trace they had cut through the woods and hurried on toward Fort Jefferson. The First Peoples' warriors pursued them for many miles but then returned to the camp, where they looted tents and tortured and killed survivors. The battle had been a great defeat for the United States Army. More than six hundred soldiers had been killed and many others gravely wounded. None of the women and children in the camp survived.

When President Washington learned of the defeat of St. Clair's army he shouted in anger. "I warned St. Clair to beware of surprise! That's how the Indians fight us. And now he has allowed our soldiers to be cut to pieces, hacked, butchered, tomahawked—the very thing I warned him against!"

President Washington demanded that General St. Clair resign from the army. He would no longer be allowed to command men in battle. Now Washington ordered General Anthony Wayne to lead the United States troops against the First Peoples of the Old Northwest. General Wayne had served under President Washington during the Revolutionary War, and Washington knew that he was a good soldier and a trustworthy officer.

Little Turtle and Blue Jacket's warriors celebrated heartily after chasing off the soldiers of the United States Army's First and Second Regiments. They were happy with the many useful items the soldiers had left behind in their tents—and the four hundred fine horses the First Peoples now added to their herds. The First Peoples had lost only twenty-one warriors, Blue Jacket crowed, while wolves would feast on their enemies' carcasses by the hundreds! The battle left Blue Jacket feeling confident that the First Peoples could stop American soldiers and settlers from taking over their lands in the Old Northwest, and many of his warriors agreed.

But Little Turtle, the First Peoples' other war captain, was not so certain. He reminded his comrades that the Americans were far more numerous than their peoples and had stronger weapons. The First Peoples would need the help of their British friends, he said, and it would be foolhardy to assume that the British could be relied upon.

General Wayne spent two years gathering and training a new army. Meanwhile, the First Peoples' warriors continued their attacks on settlers, and they harassed the soldiers who had been ordered to stay on at Fort Jefferson. The settlers put out a reward for killing the First Peoples. They promised one hundred and thirty dollars for each Indian scalp that was delivered.

General Wayne was determined not to be defeated as General St. Clair had been. His army was larger than St. Clair's, and their training long and difficult. They practiced with rifles, learned to build defenses for their camps, and fought mock battles in the forests, with some of the men playing the part of the First Peoples' warriors. The new army was called the Legion of the United States. There were four sub-legions within the Legion, each distinguished by differently colored horses: sorrels, grays, chestnuts, and bays.

When General Wayne felt that the Legion was ready for battle he and the troops set out from Fort Washington. He took precautions to make sure that his army would not be surprised. They made camp early each afternoon to allow time to build good defensive works before nightfall; and reveille was sounded an hour before dawn, so the soldiers could be at their battle posts at the first light of day. The army's destination was a place deep in the Ohio country called the Grand Glaize, where the Auglaize River joins the Maumee on its course toward Lake Erie. The First Peoples' warriors had gathered at the Grand Glaize, alongside a regiment of British soldiers. The British were building a new fort there on the banks of the Maumee River.

General Wayne was determined to attack the First Peoples' villages at the Grand Glaize. He would scorch the earth, burning homes and crops so that the First Peoples would have nothing to eat and nowhere to live. Then they would have to make peace on the United States government's terms—by giving up their land. General Wayne did not wish to start a war with the First Peoples' friends the British, but he would not let the new British fort at the Grand Glaize stand in his way.

After many days marching, General Wayne's soldiers stopped to build a fort at the place where General St. Clair's army had been defeated two years earlier. General Wayne named this stockade Fort Recovery. He sent messengers to Little Turtle and Blue Jacket to say that he would not attack them if they would give up their lands. But the Indian leaders would not consider the general's proposal. "We have no place left to run to," Little Turtle said, "and we are determined to stay here, even if we must die." Little Turtle knew that his warriors were not numerous enough to defeat General Wayne's troops, and he was not at all certain that his British allies, at their new fort, would protect them. Yet he felt that he and his fellow warriors had no choice but to fight for their homes.

On learning that the Indian leaders would not yield to his demands, General Wayne attacked the First Peoples' villages. The villagers fled, leaving gardens overflowing with corn, beans, and squash. In one village after another General Wayne's men destroyed crops and burned wigwams to the ground. Then they marched toward the British fort, where the First Peoples' warriors had gathered nearby.

Little Turtle and Blue Jacket's warriors met General

Wayne's Legion in a tangled forest of fallen trees and thick brush. The Battle of Fallen Timbers was brief but bloody. General Wayne's forces were far more numerous, and within an hour they had sent the First Peoples' braves fleeing toward the British fort. To their dismay, Major Campbell, the commander of the fort, refused to open the gates when they arrived. He had been willing to give arms to the First Peoples and encourage them in their attacks against the Americans. But he was not prepared for Britain to begin another war with the United States. The First Peoples' shocked and angry warriors ran on past the fort and fled across the river to safety. General Wayne's Legion spread out. They destroyed all of the First Peoples' villages within fifty miles of the Grand Glaize.

Little Turtle and Blue Jacket knew that they were defeated. Their villages were destroyed and they had no food for the winter. Realizing that the British could not be relied upon to protect their people from the American soldiers, they agreed to parley with General Wayne. They sold the better part of the Ohio Country to the United States for a small amount of money. President Washington was very happy with General Wayne, but the First Peoples were dejected. They would no longer be able to roam through their old hunting territories, taking game to feed their families.

After the defeat of First Peoples at the Battle of Fallen Timbers, settlers flooded into the Ohio Country. They built towns and established farms all across the land. Some of the First Peoples of the Ohio Country "took the white man's road." They quit wandering and learned to farm the land like the American settlers, staying in one place. Others moved further west to the Indiana and Illinois territories, where the forests and plains were still open and free.

Before very long the settlers wanted yet more land, and they continually pestered the government to send soldiers to make the First Peoples give up the rest of their hunting grounds. Now it was General William Henry Harrison, who had been appointed governor of the Indiana Territory by President John Adams, who threatened the First Peoples. He told them that if they would not sell their lands in Indiana and Illinois to the United States, the army would come and take those lands by force, just as General Wayne had done in the Ohio Country.

The First Peoples resented General Harrison's threats and attacked American settlers in retaliation. And two new leaders now arose among the First Peoples of the Old Northwest. One was Tecumseh, who had been a scout for Little Turtle when the First Peoples defeated General St. Clair's army on the banks of the Wabash River. The other was his brother Lalawethika, which means "Noisemaker" in the Shawnee language.

One autumn Lalawethika became very ill. When he was near to dying, he had a vision. In his vision Great Spirit, or Master of Life, spoke to him. The Great Spirit told him that the First Peoples should not give up any more of their lands to the American settlers. Great Spirit said that the First Peoples should not "take the white man's road" but should live in their ancestors' way, hunting the forests and moving their villages to follow the game. In his vision, Lalawethika was told by Great Spirit that if the First Peoples clung to their traditional customs, Great Spirit would help them drive the American settlers out of their lands. After this vision, Lalawethika called himself Tenskwatawa, which means "Prophet." A prophet is one who brings messages to people from the world of Spirit.

The Prophet began to preach to the First Peoples of the Old Northwest. Many gathered round to hear him speak. He told them that Great Spirit wanted them to live off the land as their ancestors had done, and not to sell the land to the United States for settlers to use. He told them to quit using alcohol, which came from the white men, and to honor Great Spirit with old-fashioned Indian ceremonies. He claimed that white men were evil. He said they were not created by Great Spirit but came from scum that formed on the first ocean at the beginning of time. So many came to hear Tenskwatawa preach that they made a special town where they all could live. They called that place Prophet Town.

While Tenskwatawa was preaching to the First Peoples,

his brother Tecumseh was gathering together warriors who would fight for their lands. Tecumseh traveled up and down the country, far and near, even down to Alabama to talk with the Creeks and Choctaws, and as far west as Kansas and Missouri. He wanted all of the different nations of the First Peoples to stand together against American settlers and armies. This way they would be stronger. He urged them to refuse to sell any more of their lands to the American government.

The British offered Tecumseh great encouragement, for they were again in a quarrel with the United States and wanted the First Peoples as allies. The British kidnapped American sailors on the high seas and forced them to serve in the British navy. The Americans were determined to make the British stop these impressments, as they were called. Many Americans wanted to march an army to Canada, which was part of the British Empire, and seize it for the United States.

General Harrison gathered an army and marched to Prophet Town. The Prophet was there with many warriors, though his brother Tecumseh was away on his travels. Tenskwatawa led his warriors against General Harrison's camp on the banks of the Tippecanoe River. They made a surprise attack at dawn, just as Little Turtle and White Jacket had done against St. Clair's troops on the banks of the Wabash. But General Harrison rallied his troops and the First Peoples were badly defeated. After the battle General Harrison's men destroyed Prophet Town, and the Prophet's followers scattered. Tecumseh was angry with his brother for attacking General Harrison's force while Tecumseh himself, and many of his best warriors, were absent.

Soon afterwards, war broke out between Britain and the United States. The First Peoples, led by Tecumseh, joined with the British in attacking American forts in the Old Northwest. They captured Detroit, the only town in the Michigan Territory, and threatened American forts in the Ohio Country. But the United States forces were stronger, and in the end they prevailed. General Harrison led an army into the Michigan Territory. They chased the British and the First Peoples' warriors into Canada. There Tecumseh was killed at the Battle of the Thames.

Once again the First Peoples had tried to fight against the Americans for their lands; once again they had been defeated. And once again, the British had been unable to help them. The chiefs of the many tribes, Wyandot and Ojibway, Shawnee and Mingo, Delaware and Ottawa, met with General Harrison in council. They agreed to "bury the hatchet," that is, to live in peace with the American settlers.

Chapter 4

Ojibway

IN THE MAPLE MOON they moved downriver toward where they had stored their canoes the previous autumn. Though the Michigan days were no longer so frozen, the ice on the river was still thick enough to walk upon. They were seven in number: Grandmother and Grandfather, Braided Waters and Singing Loon, Talks Too Much, who was Singing Loon's brother, Morning Star, who was eleven years old, and Wind-in-Grass, only two-and-a-half and who rode in a papoose on Morning Star's back. Normally Wind-in-Grass was carried by his mother, but today Braided Waters had a heavy pack on her back, filled with deer skins. They were Ojibway, the First Peoples of the Michigan country.

They had spent the winter not far from the headwaters of the Cedar River, hunting and trapping at their winter camp, as was the custom of the Ojibway people. In the summer they gathered in large villages with all their clan, on the shores of lakes and rivers where they fished, planted gardens, and held feasts and dancings together. But during the winters, when they could not grow crops, and when the rivers and lakes were frozen over, they spread out to hunt game in the forests. Each family went to its separate hunting camp, well spaced so that there would be enough game animals to go around for everyone.

It had been a good winter for hunting and trapping. In January the strong winds had come, making a hard crust on the deep snow. Singing Loon and Talks Too Much, and Grandfather too, stalked deer and elk through the forest. While they glided quickly over the surface on their wide snow-shoes made of ashwood and birch bark, the animals, punching through the crust with sharp hooves, could not escape. They had collected many deer skins, and Braided Waters and Grandmother had dried a good quantity of venison meat. At the same time, the winter had not been so cold as to make the bears hibernate too deeply, so the big furry beasts made easy prey. The family had twelve porcupine skins filled with bear oil, which would fetch a good price from Thomas Campau, the trader at Saginaw Bay. Their traps had not been so successful, however; it seemed that every year there were fewer small animals to capture. They seldom found beaver anymore, and had to be content with the less valuable furs of muskrats.

The day was cloudy, with a rambunctious wind that rustled the tree tops as it came whistling down the frozen river. Every now and again the sun would break through the clouds and send a shaft of bright gold through the forest to glint on the river ice. All of the adults in the party carried deerskin bundles on their backs. Morning Star carried Wind-in-Grass in a papoose. Two dogs wove among the legs of the Ojibway family, sniffing the ground and wagging their tails.

"It was a good season for hunting," said Talks Too Much.

"And a lot of hauling to do," said Singing Loon, grunting and shifting his heavy load.

"It's better than having nothing to haul," said Grandmother, crunching carefully through the snow.

"Hmm," Singing Loon said. That meant that he agreed.

"The Owners of the Animals have been kind to us," said Grandfather. "We did not know hunger all winter long."

Grandmother began to hum a song, a song she had known since she was a little girl.

Morning Star looked through the trees. The sun peeked out from the edge of a cloud. A crow squawked as it flapped across the sky. Though everything seemed peaceful around her, she felt oddly sad. Wind-in-Grass fussed behind her. She bounced the papoose gently and he quieted.

When sun shafts fell so low in the sky that they barely

broke through the forest to the river, the family stopped. The dogs ran about in circles. The adults laid their packs against tree trunks. Talks Too Much and Singing Loon went into the forest and began to cut trees, strong and straight but not too big around. Braided Waters tended to Wind-in-Grass, and then she and Grandmother made a fire and began to prepare a meal. Morning Star watched silently, her thoughts far away. Singing Loon and Talks Too Much stripped the trees they cut of their branches, brought them to where the women were cooking, and laid them in a pile. When they had collected a couple of dozen they began to build a scaffold. They lashed the posts together with rawhide strips and raised a platform fifteen feet above the ground. They would store the packs they carried upon it while they went back to the winter camp to collect other packs; for they had piled up more winter stores than they could carry in one trip.

Talks Too Much stood back and looked at the scaffold. "You shouldn't be able to get to that, Brother Wolf, clever as you are!"

"Let us hope," Singing Loon said.

Grandfather smiled.

Once they had lifted the packs up onto the scaffold, the family used limbs and branches to build a small wigwam they covered with birch bark strips they had carried in their packs. Morning Star helped layer the ground with skins and furs the men of her family had hunted and trapped, and also with blankets they had bought from the trader. They ate the meal that Braided Waters and Grandmother prepared (venison seasoned with last year's maple sugar, and some little bit of corn hominy) and then all, exhausted by the day's labors, fell fast asleep. In the morning they went back up the river to collect the rest of the packs from the winter camp, which they had left on a scaffold just like the one Singing Loon and Talks Too Much built the evening before. They brought the rest of the things down the river, two more times stopping to build scaffolds and backtrack, until they reached the place where the Cedar River flows into the Grand. This is the place where they had stored their canoes last autumn.

Not far away was the family's sugarbush. Every spring, in the month of the Maple Moon, the family tapped the tall maple trees for their sap and boiled it down into sugar. Here they brought their packs of winter stores. The sugarbush wigwam had suffered much damage through the icy winter, and they made repairs right away. Morning Star helped Grandmother unwrap caches of food they had left at the sugarbush camp in the autumn. There was wild rice, cranberries sewed up in packages of birch bark, dried apples, and potatoes strung along a deerhide cord. Morning Star then helped Grandmother and Braided Waters make a special meal.

"Mmm," Talks Too Much said, "we haven't had cranberries for two moons."

"It is good to eat fruit again," said Singing Loon.

Grandfather smiled and chewed a slice of dried apple.

"Why aren't you eating your cranberry sauce?" Braided Waters asked Morning Star. "I thought it was your favorite, just like Talks Too Much."

The sound of her mother's voice startled Morning Star, for she hadn't been paying attention. She was aware again of the crackling fire and the faces of her family seated around. She couldn't think how to answer.

"Can't you hear me?" Braided Waters said. "Why aren't you answering me?"

"I don't know."

"What's the matter, little Star," said Singing Loon. "You've been so quiet today."

No one spoke. The fire crackled.

"Of course she doesn't want the cranberries," Grandmother said abruptly.

Morning Star looked into the fire, watching the flames leap and play through the dark. Everyone seemed puzzled by Grandmother's remark, but Morning Star knew what she meant. Last fall, when her brother Fleeting Elk was ill and feverish, she had made a special cranberry sauce sweetened with much maple sugar. She thought that his happiness at her gift might make him well. But it had not, and he died before the family moved to the winter camp.

"She's been like this ever since," Grandmother said. "Haven't you noticed?"

Braided Waters had to think. She'd been so busy at the winter camp, dressing the deer skins the men brought in from the woods, making meals, and looking after little Wind-in-Grass. Morning Star had helped with the women's work without complaint, and Braided Waters had been pleased with her daughter. She looked at her across the light of the fire.

"You don't have to eat them if you don't want to."

"Give them to me," Talks Too Much said. "I'll take 'em."

Everyone ate in silence. In the distance, a pack of wolves began to howl. Starting and stopping and starting up again, answering and overlapping one another; some high, some low, yipping and yapping. The dogs roused themselves from where they lay and joined in. The Ojibway family looked at one another. Grandfather began to sing an old song, both mournful and beautiful at the same time . . .

Here comes the spirit of the wolf,
Here comes the spirit of the wolf,
Here comes the spirit of the wolf,
Here is the spirit of the wolf. . .

He repeated these simple lines over and over, his voice rising sometimes until it cracked, or sinking so low that his family had to strain to hear him over the crackling of the fire. He sang on even after the wolves and dogs had ceased their howling. When he was finished, he rocked his head slowly back and forth with his eyes closed.

"Let me tell you a story," Grandmother said. Though she spoke to the whole family, she cast her gaze especially upon Morning Star.

Everyone lay their birch bark dishes aside and listened.

"Once, before time was," Grandmother began, "their was a young girl. She was a good girl, but she became easily distracted, and sometimes she failed to do her chores. Her mother had died, so it was her job to take care of her father. She mended his clothes, cooked his meals, kept the wigwam tidy, and did all the other women's work that her mother had done while she was alive.

"It so happened that one day, when she and her father were at their winter camp, the father went out to hunt. It had been icy cold all that long winter. The furry animals had hibernated deep in their dens and refused to come out, and hunting hadn't been good. Now winter was nearing its end, and the stores of food left over from the autumn were nearly gone. As on many days that winter, the father returned from his hunt empty-handed. He knew that there would be nothing for supper but some stringy, dried up old deer meat. Angry and frustrated, with a low grunt he sank his tomahawk deep into a maple tree that stood near the lodge.

"The next morning the father rose and went out again to hunt. With difficulty, he pulled his tomahawk from the maple tree as he passed. He was so downhearted that he didn't notice the new feeling in the air. The sun was a little brighter, the breeze a little milder.

"Spring was on its way.

"After his daughter finished her lodge chores she came outdoors. She carried a birch-bark pail, for she needed to collect water to fix the evening meal. To collect water she would have to travel to the stream, some distance away. Unlike her worried father, she immediately noticed how the season was beginning to change. The warming sun was high in the sky. A bird sang from somewhere in the distance. The coming spring filled her heart with such joy that she rested her pail against the base of a tree and began to play in the sunlight.

"She sang all the old songs she could remember and danced with the shadows of the trees. She made the cloud shapes into things she knew and hollered at the crows that passed overhead. She was having so much fun that she didn't notice how the day was slipping away until she saw, with alarm, that the sun was rapidly sinking into the forest. Her father would be home soon, she realized, and she had not made the evening meal! He would be tired, hungry, and very disappointed. She ran for the pail, wondering how she could get to the stream and back in time for the water she needed to cook supper. She silently prayed to Great Spirit to help her out of her difficulty.

"When she came to the tree where she had left her pail, she saw that it was filled with a liquid that dripped from the tree; for this was the maple where her father had planted his tomahawk the day before. The warm spring sun had played against the tree's stout trunk all day long and had made the sweet sap start to run. The girl thanked Great Spirit and rushed home to make Father's evening meal. She used the liquid from the tree to boil the dried meat and the few grains of corn that were still left in their winter stores.

"Soon Father returned, exhausted and hungry. He plopped down on a bench against the wall of the lodge and asked his daughter for his supper. She brought him a plate filled with the venison and corn. She watched her father closely, hoping the meal, cooked with the strange liquid, would please him. His face lit up with a smile at the first bite and he rapidly ate more. With each bite his weariness seemed to melt away. When he was finished he stood up, rubbed his stomach with satisfaction, and complimented his daughter on her fine cooking.

Grandmother looked at Morning Star. "Ever since, we Ojibway have used the sap of the maple tree to sweeten our food."

"And tomorrow we begin," said Braided Waters.

"Another sugar making season has come," said Grandfather.

"I love sugar," said Talks Too Much.

"Me too," said Morning Star.

In the days to come the women of the Ojibway family worked the sugarbush. The men helped them drive new taps into the trunks of the maple trees and then passed their days fishing for sturgeon in the river. Braided Waters and Grandmother placed pails below each of the taps, and when the sun struck the trees, the sap flowed from the taps into the buckets. The women were very busy, carrying full pails to the fire where they boiled the sap until the sugar syrup formed. The syrup was then poured into a wooden trough carved from a tree trunk. Morning Star stirred and stirred the syrup until the sugar formed into grains. Some of the sugar would be made into sugar bricks, and some formed into the shapes of turtles and birds and elk and beaver for special gifts to friends and loved ones.

One day Morning Star stirred at the trough. Braided Waters watched from where she and Grandmother were making sugar bricks.

"You're right," Braided Waters said. "She has been awfully quiet lately, ever since Fleeting Elk died. I guess I was so busy with our work, I failed to notice."

"That's understandable," Grandmother said.

"I feel a great sadness too," said Braided Waters. "But I guess Great Spirit had other plans for my son."

"Yes," said Grandmother, "in naming him Fleeting Elk, you chose wisely. His time in this world was brief."

The women sat in silence for a moment. Braided Waters' eyes teared up. "I don't know what to do to help my daughter. We share the same grief."

Grandmother hummed low for a while, an old song. "They used to love to play together," she finally said. "Remember how their excitement would grow at picking time, when they searched in the marshes for the cranberries?"

Braided Waters nodded.

Grandmother watched Morning Star for a moment. She was stirring and stirring the syrup with great intentfulness, her gaze lost in its brown sweetness.

"A part of her has died," Grandmother said.

"Yes," said Braided Waters.

"Only Spirit can help her now."

"She's starting to become a woman," Braided Waters said.

"That's right. She will need a vision to guide her life."

"Do you think it's time?"

"Why don't you talk to her," Grandmother said. "See how she feels. If she is ready, she can seek a vision before we leave this place."

Braided Waters watched her daughter working at the trough, steady and true. "Okay," she said, "I will speak with her."

When an Ojibway boy or girl began to grow older, around

the age of eleven or twelve, they would make a vision quest. Their elders would take them to a quiet place, well removed from their village or camp. The boy or girl would remain alone at that place for many days. They would not eat, but fast, and pray for a vision from the world of Spirit.

The Ojibway believed that Spirit could come to them in many forms, as Spirit Beings called *manitous*. Some of the different manitous were the Owners of the Animals (one for each species), the Four Winds, the Thunder Beings, Nanabush, who taught the original people how to live, and shining Star Beings who could guide a person's life. There was also *Kichi-gami*, or the Master of Life, one great spirit who made all things possible.

The Ojibway believed that without a vision from the world of Spirit, a person would not be able to live a good life. A man would not enjoy success in the hunt, and he and his family might starve. A woman needed a vision to raise her children and to keep her family strong. Some Ojibway received visions that taught them about the herbs of the forest, especially ones that could be used to cure sickness. Such people used their knowledge to become healers. Others might receive a vision teaching them how to contact the world of Spirit for their community. Such a person would lead the shaking tent ceremonies, where Spirit was brought forth to help the people make difficult decisions for their villages and clans.

A person never told anyone, except their parents and grandparents, about the vision they received during the vision quest. They never forgot it, but remembered the things they had learned from Spirit throughout their lives. Once each year, each Ojibway would make a special offering to the Spirit Being who helped them.

It was late in the day. The men had returned from the river with a good catch of sturgeon. Grandmother looked after Wind-in-Grass. Morning Star helped her mother cook a supper of fresh sturgeon, wild rice and cranberries, and some boiled potatoes.

"Grandmother and I were talking today," Braided Waters said.

Morning Star nodded as she cleaned a potato.

"You are growing up."

Morning Star nodded again.

"You are becoming a woman."

The previous summer Morning Star had had her first menses. She had stayed in a special hut for three days, while Braided Waters and Grandmother made a ceremony. Her body was changing, but she wasn't sure what it all meant. She felt excited, but also a little scared.

"Have you thought about your vision quest?" Braided Waters said.

"Yes," Morning Star replied. "When I do my work, I sometimes picture the Spirit Beings. Sometimes I dream about them, and I pray to the Master of Life."

"Grandmother thinks it may be time," Braided Waters said.

Morning Star dropped the potato into the boiling pot that hung over the lodge fire by a pole.

"Your brother would have made his vision quest soon."

Morning Star was quiet.

"Do you miss him?"

Morning Star looked down. "Yes."

I hope he has made his way to the West," Braided Waters said, "to the land of the Blessed Ones."

"I think he has." There were tears in Morning Star's eyes.

"But if he hasn't," Braided Waters said, "if his spirit is still struggling to find that place, you may be able to help him. When someone seeks a vision from Spirit, it can serve as a benefit to all their relations."

Morning Star nodded.

"I miss him too," Braided Waters said.

They worked in silence for a while.

"Grandmother thinks you should make your vision quest before we leave the sugarbush," Braided Waters said. "Do you think you are ready?"

"I want to. But how will you and Grandmother finish the sugar-making without me? Who will look after Wind-in-Grass when you are busy?"

"Don't worry about us. Grandmother and I will manage."

Braided Waters and Morning Star finished preparing the evening meal. Everyone gathered around the lodge fire to eat.

"Talks Too Much and Grandfather and I were talking at the river," Singing Loon said. Then he fell to silently eating, leaving everyone waiting for his next words. Finally Braided Waters spoke.

"Singing Loon, are you going to tell us what you men were talking about, or would you rather eat than sing right now?"

"Mmm," he said, too busy enjoying his food to supply any further reply.

Talks Too Much cleared his throat and looked up from his dish. "We were talking about where we will go when the sugar-making is finished," he said.

"We will go to our village on Saginaw Bay with the rest of Singing Loon's clan," said Braided Waters, "like we do every summer."

Singing Loon didn't speak. Nor did Talks Too Much say anything. Then Grandfather cleared his throat. He spoke softly, looking ahead as if he could see very far, though he was only staring at the wall of the narrow wigwam.

"Many changes are coming," he said.

"Do they ever stop?" Grandmother replied.

"Truly, many have come already," Talks Too Much said.

Two years earlier, the Ojibway chiefs around Saginaw Bay had sold their hunting grounds to the United States government. They had agreed to live on small areas of land called reservations. In return the United States government promised to pay the tribe two thousand dollars each year, and to send farmers, teachers, and blacksmiths to help them learn to live as farmers instead of wandering hunters.

"The white men will never stop coming," Grandfather said.

"They say there are as many white people as grains of sand on the beaches of the Great Waters," Talks Too Much added, "—maybe even more."

Everyone was quiet.

"First they promised to stay on the other side of the big

mountains," Grandfather took up again. "Then, after they beat the English Father in the long war, they forgot their promise and began to settle the land on this side. And after General Wayne beat our peoples at the Grand Glaize, they took the entire Ohio Country for themselves."

Morning Star had heard these stories before. Her grandfather had fought against the Americans with Little Turtle's men when he was young

"Little Turtle and Blue Jacket were good leaders," Grandfather said, "but we were too few, and they were too many."

"Fate was not on our side," Grandmother put in.

"Tecumseh also was a brave chief," Talks Too Much said.

"Hmm," added Singing Loon. He and Talks Too Much had fought with Tecumseh's men during the War of 1812.

"A brave chief," Grandfather said, "but his brother—"

"The Prophet had a good vision," Grandmother said. "But he got carried away with himself. He attacked Harrison's men at Tippecanoe before the people were ready."

"Many brave warriors sang their death songs that day," Talks Too Much said.

"In any case, nothing can be done now," said Braided Waters. "We must live as best we can with what we have left."

Singing Loon put down his plate of food, now wiped clean. "Grandfather says that soon they will make us stay on the reservation. The settlers will come into our land. They will fill our hunting territories with farms and roads and towns . . ."

"The settlers grow like weeds," Grandfather said. "Now you see only a few of them, like Trader Campau at the Bay. But look at the Ohio Country. I have heard you cannot walk a full morning without meeting them."

"So have I," Talks Too Much said.

"And when they come, they will bring more sickness," Grandmother said now. She looked sadly into the fire.

The settlers carried European germs against which the Ojibway people had no immunity, germs that caused diseases like measles, smallpox and typhoid fever. Many Ojibway had died from diseases settlers had brought among the First Peoples. Morning Star's brother Fleeting Elk had contracted such a sickness at Thomas Campau's trading station.

"They will bring their firewater, too," Talks Too Much said.

The settlers had also brought in whiskey and rum, and too many First People had ruined their lives with alcohol addiction.

Singing Loon stared silently into the fire while Grandmother hummed softly. A crow cawed outside. The wind rustled through the pines. Everyone had finished eating.

"So, the white people will come, but what can we do?" Braided Waters said.

"We can live among your clan relations in the north," Singing Loon said, "across the straits of Mackinac. Surely they will help us."

Braided Waters grew thoughtful. "I never thought I would live among my people again." She had left Michigan's Upper Peninsula when she married Singing Loon and come to live among his people around Saginaw Bay. "But what will become of our sugarbush," she went on, "and our winter camp?"

"Sooner or later the land will be bought by some settler anyway," Talks Too Much said, "and they will run us out."

Grandmother gasped. She had worked the sugarbush for more years than she could count.

"It's hard to leave what is familiar," Grandfather said, "but we cannot stay here any longer."

"Not unless we want to walk the white man's road," Talks Too Much put in, "and learn to be farmers."

Singing Loon's face grew stern. "Never! We would miss hunting, sugar making, and taking sturgeon from the river. The settlers will kill all the animals, and there will not be enough game to go around."

Morning Star felt sad at the thought of leaving the places she had known. She thought of her brother and all the happy times they had shared. Then Grandmother spoke, as if she could read Morning Star's mind.

"When the settlers come, there will surely be more sickness," she said. "We must keep Morning Star and Wind-in-Grass safe."

Braided Waters looked at her children. She knew that what Grandmother said was true, and the safety of her children was the most important thing in the world for her. Still she felt reluctant to agree to any rash plans. Braided Waters was the type of person who liked to think things through carefully, especially big decisions with powerful consequences. "How much time have we got?" she asked. "Must we leave this year? The settlers have not yet come. Perhaps we could wait until next year, or the next."

Singing Loon shrugged.

Grandmother began to quietly hum, one of her old songs.

"Tomorrow Morning Star will make her vision quest," Braided Waters announced suddenly. "Grandmother and I will take her into the forest very early. Let us not decide until she returns."

"That is a good plan," Grandfather said. "We will fish the sturgeon, and you women can finish making your sugar. My granddaughter, I am very proud of you. You are growing up so nicely."

Grandmother, who sat beside Morning Star, patted her leg. In the distance the wolves began to howl. Starting and stopping and starting up again, answering and overlapping one another, some high, some low, yipping and yapping. Outside the lodge the Ojibway family's dogs joined in. Grandfather began to sing his wolf song:

Here come the spirit of the wolf,
Here come the spirit of the wolf,
Here come the spirit of the wolf,
Here is the spirit of the wolf.

Morning Star watched the firelight, and its shadows playing across the faces of her family, and thought about starting her vision quest in the morning. She wondered what it would be like to go without food day after day, and she hoped she would be strong enough to bear it. She felt a funny feeling inside. Memories of Fleeting Elk filled her mind. She pictured him traveling over a broad landscape, vast as the sea, seeking the land in the West where the Blessed Ones go when they die. Visions of Spirit Beings passed over her mind's eye, until she was only vaguely aware of the flickering faces of her family seated around. Finally the wolves quieted. Grandfather sang a while longer, and then Grandmother spoke.

"I will tell you a story," she began . . .

Chapter 5
A Boy and His Father

Six hundred miles to the east of the Michigan territory, the bustling city of Albany, New York, stretched along the western bank of the Hudson River.

The First Peoples once had a settlement here they called Penpotawotnot. But in 1609 the English explorer Henry Hudson sailed up the river that bears his name, and soon afterward the Government of the Netherlands built a fort to protect the Dutch traders who bartered with the First Peoples for furs. And by the time of our story, in the year 1823, the First Peoples of Penpotawotnot had been driven out by European settlers and Albany had grown into a thriving city. Its merchants provided for the needs of families who farmed the land all around, and ships sailed daily to New York City from its riverfront docks bearing the bounty of the fields, and also timber and furs from the surrounding forests.

Wide State Street ran away from the river and up through the town. It was lined with the grand homes of the city's most rich and powerful citizens. Pearl Street crossed it before running out of town to the Pastures, where the townspeople took their cows to graze. Along the riverfront ran Quay Street, noisy and crowded with ships being loaded and unloaded. In the middle of Market Street was the Market House, where farmers came in from the countryside to offer the fruits of their labors, and where seafaring traders sold their wares to the highest bidder.

There were many smaller streets in the city, narrow tracks hardly more than paths, back alleys behind the grand avenues, and dirt lanes where the common folk lived and worked. On one of these streets lived a boy, Caleb Jordan, and his father Daniel. Daniel Jordan was a blacksmith. His workshop, the smithy, was located in back of the house across a wide yard. Caleb Jordan, who was twelve years old, worked there with his father in the afternoons. In six years his apprenticeship would be done and he would become what was called a journeyman blacksmith. Then he would travel to farms all around the area, shoeing horses and oxen and repairing tools and farm machinery. After five years as a journeyman he would be able to set up his own smithy.

Caleb's mother and sister had died the year before, when a strange sickness visited the city. No one knew where the germs had come from, probably from one of the ships that anchored at the city's docks, ships that arrived all the way from New York City, London, and even as far away as China. Caleb too had been sick with the disease. Like his mother and sister he had grown weak and feverish. His muscles hurt, he was nauseous and couldn't eat, and he had the shivers so badly that he couldn't rest. He lay in bed with an aching head for three days, but after the fourth day he felt better and was able to move about again. His father said that Mother and Emily would also soon be well but instead their conditions worsened. They sweated with fever and complained of awful stomach pains. They vomited, and the vomit had blood in it. Emily died first, in the second week, and then Mother.

Ever since then Caleb hadn't felt the same. Things that used to give him pleasure, like seeing cows being driven to the Pastures, or going to Foxes Creek with Thomas to watch men working in the tanning pits, were hardly fun anymore. The hustle and bustle of the Market House wasn't really exciting, and even hanging around the waterfront, seeing tall ships offloading at the docks, or catching the wind as they embarked downriver toward New York City, brought him no joy. The sight of their sails reminded him that one of these ships had brought the germs that killed Mother and Emily.

One of the few things that gave Caleb comfort was playing with his toy soldiers, for then he could lose himself in a world of his own imagining. It was a world where there was no sickness and where even death was not real, for after shooting one another the soldiers could be made to stand up and start over again. He also had figures of Indians and frontiersmen. When he played with these he imagined that they were characters from his book about Daniel Boone. Boone had lived among the First Peoples of the Ohio Country, sometimes as a friend but just as often a mortal enemy. Caleb sometimes daydreamed about living among the Indians himself, and once he made a wigwam from branches and twigs, where he smoked an imaginary peace pipe with his friend Thomas.

It wasn't that Caleb had that much time for play. In the mornings he went to a one-room school run by Widow Chambers, where he learned reading, writing, and arithmetic. A blacksmith's son would not require much learning, but his mother, who had been raised in the Quaker religion, was determined that he read well enough to understand the Bible. She believed that a person could not live well in this world without a connection to the sacred, and she believed that if a person sincerely sought communion with God, by whatever means, God would respond. She also loved poetry, as she loved all things beautiful, and believed that words had the power to bring people closer not only to God, but also to one another and to their truest selves. As for Caleb's father, he would remind Caleb that a blacksmith had to make many calculations in a day's work, and he encouraged his son to study hard at doing figures and sums.

After school Caleb came home to help his father in the smithy. They usually worked until sundown; afterward they had to fix supper and clean up. In the brief time left before bed Caleb could play with his soldiers or read about Daniel Boone by the light of an oil lamp, while his father played folk tunes, or an occasional hymn, on an old violin. Before they put out the lamp to go to sleep they would bend on their knees to pray. They would pray for God's guidance in their lives and that the souls of Mother and Emily were peaceful and at rest. Sometimes Caleb's father would take the family Bible from a sideboard where it lay open. He would read a passage, one of Caleb's Mother's favorites that she had marked with pale blue ribbons.

And so they lived.

One afternoon Caleb was helping his father make an ax in the smithy. Caleb worked the bellows that pumped air into the forge to bring the fire to its greatest heat, so that when his father drew the red-hot metal from the fire it would be soft enough to hammer into shape on the anvil. Caleb pulled very hard on the lower handle of the bellows, bringing it up swiftly, and then let the handle drop so that the bellows could once again fill with air. Though it was cold outside on this February day, it was warm near the forge, and Caleb felt sweat beading up on his face as he worked. His father hummed a tune from time to time or became silent with concentration as he pounded iron to a perfectly tapered wedge. He would place it again and again into the forge to keep the metal soft, or dip it in the water pail to make it set stronger, which would cause a great cloud of stream to rush through the smithy.

When the ax was finished; when both sides of the blade had been shaped from iron, with a sliver of the strongest steel inserted along its edge; and when a hole had been pounded out to fit the ashwood handle, Caleb's father motioned to Caleb to stop the bellows. Caleb came around the forge to see the work that had been done. His father let him examine the ax blade and then took it to the work bench, where he showed Caleb how to use files to smooth the rough edges. They inserted the handle and stood back to admire the new tool they had made. It had already grown dark outside. They had finished the work by the light of oil lamps that hung from the smithy's rafters.

"That should do it," Daniel Jordan said.

Caleb nodded. His father lifted the ax and held it at arm's length.

"A fine looking ax, if I might say so myself. Farmer Schuyler should be well pleased."

"How much will he pay us?" Caleb asked.

"Three farthings, and it's worth every penny."

He lay the ax on the work bench and took off the heavy

leather apron he wore when he worked. Caleb too removed his apron. He was walking toward the door of the smithy when his father spoke.

"Son."

Caleb turned.

"You did a good job today."

Caleb nodded.

"You're getting stronger. You don't tire so easily when you pump the bellows. Soon you'll have enough strength in your arm to handle the hammer. Then we'll start you at the anvil."

"Yes, sir."

"How do you like the blacksmith trade so far?" his father asked. Caleb had begun working as his father's apprentice after his mother died.

"I like it, Father."

"I like you working with me, too. I'm proud of you," his father said. "You don't miss your boyish games?"

"Not really."

"Let's sit down a minute before we go in for supper."

They sat on a couple of stout tree stumps that served as chairs in the smithy. The oil lamps cast a watery light on their faces. Caleb's father looked at him with concern in his eyes.

"I've noticed," Daniel Jordan began slowly, "that even on Sundays, when you have all the time in the world, you don't go out anymore. I can't think the last time you told me you'd gone to the Pastures, or watched the men at the tanning pits. Why, last Sunday Thomas came by for you, and you turned down his invitation to go to the docks, even though the *Adventurer* was arriving from India. They say half the town turned out to see her come to port."

Caleb didn't say anything but just shrugged his shoulders a little.

"It seems the only thing you do nowadays is play with your toy soldiers and read your storybook. I'm a little concerned about the way you've turned in upon yourself."

Caleb remained silent. He was afraid his father wasn't pleased with him, and it made him squirm where he sat.

"Now," his father said, "it's natural you not feeling so

happy-go-lucky, what with losing Mother and Emily last year." He looked away a moment, and Caleb thought he saw a tear in his eye. "I'm not feeling so great myself," he went on as he turned back to Caleb. "But we've got to keep on living. You know that's what Mother would want."

He looked around his smithy. Caleb squirmed again.

"Sometimes I wonder," Daniel Jordan said, "if I shouldn't have sent you to live with Aunt Elizabeth in Boston like she wanted me to. She said you needed a woman to take care of you. Said I wouldn't be able to handle the smithy and keep house and take care of you all by myself."

"I want to stay with you."

"I like your being here." Daniel Jordan patted Caleb's knee. "Do you reckon we're making a decent go of things, then?"

"Yes."

Caleb's father looked off, as though he weren't quite sure himself.

They put out the oil lamps, left the smithy, walked across the yard and went into the house. It still seemed funny to Caleb how quiet it was when they came in, without Mother and Emily there. They made their supper and cleaned up. Then Caleb sat by the fire and read his storybook while his father stood nearby playing his violin. Sometimes Daniel Jordan would say, "Remember this one?" or "This one's for Mother." Then he would play an old tune that was one of her favorites. When Caleb began to look glum, Daniel Jordan tried dancing, clacking the heels of his boots on the wooden floor to make his son laugh. But all he drew from Caleb was a weak smile.

Finally he put down his violin, sat in a rough-hewn wooden rocker, and stared into the fire. From time to time he glanced at Caleb.

"What are you reading?" he asked.

"It's about how Daniel Boone was captured by the Shawnees. They made him run the gauntlet!"

When Daniel Boone was captured by First Peoples of the Shawnee Nation, they made him run between two rows of warriors who each struck him with a thick and heavy club as he passed. In this way they tested his toughness, courage, and endurance. This was called "running the gauntlet."

"I see." Daniel Jordan stared into the fire again and grew thoughtful. He sat this way for a long while. Then he rose from his chair. "Maybe we need a change of scenery," he said.

Caleb looked up at his father. He wasn't sure what he meant, but he didn't ask. His father said it was time to turn in, and they read a passage from the Book of Proverbs. It read like this:

Let not steadfast love and faithfulness forsake you; bind them around your neck; write them on the tablet of your heart. So you will find favor and good success in the sight of God and man.

They put out the oil lamps, banked the fire, said their prayers, and climbed into their beds.

Chapter 6

A Vision

MORNING STAR'S MOTHER woke her very early. During the night Spirit Beings had floated in and out of her dreams, beckoning her toward a world of light more bright and shadows more deep than any she had ever seen. Shreds of those dreams still occupied her mind as she watched her mother revive the dying fire in the center of the cramped lodge. Grandmother was also awake. She crouched beside Morning Star and spoke in a low voice. She spoke the ways of the vision quest, ways handed down by her people through untold generations.

A human being, Grandmother said, was a small and fragile thing, powerless to create her own destiny. She said that only Spirit can guide us toward happiness, and that is why, when she sat alone in her vision lodge, Morning Star would beseech Spirit Beings to come to her aid.

"They will teach you your destiny," Grandmother said, "as they did for me. Then you will know how to live. You will be confident in your spirit. Before I had my vision quest," she said, "I felt afraid and alone. I felt that no one understood me."

"But how can I make the Spirit Beings help me?" Morning Star asked.

"You cannot *make* Spirit Beings do anything," Grandmother said. "No one can control Spirit. You can only invite them to your vision lodge. Call them with prayers and with the spirit songs I have taught you. But you must ask with sincerity, and you must be prepared to listen to what they tell you."

"Why can't I eat?" Morning Star asked.

"Some say we fast to make Spirit pity us. They say that when the Spirit Beings see that we are suffering and helpless, they will be moved to relieve our distress."

Morning Star tried to fathom everything her grandmother was saying.

"But," Grandmother continued, "we also fast to clear the mind. You may find that when you are no longer thinking of filling your stomach all the time, you will begin to see more into the heart of life, where Spirit lives."

"How many days must I fast?"

"Until Spirit comes to you, or until you can bear it no longer. But for now, you will eat one last meal. I see that your mother has it ready."

Morning Star ate a large breakfast, and then Braided Waters and Grandmother hoisted deerhide packs onto their backs and led her into the forest. Morning Star carried Wind-in-Grass on her back in his baby board. They followed trails that had long been used by the Ojibway to travel through the forests of the Michigan country, then they left the trail and wove through the woods until they came to a swiftly running brook.

Grandmother and Braided Waters took the packs from their backs. From them they removed strips of birch bark to make a wigwam for Morning Star's vision quest. Morning Star helped them gather branches to make the framework of the lodge. They covered it with the birch bark strips, leaving a hole in the roof for fire smoke. They then collected a good quantity of firewood from the forest and laid it by the vision lodge's door. Braided Waters said that she would come in a few days to check on Morning Star. She told her that she should not leave the lodge except to relieve herself or to fill her birch bark jug with water from the stream, and that she should spend her time praying, singing spirit songs, and beseeching Spirit to bring her a vision to guide her life. Morning Star helped her mother put Wind-in-Grass on her back in his baby board. Then Braided Waters said goodbye, and she and

Grandmother walked off together.

Morning Star didn't know what to feel as she watched Braided Waters and Grandmother disappear into the forest. She felt terribly alone—almost abandoned—but at the same time, deep inside, she sensed that a beautiful adventure awaited her. She longed to meet Spirit Beings face to face, though she feared them just a little. The forest was very quiet; there was no sound save the stream and the wind moving through the branches of the evergreens. She thought back over things Grandmother had told her that morning, how she would grow in Spirit and become a woman. She remembered her favorite spirit song, went into the lodge, wrapped herself in a bearskin robe, and began to sing.

And so Morning Star passed the day, singing sacred songs, beseeching Spirit to send a vision to guide her life, and watching the crackling fire. When the light outside grew dim (about the time she would normally be helping her mother prepare the evening meal) her stomach began to gnaw at her fiercely. No matter how hard she tried, she couldn't keep from thinking about the tasty things her family must be enjoying at the sugarbush camp, all seasoned with newly made maple sugar! She grew so distracted thinking about food that she quit singing sacred songs and praying to Spirit for a vision. Outside the entrance to her wigwam she watched darkness descend upon the forest. The wind had died down; all she could hear was the low crackling of the fire. She wrapped her arms around her stomach to soothe her hunger pangs, fell over onto her side, and went to sleep.

She was awakened by the sound of wolves howling. They seemed closer than when she had heard them at the sugarbush camp. She sat up and listened. Starting and stopping and starting up again, answering and overlapping one another, some high, some low, yipping and yapping. She thought of grandfather's wolf song and began to sing:

Here come the spirit of the wolf . . .
Here come the spirit of the wolf . . .
Here come the spirit of the wolf . . .
Here is the spirit of the wolf.

She sang and sang until she fell asleep again. In her dream she was among the wolves. She heard a strange but beautiful song, and when she awoke she was humming that very same tune. Outside the wigwam dawn was coming to the forest. Her mouth was parched and her water jug empty. She walked to the stream and filled it. She stood and listened a moment. She heard squirrels chittering somewhere off in the woods. She returned to the lodge.

She spent the second day much as she had spent the first, singing sacred songs, praying, and watching the flames leap against the walls of the wigwam. Sometimes the melody she had heard in her dream came to mind, and she would sing that too, though there were no words. That afternoon her hunger was greater but she noticed it less. It seemed ages since she had eaten, and she was beginning to forget what food tasted like. She felt quite good, actually, and when darkness came to the forest she sat facing the fire, wrapped in her bearskin robe, and sang her sacred songs with a soft smile on her face. When the wolves began to howl she sang with them, too. She then fell silent and sat quietly, feeling that a great space had opened up inside her.

It was just before daybreak. She had gone to the stream to fill her water jug, and upon returning sat again before the fire. She must have dozed off, because she was suddenly startled by the sounds of wolves howling very close. She peaked outside and, much to her surprise and apprehension, saw a pack of wolves lying in the clearing near the lodge. She froze in fear, hoping they would not notice her. But suddenly one of them, the largest, turned its gaze in her direction, and it began to speak!

"Do not be afraid," it said. "We are Spirit Wolves. Kitchi-gami, the Master of Life, has sent us to you."

Morning Star was so astonished that she could neither speak nor move. She considered grasping the end of a burning log with which to frighten the wolves when another wolf rose and came near to the one that had spoken. It looked at her with the friendliest of eyes, eyes that she had seen before. And then she realized—they were the eyes of her brother!

This wolf soon began to howl the song that she had heard in her dream.

"Come and join us!" it said. At that the entire pack rose and began to dance, all the while howling Morning Star's dream song; she left the lodge and joined them. While they danced, the wolves began to speak to her, not with words, but as though they could speak directly to her mind.

"We have come to prepare you to meet Everlasting Shining Woman," they said. "Gather cedar boughs. Place them around you while you sing in your lodge. Pull pieces from the fragrant cedar bark and burn them in the fire. Its delightful scent will rise up to Everlasting Shining Woman, and she will be called to visit you."

They taught her words to go with her dream song and she sang them. They covered her shoulders with a cape of wolf-skin and said that they would always help her if she should call on them with her dream song.

When next she knew, Morning Star was in her lodge, sitting before the fire. She did not remember taking leave of the wolves or entering the lodge. She stood up and rubbed her eyes. It was light outside. Though she did not really understand the vision of the wolves, she felt that she must follow their instructions. She went into the forest to search for cedar boughs as they had told her to. She soon found a suitable tree and cut off a good number of branches. She returned to the lodge and lay them in a circle around where she sat. She sang her dream song while she burned cedar chips in the fire, calling for Everlasting Shining Woman to visit her lodge.

She passed the day this way. Her hunger became almost unbearable now, but she sang and prayed to keep her mind off her stomach. Late that afternoon her mother appeared at the entrance to the wigwam. She crawled through and came to Morning Star. She took her face in her hands, looked deep into her eyes, and asked if she was alright. Morning Star nodded and her mother left. She heard her bringing firewood and stacking it outside the lodge. After this was done, Morning Star heard the faint sounds of her mother's footsteps disappearing through the forest.

That evening Morning Star sat quietly by her fire singing her dream song, and now and then casting a few chips of cedar into the flames. After a while she became so absorbed in her song that she ceased to be conscious of where she was. It was as if she were floating in space. Then she heard a voice inviting her to walk the Shining Trail, which leads from earth to the heavens. She rose and began to walk. She climbed and climbed along the Trail, surrounded by stars and galaxies, until at last she came upon Everlasting Shining Woman. Everlasting Shining Woman was clothed in cloth as bright as the brightest stars; her face, her hair, and her eyes shone with double brightness. She took Morning Star by the hand and smiled at her.

They walked along, deep into the sky, until they came to a place beyond the stars. There were meadows, and brooks, and green-clad hills. Everlasting Shining Woman led Morning Star to a place high on a bluff. Vast lakes and oceans stretched as far as the eye could see. Everlasting Shining Woman directed Morning Star to look back down the path they had traveled. Down that path Morning Star saw everything her life had been until that time, her birth, her infancy, and her childhood. She saw many happy times with her family all around her, surrounded by the beauty of forest and stream, joyful in the bounty of Mother Earth. But she also saw the death of her brother and was gripped by a terrible sadness. Thunder crackled, and lightning lit up the sky.

Suddenly Little Spirit Man appeared. He was as round as a ball and had no legs. He and Everlasting Shining Woman led Morning Star to the Abiding Place of Bright Blue Sky.

Bright Blue Sky spoke to Morning Star. It said:

You will speak in other tongues

You will bridge two worlds

You will see into the heart of life

You will be a woman

Morning Star looked at Everlasting Shining Woman. Everlasting Shining Woman smiled at her and nodded. Bright Blue Sky spoke again:

You will know sorrow and joy

You will carry your mother's medicine
You will see the great waters
You will grace the earth with your sacred spirit

Morning Star was awake in her lodge, sitting in front of the fire. She was filled with great happiness that Spirit Beings had come to her and for the things they had shown and told her. She felt a new kind of strength, and she was deeply grateful that Spirit had given her a vision. She did not understand the meaning of everything Bright Blue Sky had said, but she felt that a plan existed for her life, one that was worthy and would bring contentment to her heart and help to her people. She sang her sacred songs and prayed throughout the day. On the morrow her mother appeared at the entrance of the lodge. She smiled at Morning Star, and Morning Star smiled back. Braided Waters knew that Morning Star had received a vision; she could tell by the glow in her face. She came into the lodge and sat down beside her daughter. They sang together, sacred songs woven into the sounds of the forest, and then Braided Waters embraced Morning Star and told her that it was time to return to the sugar camp. She handed her some dried deer meat.

"Eat slowly at first," she said. "Your stomach must get used to food again."

They packed their things into deerhide bundles, hoisted them onto their backs, and returned to the sugarbush.

Chapter 7

A Strange Visitor

Caleb Jordan had finished school and was helping his father in the smithy. He had gone into the yard to fetch some wood for the forge when he noticed a stranger coming through the gate. The man was tall and square in a loose-jointed way. He wore a coonskin hat. His thick coat was also made of animal furs. Caleb hurried inside with an armload of firewood.

"Somebody's coming across the yard," he told his father.

"Good," said Daniel Jordan. "Let's hope it's a customer. After we finish mending this anchor, we'll need more work."

"He looks like Daniel Boone!" Caleb said.

Daniel Jordan put down his hammer, removed his thick leather gloves, and laid them on the work bench. He stepped toward the open door of the smithy. Caleb stood beside him. The stranger was only twenty paces away.

"How do?" the man said, raising his hand in a sort of salute.

"Well enough," said Daniel Jordan. "What can we do for you?"

"I've got a proposition I'd like to talk to you about," the man began as he approached them, holding out his hand, "—if I might ask a minute of your time . . ."

"You might," said Daniel Jordan, shaking the man's hand. He stepped back from the door so the man could enter the smithy. He offered the stranger the best seat in the place—the stoutest of the old stumps they used for chairs—and stood against his work bench.

"I'm Daniel Jordan," Caleb's father said, "and this is my

son, Caleb."

"Pleased to meet you both," the man said. "My name is Josiah Strong. I'm an Indian agent for the government of the United States of America."

"Glad to know you," Daniel said while Caleb stood by, staring with great interest at this curious visitor. The man sat squarely on the stump with his long legs spread some distance apart. He took off his coonskin hat and held it against one leg.

"You said you had a proposition for us," Daniel said. "Is it smithy work?"

"You might say that," the man said. "It's a rather . . . involved job."

"After we finish up this anchor here," Daniel said, "we'll be in a position to take on any piece of work you've got for us. As long as you're willing to pay us fair, of course . . ."

Caleb tugged quietly at his father's sleeve. His father, anxious to make a deal with Josiah Strong, tried to ignore him. But Caleb kept tugging, and Strong began to stare at Caleb in such a quizzical way that Daniel Jordan had no choice but to attend to his son.

"What is it, my boy?" Jordan said. "You better tell me before you pull the sleeve clean off my coat!"

Caleb was a little embarrassed, but his curiosity was greater still. "I just wanted to ask, Father, what is an Indian agent?"

His gaze had not moved from their visitor.

"An Indian agent . . ." his father began, but while he hesitated, Strong answered for him.

"An Indian agent," Strong said, "is authorized by the government of these United States to treat with, make contact, and do all within my power to better the condition of the native inhabitants of the continent, materially, socially, and spiritually. Least ways that's the official story."

Caleb looked at his father. He wasn't sure what the visitor had just said.

"Are you saying you deal with the Indian tribes on behalf of Uncle Sam?" Daniel Jordan asked.

"That's right."

Caleb stared even harder at the man.

"What is it, son?" his father said. "If you stare any harder I'm afraid you're going to knock the good gentleman clear off his stump."

"Do you know any real Indians," Caleb asked Josiah Strong, "like Daniel Boone?"

"I wouldn't draw any comparisons between myself and Mr. Boone," the man said with quiet laughter in his voice. "But I know more Indians than I could tell. I count some among my best friends. I've often broken bread with them and shared their hunting trails."

Caleb's eyes were wide with wonder. "Have you ever run the gauntlet?"

"The Indians in my territory are pretty peaceful lately," Strong said, "though some of them did fight with the British in the last war. But that brings me around to the purpose of my visit . . ."

He paused.

"You had some work for us, I believe you said," said Caleb's father.

"Yes, that's right." Strong hesitated again before continuing. "But I have to tell you, it's not a job for . . . just anyone."

"If it's smith work, I'll wager we can handle it," said Daniel Jordan.

"Have you ever heard of the Ojibway Indians?" Strong asked.

Jordan looked to his son, who returned a questioning look, and then turned back to the Indian agent. "I don't suppose we have."

"How about the Chippewa?" Strong said. "People call 'em by different names."

Again Daniel Jordan looked toward his son. "I know about the Shawnee Indians," Caleb said excitedly. "They captured Daniel Boone and made him run the gauntlet. Pretty near killed him! But he escaped and ran all the way back to Kentucky, with a band of Shawnee warriors hot on his trail!"

"That's right, my boy," said Strong. "But those days are gone. All that business with the Ohio Indians got settled at the Battle of Fallen Timbers." The man's expression turned wistful. "The Shawnees, along with all the rest of what used to be Ohio Indians, are pretty much cleared out of the Ohio Country. They had to make way for American settlers, like it or not."

The man sat quietly for a moment.

"But what about this piece of work?" Daniel asked.

"Are you familiar with the Michigan Country?" asked Strong.

"A little," Jordan said. "A few folk from here in Albany have pulled up stakes and journeyed out there to try their fortunes, they say. From what I've heard, it's still right wild."

"That's pretty much the size of it. There's the city of Detroit, but it's not much more than a riverfront settlement. Elsewise it's nothing but endless forests, nary a road to speak of. There's no way to get around except old Indian trails—or in canoes, if you're near a river or lake. But I reckon those woods will soon be filled with the sound of the settler's ax. The territory governor, Governor Cass, is determined to bring new citizens into Michigan, until the state's just as crowded as New York."

"That I'd like to see," said Daniel Jordan.

"He's a determined man," Strong replied.

"Who are the Ojib, Ojib—?" Caleb asked, unable to contain his curiosity any longer.

"Ojibway?" Strong replied. "I'm glad you asked, my boy. I was just getting to that. They're the native people of the Michigan Country. They've kept their fires there since time before memory. Yep, they call those northern forests their home, along with the bears, the elk, the wolves . . ."

"Wolves?" asked Caleb, a little astonished.

"That's right, my boy. That country's teeming with them. But it won't be for long. Every state in the Union has passed a wolf bounty, and I imagine it won't be long before Michigan follows suit. Do you know what a bounty is?"

"Is that where they'll pay hunters to bring them in?"

"That's right," said Strong. "These law makers figure they're going to have to clear the country of wolves if they expect settlers to move in. Wolves and human civilization don't mix, especially when the humans have livestock. A wolf will just as soon eat a cow or a sheep as it will a deer."

"Do the wolves eat the Indians' cows and sheep?" Caleb asked.

"Oh, no," Strong said with a touch of laughter in his voice. "The Ojibway don't keep livestock. In the wintertime they live in hunting camps, deep in the woods. They roam the forests stalking game, just like their wolf brothers. In the summertime they congregate along the shores of the lakes and rivers, where they have great dancing feasts, plant gardens of corn and beans, and hold their sacred mysteries."

Caleb was silent. In his mind he pictured the Ojibway people, and he wished he could stalk through the forests with their hunters, or see their feasts on the shores of the broad lakes.

"But about that piece of work you mentioned?" Daniel Jordan asked again. He could see the light outside softening, and he wanted to get back to work on the anchor before the day had fled.

"Certainly," Strong said. "Like I just remarked, Governor Cass is keen on developing the Michigan Country til it's just as settled as any state in the East. He's determined to get possession of the Ojibways' land so he can open it up to settlers. A couple of years ago there was a big parley up at Saginaw Bay—that's about sixty miles or so north of Detroit—and the Indians, at least some of the chiefs, agreed to sell a good piece of Michigan's Lower Peninsula."

"Lower Peninsula?" Jordan asked as he moved toward the forge.

"Here, let me show you." Strong got down off his stump and knelt on the dirt floor. He gestured to a chisel hung from a hook on the wall.

"Do me a favor, would you, my boy? Fetch that chisel."

Caleb looked at his father. Daniel Jordan nodded yes , and Caleb reached up to the chisel and handed it to Josiah Strong.

"Alright now," said the stranger, "here's the Lower Peninsula of Michigan." Strong began to draw on the floor with the chisel. "This is Lake Michigan to the west, and here's Lake Huron on the east. Right here is the Straits of Mackinac. Just above that is the Upper Peninsula—wildest country imaginable! Sitting up here on top of everything is Lake Superior, what the Indians call *Kitchi-gami*, the Great Water."

Caleb knelt on the floor beside Strong and examined the map. His father bent over the two of them, sorting out, in his mind, the geography of it all.

"Now," Strong continued, "this here is Saginaw Bay. There are quite a few Indians, Ojibway, who live around the Bay's shores. These are the folks that just sold their land to Governor Cass. Here's the area they sold."

Strong used the chisel to mark a deep line across the Lower Peninsula of Michigan.

"That looks like a considerable piece of land," Daniel Jordan said. "They must have gotten a pretty penny."

"Not near enough, truth be told. No, the Indians, I'm afraid, aren't much experienced in land dealing. To them, you see, land isn't something a person can own. They believe that each generation just sort of uses the land while they're here, alive on this earth. Then the next generation comes along, and they use the land while they're here, hunting the forests, fishing in the streams and lakes, planting gardens of corn and beans at their summer villages. They don't each own their separate parcels, the way we do. So, not really understanding these kinds of transactions, the Saginaw Bay Ojibway sold their lands for considerably less than they're worth. In any case, they didn't have much choice. If they didn't sell their land to the government, the government would have taken it by force, just like they did the Ohio Country. What the government really wants, you see, is for the Indians to settle down and live like us white folk, farming in one place, not roaming among the woods hunting and fishing."

Josiah Strong directed his gaze upward toward Daniel Jordan. "And this, my friend," he said, "is where you come in."

"Me? What do you mean?" asked Jordan.

"Well," Strong replied, "when the Ojibway people at Saginaw Bay sold their land to Governor Cass, Cass created a reservation. That's the place where the Indians will live, this piece of land right around here." Strong took the chisel and scratched an X over a place near the head of Saginaw Bay. "To help the Ojibway learn to be settled folk, the government's supposed to send a couple of regular farmers to help them plant their crops, and also a couple of teachers to teach them to read and write. Governor Cass also promised to supply a blacksmith, so as they'll have someone to mend their farm tools and such."

Strong then straightened up and looked directly into Daniel Jordan's eyes. "Do you suppose you'd be interested in the job?"

Jordan was stupefied. "Are you saying you want me to go to Michigan and blacksmith for the Indians?"

Caleb's eyes grew wide as he looked between his father and Josiah Strong, listening eagerly to each word.

"That's precisely what I'm saying," Strong replied. "It's good, regular pay, backed by the Government of the United States. They'll pay your travel expenses as well, and also help with the building of your cabin. And should you need anything, I'll be at the Indian Agency right down in Detroit."

"I don't know," Jordan said. "I never really considered leaving Albany . . ."

Caleb spoke out excitedly. "Do the Indians live in wigwams, Mr. Strong? Do they paint their faces with war paint and take scalps?"

"Most of the Ojibway do still live in birch bark wigwams," Strong replied, turning to Caleb, "though a few of the more successful among them—those who've made good in the fur trade, particularly—have built themselves regular timber cabins. As for war paint and scalp-taking, that would depend on whether they're at war. For now, the Ojibway have agreed to bury the hatchet—that is, live in peace—with the people of the United States. The ones on the reservation will be just like regular folk, tending their farms and such."

Caleb preferred to picture the First Peoples hunting and trapping, deep in Michigan's endless forests; or on the warpath, slaying their enemies and taking scalps.

"It's a lot you're asking," his father now said, speaking to Josiah Strong. "After all, we'd have to pull up stakes, leave behind everything we own. And I've got my son to think about. How did you find us, anyway?"

"I had to come through Albany on my way to New York City, took the new steamship line across Lake Erie. Quite a contraption, that. I thought while I was here I may as well try and find a blacksmith. I asked around at the market, and they said you were as good a blacksmith as they come." Strong paused a moment and then spoke more quietly. "I was told you lost your wife recently."

"That's right," Jordan replied, "—and our Emily."

"I'm terribly sorry."

Daniel Jordan stared out the window at the gathering dusk.

"It may not be my business," Strong said after a moment, "but you know, going to a new country might do you some good . . . give you a new start."

Jordan stared into the forge. "I'll think about it," he said. "How long will you be in town?"

"I'll be here for two days. Then I leave for New York on Mr. Fulton's steamboat line."

"When would we need to start?"

"We'd like to have someone out there before planting season begins, not more than a month or two."

"I see. Come and see me before you go. I'll give you an answer then."

"I'll do that," Strong said as he placed his coonskin cap on his head. He shook Daniel Jordan's hand, tipped his cap to Caleb, and walked out the door. Daniel Jordan looked back toward the forge. The fire had gone out. "Oh well," he said. "I guess we'll finish that anchor in the morning." He looked around the smithy, nodded to himself, and laid an arm across his son's shoulders. "If that ain't something," he said as he and Caleb walked out of the smithy and toward the house.

Chapter 8

Two Decisions

The sugarbush lodge fire burns brightly. Morning Star's family is gathered together, speaking in low voices. They speak quietly so as not to awaken Grandfather, who is propped near the fire where it is warmest. Sweat beads up on his forehead; his breathing is heavy and labored. Grandmother sits beside him, holding his wrist, or at times wipes his forehead with a moistened scrap of deer hide.

There was an accident while Morning Star was away on her vision quest. Braided Waters told her about it as they returned through the forest to the sugar camp. Talks Too Much had broken through the ice while the men were fishing at the river. Grandfather had warned him not to go onto that section of ice, but Talks Too Much hadn't listened. He was always taking chances and thought his luck would never run out. When he broke through, Singing Loon was not there. He was at the fish-drying racks that the men had set up some distance away. Grandfather seized a branch to save his son. But the branch was not long enough to reach Talks Too Much from the bank, and Grandfather had had to wade into the river. The cold water soaked right through him, and when Talks Too Much and Singing Loon brought him back to the lodge, he was pale and shivering.

"His fever is still high," said Braided Waters. She held Wind-in-Grass in her lap.

Grandmother nodded.

"I will go into the forest tomorrow for herbs," Braided Waters said. She was gifted with healing medicine, and she was familiar with all the many plants of the forest that carried curative properties.

"Is he going to be alright?" Morning Star asked.

"Only the Master of Life knows the length of a man's days," Singing Loon said sternly. He stared straight ahead into the fire.

"I'm such a fool," Talks Too Much blurted out. "It's all my fault!"

"Maybe you will learn to be more cautious," Grandmother said, "and heed the advice of your elders."

She patted Grandfather's hand softly.

Talks Too Much didn't reply.

"We all make mistakes," Braided Waters said.

"Will we make sugar tomorrow?" Morning Star asked.

"No," Braided Waters replied. "The sugar making is done. We finished while you were away."

"Tomorrow you can see all the sugar bricks we made. We also made many treats for our clan relations," said Grandmother.

"Maybe white man's medicine can help," Talks Too Much said excitedly. "We can take him to Tom Campau's trading post. I know he sells medicines there."

"Speak more softly," Grandmother said. "He's in no condition to travel. Can't you see?"

"I could go myself," Talks Too Much replied, whispering now. "I will run. I could be back in five days' time."

"I would rather treat him with my own medicines," Braided Waters said.

"Wait a minute!" It was Grandfather's voice. It sounded weak and hoarse. He opened his eyes and shifted toward his family. With difficulty he slowly turned his head, staring softly for a moment into the eyes of each of his relations. Then he lay back and spoke quietly.

"You must not waste time seeking medicines. I am an old man. My days are full."

"No, Father," Talks Too Much said. "You are still strong!"

Grandfather stared straight ahead as he spoke. "I had a dream. I was traveling through a strange country. Hawks and eagles flew overhead, and the sun was as big as a mountain . . . and very strong. The wolves ran before me and I followed them. I didn't know where we were, or where we were going . . .

"In the distance I could see thunder clouds. We approached a river. Fleeting Elk was there, standing on the bank. He waved to me and greeted me . . . my mother, my father . . ."

Grandfather began to cough. He held his chest and heaved forward and back. Grandmother lay a hand on his back to soothe him. Finally he quieted, and then he began again to speak.

"It is time to move on. After holding my funeral fire, you must pack up and travel to Campau's trading post. Make sure he gives you the best price for our furs and oil."

He was out of breath. He lay back and closed his eyes. His relations gathered round him, waiting for him to speak again. He coughed a couple of times and opened his eyes again.

"Do not linger at Saginaw Bay," he started up again. "You must journey north to Braided Waters' clan relations. It will be a long journey, and you will want to arrive in time for her to plant her garden. They will welcome you. This is no place for we Ojibway any longer. They have sold our lands, and the settlers will soon be here in swarms. Do not delay long . . ."

He lay back again and was quiet. He seemed to sleep.

The family sat staring at Grandfather. Suddenly he opened his eyes.

"Help me to sit up."

They looked at Grandmother and she nodded. Talks Too Much helped her push Grandfather into a seated position, and Braided Waters placed a deerhide bundle behind his back to support his weight. He exhaled, and a smile of contentment passed across his face. He looked around at his relations one more time, gazing into each of their eyes in turn. Then he closed his eyes and began to sing. Though his voice was hoarse and weak, Morning Star thought his song more beautiful than she had ever heard it:

Here comes the spirit of the wolf
Here comes the spirit of the wolf

Here comes the spirit of the wolf
Here is the spirit of the wolf

Grandfather sang and sang. The fire crackled. There were tears in Braided Waters's eyes. Another sound arose in the distance. The wolves had begun to howl. Starting and stopping and starting up again, answering and overlapping one another, some high, some low, yipping and yapping. The dogs rustled about but did not join in; they just cocked their heads and whined softly. Suddenly Grandfather stopped singing and slumped forward. The distant wolves continued their howling.

&&&

After Josiah Strong left the Jordans' smithy, Daniel and Caleb Jordan went into the house. Daniel sent Caleb out to the well to fetch water and they made supper. After supper they banked the fire with good logs and sat together in the parlor. Caleb played on the hearth with his Indian figures while his father sat in the wooden rocker. Daniel Jordan was quiet this evening; he neither played his violin nor sang, but just sat staring into the fire.

Josiah Strong's visit of the afternoon was very much on his mind.

Indian Agent Strong's visit was much on Caleb's mind too as he sat near the fire. Up until now the Indians were just characters in his Daniel Boone book, or the toy figures he now moved back and forth before the fireplace as though they were hunting elk or going on the warpath. But with Mr. Strong's visit the Indians had become as real as the very people of Caleb's town. After all, hadn't Mr. Strong said that he knew many Indians personally? That he had broken bread and hunted with them? And didn't he tell Caleb's father that he wished for he and Caleb to come and live among the Indians as well? As Caleb slid his toy figures across the hearth he pictured himself among them, as one of them, hunting or raiding, or dancing together at a great feast.

The sound of his father's voice interrupted his fantasies.

"What did you think of our visitor today?"

"He's almost as grand as Daniel Boone," Caleb said. He made one of the Indian figures shoot his bow at a running elk.

"Did you understand his proposition?"

"His propo . . . sition?"

"Yes. Do you know why he came, what he was asking us?"

"He wants us to move out and live with the Indians, and do their blacksmith work," Caleb replied. He leapt up and began to run in small circles, making exuberant war whoops as he pumped his arms up and down.

"Okay, okay," his father said, "settle down. I want to talk to you seriously."

Caleb stopped, looked at his father, and slipped down onto his knees.

"You know," Daniel said, "we're not talking about a game. Mr. Strong's a real Indian agent, and his was a serious proposition. You know what it would mean, don't you, moving out to the Michigan Territory to work on an Indian reservation? That's a long way from here. It's a long way from everywhere, for that matter. We'd be giving up our home, all the things we're familiar with . . ."

Caleb tried to conceive what his father was saying. Giving up everything they were familiar with? It seemed like a big thing, but he couldn't quite wrap his mind around it.

"The living arrangements would be on the rough side, I'm sure of that. We'd probably have a simple crude cabin, with one or two rooms at best. There'd be no town, no marketplace or docks. It's just woods and woods and more woods, filled with Indians and wolves, and barely another Christian soul around. It sounds more like the job for a young man just starting out, or someone down on his luck with no place else to go. I don't know if it's the place to finish raising up a young man like you, that's for sure."

In reality, Caleb thought it all tremendously exciting. "Could I go hunting with the Indians?"

His father laughed. "I suppose you might be able to now and then, if you got to know them. But listen," he added, "have you thought of the fact that you would not be seeing your friend Thomas anymore, probably never again in all your born days?"

Indeed, this was something Caleb hadn't thought about. Thomas was his best friend in the world. They had even become blood brothers, and swore to always back each other up and never tell one another's secrets. Caleb became very quiet. He turned toward the fire, where his Indian figures glowed with firelight, casting twisting shadows on the hearth.

"Couldn't he come to visit?"

"I doubt it," his father said. "Michigan Territory is half a country away from here."

Caleb's expression grew glum, and he cast his eyes to the floor.

They were both quiet now, each lost in his own thoughts. After a while, Daniel Jordan spoke again.

"There's something I must tell you about, my boy, because it has some bearing on all of this."

"What's that?"

"It's about our business." Daniel spoke slowly and carefully. "The thing is," he said, "the smithy trade has not been all that good of late. You know Mr. Francis? His carriage shop has always been one of our best customers. You remember all the wheel rims we used to make? "

"Yep."

"Then you probably noticed that we haven't been making any lately. And why is that? Well, now he gets them from a factory where they're made by machines. They're cheaper that way. I'm afraid that'll soon be the way of much of our trade, factories where the work is done by steam engines instead of a man's strong arm. I met a man in the marketplace the other day from New York City. He talked real fine. He said that someday everything will be made in such places. Tools, pots and pans, even horseshoes! Why, if that were to happen, there would hardly be any need for smiths like us at all. All they'll need is folks to stand by and tend the machines."

Caleb was shocked at the idea that the world would have no need of blacksmiths. Blacksmiths had been around since the beginning of time, hadn't they? In Widow Chambers' school he had learned that the ancient Greeks and Romans even believed that one of their gods, Vulcan, was a black-smith. "You don't suppose that could really happen, do you?" he asked his father.

"I can hardly imagine it. But there were many said a country could never survive without a king, and look at these United States, still going strong after nearly fifty years."

Caleb looked down at his toy Indian figures. They were arrayed across the hearth where he had left them. Further along, at the hearth's edge, his toy soldiers stood at the ready. They all seemed to be waiting for something.

"Perhaps I depended too much on Mr. Francis's business." Caleb's father stood up and began to pace around the room. "I never thought it would go away. I suppose we could go out and hustle up some more steady customers. There's probably someone else out there who could use a good smith or two. We could take on more of the household work around here, mending the ladies' pots and pans and such. For that matter, we could travel out to the farms and repair tools, shoe horses and oxen . . ."

Daniel Jordan stood still a moment, holding his chin in his hand. Then he walked to the fire, stood beside Caleb, and grew thoughtful. "You know something, though," he said, "none of those ideas strikes me just right. I don't know what it is." He stared into the fire a moment. "The fact is, ever since we lost Mother and Emily, nothing seems quite right. But then, I suppose that's the way we should expect things to feel . . ."

Caleb watched his toy Indians and soldiers. His mind began to drift until he was standing among them, deep in the forests of the frontier. He didn't notice Daniel Jordan crouch down beside him until his father's voice startled him from his daydream.

"Perhaps we should give Mr. Strong's offer some consideration," his father was saying. "I know it sounds crazy, the idea of going off to the woods to blacksmith for those Indians—the Ojib . . .way—I believe he called them. But there's something about it that, for some reason, seems to make sense. I mean, those Indian people have had their lands taken away, and now they've got to learn to be farmers. They're going to need a couple of good blacksmiths. Maybe more than we'll be needed around here, with all these factories coming in . . ."

Caleb grew thoughtful himself. "I'd miss Thomas awful bad."

"Of course you would." Daniel Jordan looked into the fire, as though he could see therein into the heart of his son. Then he took Caleb by the shoulders. "Look at me."

Caleb turned toward his father and looked into his eyes.

"I've been saying we could use a change of scenery, haven't I? I was just saying so the other night, in fact Business hasn't been so good, and it looks to maybe get worse. And everything seems so dull and drab around here anymore . . ."

Caleb knew that what his father said was true. His father released his shoulders, looked back toward the fire, and went on.

"Now this Indian agent—this Mr. Strong—comes along, offering us to move out to the frontier and help the Indians. Mother always used to say that if your heart is willing, God will find a place for you to be of service. I wouldn't doubt but that, if she was here, she'd say the Lord was trying to tell us something; you know, offering us a change just when I've been thinking we need one. Maybe He knows our needs better than we do ourselves, just like she always said."

Being reminded of his mother made Caleb both happy and sad at once.

"Sure, it's a little scary. But look at it this way. If we don't like it, we can always come back. Least ways after we fulfill our obligation. One thing's for sure. I'll bet we won't need to worry about no factories coming in to take our work, way up in the woods like that."

Caleb didn't say anything.

"Of course we wouldn't sell our house right away," Daniel went on. "We'd just board it up. That way we'll always have a place to come back to if we wanted."

Caleb still remained silent.

"Tell you what," his father said. "Remember what Mother

used to do when she was pressed by a difficult decision?"

Caleb remembered well. When something weighed on his mother's mind, something about the family, or a neighbor, she would take out the family Bible, hold it in her lap, and close her eyes. She had been raised as a Quaker and believed there is an Inner Light within each of us, a Light that can guide us to what is true and right. And when she sat with the Bible in her lap, she let her mind go inward toward that Light. Then, when she felt settled and empty, ready to receive Truth, she would open the Bible. Wherever her eyes landed she would read, and the words from the sacred scripture would help her decide which way to go.

"Can the Bible really tell you what to do?" Caleb asked.

"That I can't tell you. I never tried it myself. Mother used to say that the guiding power wasn't in the Bible itself, but in your willingness to be guided by a higher power. She said that the Almighty can choose all kinds of ways to speak to people, if we're willing to seek them out. She said you just had to quiet your mind, and then let yourself be open to Spirit."

Caleb's father walked to a sideboard where the family Bible lay. He took up the thick book and an oil lamp and came to where Caleb sat at the hearth. He crouched to the floor and laid the Bible between him and his son. "Okay," he said, "let's close our eyes and give it a try." They placed their hands on the Bible's cover and lowered their heads in prayer. They were silent for some time; there was no sound save the crackling of the fire. Behind closed eyes Caleb saw an image of his mother, with her lovely, glowing face and the golden hair that lay across her shoulders, holding out a flower to him when they walked in the Pastures when he was small. Finally Caleb's father opened his eyes and tapped his son on the shoulder.

"Okay," he said, "let's open her up and see what she says."

He ran his fingers along the edges of the Bible's pages and opened the book. He placed his hand upon the page, held the oil lamp over the text, and where the tips of his fingers rested, he began to read.

A man who hardens his neck after much reproof will suddenly be broken beyond remedy.

After staring thoughtfully at the page for a moment Daniel Jordan turned to Caleb.

"I'm not sure I can make any sense out of this one," he said. "I mean, I can't see as how anybody has been reproved . . ."

Caleb stared at the words a long moment, but he could make no more sense of them than could his father. "Maybe we should try again."

Daniel thought for a moment. "I'm not sure that wouldn't be cheating," he said, looking doubtful. "But then again, we're just beginners at this. We're not used to prophecy, the way your Mother was . . ."

The fire crackled. "Okay," Daniel said suddenly, "we'll give it another try."

He placed a hand on the edge of the Bible's pages and, at random, opened it to another section. Looking down into the book, he read the following:

And not only this, but we also exult in our tribulations, knowing that tribulation brings about perseverance, and perseverance proven character, and proven character hope.

Daniel Jordan looked toward Caleb, his expression quizzical. "I get what it's saying, about how our struggles make us stronger. But does that mean that if we take up Mr. Strong's offer, and go to live among the Indians, we're going to have nothing but tribulations?"

"I guess it could get pretty rough, living out on the frontier," Caleb said.

"I don't know," Daniel said after the two sat silently for a moment, "let's try it one more time, then we'll quit no matter what. Third time's a charm, like they say. But this time," he added, "pray real hard."

Again Daniel Jordan turned over the thin, airy pages of the family Bible. While he did so he pictured Caleb's mother, his late wife, in his mind, and he silently asked her to help him. He placed his hand among the letters on the page and again he read aloud:

Now it came about when the king lived in his house, and the Lord had given him rest on every side from all his enemies, that the king said to Nathan the prophet, "See now, I dwell in a house of cedar, but the ark of God dwells within tent curtains."

And Nathan said to the king, "Go, do all that is in your mind, for the Lord is with you."

Daniel Jordan softly closed the book upon itself, glanced toward Caleb, and sat staring thoughtfully into the fire. This last verse was almost as mysterious to Daniel as had been the first two, but somehow it spoke to him. The "house of cedar" reminded him of the house of wooden planks in which he and Caleb lived, and the "tent curtains" made him think of the wigwams and tipis of the First Peoples. When he thought of the final line of the verse, "do all that is in your mind, for the Lord is with you," he realized that, deep in his heart, he felt a powerful attraction to the Michigan country and, for reasons he could not entirely explain, wanted to accept Josiah Strong's offer. Caleb, who watched his father's face, trying to discover what he might be thinking, noted a sudden look of wonder, as though a troupe of angels had just passed through the house. Daniel Jordan reached out and took his son's hand, never taking his eyes from the fire.

"I can't say as I understand it all," he said, "but I can't help feeling like the Michigan Country is the place for us."

When Caleb returned from Widow Chambers' school the next afternoon he went out back as he always did. But his father was not working at the forge, as Caleb expected, but moving about the smithy, taking things down off of hooks and shelves.

"We've got to start packing up," Daniel said without ceasing his labors. "Mr. Strong came by here this morning, and I told him that we decided to take him up on his offer. We're to take the stagecoach out to Buffalo next week and ride on a steamship across Lake Erie to the Michigan Territory. We won't be able to take the anvil, of course. It's much too heavy to travel with. Mr. Strong said they'd have one for us in Detroit, and that he'd take care of getting it to the Indian reservation. We're going to have to collect up our other tools and pack them in that big trunk. We'll also have to pack up our clothes and a few other personal things. We won't be able to take much with us. The rest we'll leave here."

Caleb stood staring at his father. They were really leaving! It all seemed so sudden.

"Well," his father said, "don't just stand there. We've got a lot of packing to do."

Chapter 9

A Journey by Land

CALEB STOOD with his father on the cobblestone paving outside the stagecoach depot, watching two men heave a trunk onto a baggage rack at the rear of the coach. It was just after dawn; Caleb and his father had gotten up two hours earlier to make final preparations for their journey. An oxcart had pulled up at the smithy, just as the first light began to paint the sky, to haul them and their belongings to the stagecoach depot. Most of their things were in the big trunk the two men were now lashing to the baggage rack. There was also a leather satchel sitting on the pavement, which would soon be placed atop the coach with the rest of the passengers' luggage.

One of the men who had just secured the trunk onto the back of the coach turned to Daniel Jordan.

"You must have filled that thing with rocks, heavy as it is," he said, trying to catch his breath.

"There are quite a few blacksmithing tools in it, Daniel Jordan replied. They must have given it more weight than you're used to. They're made of good sturdy iron, every one of them."

"That would be it, no doubt," the man said. "Not that I can't handle it, mind thee," he hastened to add as he bent over to pick up the satchel. "But I wouldn't think of putting it up top with the rest of the things. These coaches are top-heavy enough as it is, they are. With all that extra load up there, you'd capsize her sure as Kingdom come."

The city was coming alive with the morning. There was the clopping of horses' hooves along the streets, pedlars hawking their wares, children cutting up on their way to school, and from down State Street toward the river, the boisterous noise of the docks. As Caleb stood and breathed in the fresh morning air, he tried to remember everything the way it was. He noted the sounds, the smells, the way the buildings looked, and the way people rushed through the town as they started their daily routines. He knew he would not see, hear, nor breath the air of Albany for quite a long time, maybe never, and he wanted to remember it all. He wanted to be able to carry it with him wherever he might go.

Other passengers for the stagecoach were beginning to congregate in the paved space in front of the stagecoach office. There were a couple of women in long woolen coats, with flowery scarves over their heads, a squat gentleman in a tight-fitting frock coat, and a thin, angular man who paced nervously across the paving. Besides Caleb and his father, these appeared to be the only other passengers for the morning coach.

One of the men who had loaded the luggage stepped out of the stagecoach office. "All aboard," he bellowed as he walked briskly toward the coach. He stood at the door and held out a hand to help the women up the high step into the passenger compartment. The four stout horses harnessed to the coach stomped and snorted in the cold morning air. After the women were aboard, the men stepped up into the coach, with Caleb and his father entering last.

The two women had taken seats on a bench at the back of the compartment and the two men at the bench along the front. Caleb and his father sat down on the remaining bench, which ran across the middle. After everyone was seated the driver closed the door. Caleb craned his neck to watch him mount the driver's seat in front. Next came the smart crack of the whip in the air, and then a great deal of clopping of horses' hooves on the paving as the coach began to wheel about. The vehicle was just starting to move down Market Street when Caleb noticed a large man in buckskin clothes and a beaver hat running towards them, waving his arms above his head.

"Why, it's Mr. Strong, the Indian agent," Daniel Jordan said.

The coach slowly came to a stop, and Caleb watched the driver step down onto the street and talk to Strong. Strong handed the driver a satchel he was carrying, the driver strapped it in with the rest of the baggage, and they both stepped toward the coach door. The driver opened it, and Josiah Strong stepped up into the passenger cab.

"Well, well," Josiah Strong said to Caleb and his father as he bent into the low space. "What a pleasant surprise. I didn't know you two were to be on the coach this morning."

"I thought you were to meet us in Buffalo," said Daniel Jordan.

"Yes, I was," Strong said, "but I finished my business here sooner than I expected. So here I am."

The crack of the driver's whip was heard again, and the coach started off with a jolt that sent Josiah Strong reeling toward the back of the cab. "Morning, ladies," he said as he braced one hand firmly on the wall above their heads. Presently another jolt sent him toward the front of the cab, where he managed to turn and plop himself onto the front bench beside the two men who sat there.

"We're off," he said with a laugh, and Caleb and one of the women laughed with him. Strong doffed his hat to the two other men and settled back. "Well," he said, "we might as well get used to the bumps. We've got six or seven days out to Buffalo, and the roads are none to good."

The coach rattled along over Albany's cobblestone streets, through Market Square, where Market Place was already full of busy activity, and then on toward the edge of town and the road to Buffalo. At Pearl Street the driver had to stop and wait for a herd of cattle being driven to the Pastures; to Caleb's surprise, his friend Thomas was there by the side of the road with his father. They had come to see Caleb and Daniel off on their journey west. While the driver waited for the cattle to cross, Caleb leapt down from the coach and said his last goodbyes. Thomas had brought him a parting gift, a gaily painted wooden top that Caleb had always admired.

As the last of the cattle crossed the street, Daniel Jordan hollered for Caleb to return to the coach, and with the driver grumping a bit about having to get down from his seat to secure the door again, Caleb climbed up, clutching Thomas's top in his hand. The driver cracked his whip, the horses began to pull, and Caleb waved furiously to his friend as the coach pulled away toward the edge of town.

Josiah Strong asked to see the top. He examined it from every angle and seemed to share Caleb's admiration. He tried to balance it on his hand as the coach bumped over the bumpy, unpaved road, but it fell and began to spin across the floor. Caleb had to scurry on his hands and knees to retrieve it from one of the women, whose boot it had run up against. She laughed and patted his hair down, just the way his mother used to do, when she returned it to him.

"That's a finely tuned top," she said. "I'll bet it'll spin for minutes on end, if you give it just the right kind of whirl."

"It will, too," Caleb said. "I've seen it."

The thin man who had paced in front of the stagecoach office stared out the window intently, as if preoccupied with some grave problem, and seemed not to notice the top at all. The other one, who sat next to Josiah Strong, glanced through a sheaf of papers and looked annoyed, as though Strong's shenanigans with the top had distracted him from his work. "Humfff!" he said, staring doubly hard at his papers.

Caleb came back to the bench beside his father. Daniel Jordan placed an arm around his shoulders. "Alright," he said, "let's settle down now." Caleb's father never liked to see anyone annoyed.

Everyone was quiet again as the coach continued on its way. It passed the last of Albany's houses, then on past farmers' fields and stretches of woods. The ride got bumpier as the wheels passed over potholes and ruts in the dirt road, and the passengers bounced along in silence, each lost in his or her own thoughts. After a little while they entered the Pine Barrens, a long stretch of sandy soil, pine forest, and marshes left by rivers that had run over the land thousands of years before, when a great lake covered the region where Albany now sat. There was a high-pitched shriek from outside the carriage, and Caleb looked up to see a red-shouldered hawk wheel away from a tree where it had perched.

As they moved through the Pine Barrens, Caleb heard

the women chatting quietly behind him. His father looked steadily out the window at the passing scenery, as did the thin man, who still looked very earnest and preoccupied. The squat man in the tight-fitting coat worked on his papers and Josiah Strong began to doze. For several miles there was no human habitation, just pine trees, meadows, and marshes. To Caleb it seemed a lonely landscape, and he began to miss his mother and his sister Emily, both of whom had died of that terrible fever a year before. Where were they now? he thought. Were they in Heaven? And why did they have to die? Why, he thought, if God loved the world, as the Bible said, and if God loved him, Caleb Jordan, as his mother used to say, would He take away his mother and sister? He loved his father, surely, but now, with Emily and his mother gone, it seemed that they were only half a family.

A painful memory then came stabbing at Caleb's heart. It was one he usually tried not to think of, because it made him sad, and a little scared. It was about something he had said to his sister not long before the sickness came that killed both her and his mother.

It was a Sunday afternoon and Caleb had been down at the docks with his friend Thomas, watching the tall ships standing in the river. He returned home a little before dinner time, looking forward to playing with his toy soldiers and Indians before the Sunday meal was set out. But when he went to the spot before the fireplace where he had left them the night before, carefully arrayed together as if to join battle, he found them scattered across the hearth in a jumble. He began to seethe with anger. Without thinking about it, he knew who was responsible. His sister, Emily. The night before she had asked if she could join him in his play, and he had refused her.

"These aren't for girls," he had said.

"Why not?"

"They're just not."

"That's not a reason."

Caleb grew annoyed, as he always did when his sister asked a question he could not answer.

"Maybe I don't need a reason."

"Maybe you just can't think of one."

"Alright," he said, a slight smile forming on his face, "I'll tell you why not. Because girls are too stupid to play with them!" He began to laugh. Emily stuck her tongue out at him. He began to get up so that he could pull her hair or twist her arm, but his mother was coming toward them.

"Caleb Jordan," she said sternly, "you apologize to your sister. What you said was very mean."

"She deserved it!"

"And why, pray tell?"

"She was pestering me and wouldn't leave me alone."

"Were you bothering your brother?" Mrs. Jordan asked Emily.

"No," she said with a pout, "I just wanted to play with him."

"Is that true?" Mrs. Jordan asked Caleb.

Caleb was already absorbed in his play again and barely listened to his mother. "She was bothering me," he said distractedly.

Mrs. Jordan's dinner pot, which she had left hanging over the fire in the big kitchen hearth, had begun to boil over with a steaming hiss, and she turned suddenly away from the children. "I need to tend to dinner," she said. "So mind! I want you both to be kind to one another. Try and remember what you learned in church this morning. Emily, you come and help me finish." She took Emily by the hand and they began to walk away. Caleb looked up in time to make a horrid face at his sister. She stuck out her tongue again.

Caleb had returned to his play and thought nothing more of the matter. In fact, he became so absorbed with the drama his soldiers and Indians were enacting that his mother had to call him to dinner three times; as soon as he finished eating, he returned again to the toy figures. He had read in one of his schoolbooks about the battle of Tippecanoe, where the Prophet's warriors had attacked General Harrison's troops. He was carefully arranging the soldiers of the United States army in their camp along Burnett Creek, with the Indians in the surrounding forest ready to attack at dawn. By the time he went to bed that night he was quite satisfied with his work; and when he returned from helping his father in the smithy on Monday evening, he was prepared to begin the battle.

But when he approached the hearth after cleaning up he was shocked to see that all his work had been ruined. Again the figures he had so carefully placed lay in a jumbled pile! He crouched over his wrecked camp and began to pick through the figures, a tight scowl on his face. Then he saw it—there in a heap of soldiers—the pink frilly cotton standing out among the dull metal of the toy figures. One of his best officers—a gallant figure holding a saber aloft, about to strike—was wearing a dress! It was one of the little outfits his mother had helped Emily fashion for some miniature dolls she had been given as a Christmas gift. Now the officer, instead of looking brave and fearsome, looked ridiculous and stupid.

This time Caleb knew for certain who had wrecked his work. What was worse, she had done it for one reason and one reason alone: to get on his nerves! He looked up, sensing that he was being watched. And there, on the other side of the room, was Emily, giggling under her breath. He rose from the floor and began to move toward his sister. He'd show her! Emily shrieked and ran outdoors.

He caught up to her about half-way between the house and the smithy. He grabbed her ponytail and tightened his grip as she screamed. Then he grasped one of her arms and twisted it behind her back; she screamed even louder. He exalted to hear her painful cries, and he bent her arm even further. But when he glanced beyond her he realized that all the noise had reached his father in the smithy, and Daniel Jordan now strode across the yard toward his children.

"What on earth are you doing?" he said to Caleb as he pulled him away from his sister.

Caleb was very excited, and he struggled against his father's grip. Emily fell to the ground, sobbing.

"Crybaby!" Caleb yelled, still trying to get at her.

"Bully!" she yelled back.

His father held him firmly until he stopped struggling. Now his mother, who had also heard the commotion, had come out to the yard. She was bent over Emily. She looked at Caleb sadly, then to his father, and then back to Caleb.

"What do we need to do to get your temper under control?" she said.

"She wrecked my camp!" he screamed. Tears had come to his eyes.

"Still," his mother said, "that's no reason to . . ."

"Come with me," his father said, and he began to lead Caleb toward the smithy.

Caleb allowed himself to be dragged along reluctantly. Glancing back, he saw his sister sobbing in his mother's arms.

"It's not fair!" he said. "She gets away with murder!" But his father seemed not to hear him.

A moment later it was Emily's turn to hear, coming from the smithy, her brother's painful cries, punctuated by the wap! of a stout switch being applied to the seat of his pants. Emily squirmed in her mother's arms at the sound of each cry, for though her brother had hurt her, she didn't like to hear him being whipped. Stifling her sobs, she asked her mother to release her so that she might run to the smithy and plead with her father to stop. But her mother refused to let her go. "He needs this," her mother said. "And for your part, you can stop needlessly antagonizing him. You know he has a temper." Now Emily began to whimper quietly, more sad for her brother's punishment than for the wrong he had done to her.

Inside the smithy, Daniel Jordan spoke to his son as he spanked him. "You are never, under any circumstances, to touch your sister, Wap! or any other member of the female sex, in anger. Do you hear me?"

"But she wrecked my camp," Caleb screeched.

"I guess we'll have to try again," his father said. "I said you are NEVER Wap! to touch your sister, or ANY OTHER MEMBER OF THE FEMALE SEX! wap! IN ANGER. Do you hear me?"

Caleb was silent.

"Do you hear me?" His father held out the switch, ready to strike again.

Daniel Jordan was a kind man and loved Caleb dearly, and he did not use even half his strength in the blows he inflicted upon his son. Caleb could take the pain if he had to, but he didn't like the feeling of helplessness, lying across a bench, awaiting the next strike. He also suspected that his father might be telling him something useful and true, and if that were the case, it wouldn't be fair to make him go through so much effort to get his point across. The real problem was that if his father was right, then Caleb was wrong, and Caleb didn't like to be wrong. He wanted to feel justified, especially in the eyes of his parents, for their approval meant a great deal to him. In the silence of the smithy he could hear his father breathing calmly above him. For now, he decided, he would give in, even if he wasn't really ready to accept that he had been wrong. After a moment he spoke, very quietly.

"I hear you," he said.

"Good."

Daniel Jordan helped Caleb up from the bench and Caleb left the smithy. His mother and Emily were still crouched on the lawn; he stalked past them on his way to the house. Emily squirmed again in her mother's arms. She wanted to go to Caleb and make sure he was alright, but her mother held her firmly.

Caleb spent the rest of the evening sulking in his room. He even declined to come downstairs for supper. That evening Emily peeked her head in his door.

"Are you alright?" she asked meekly.

He didn't bother to look up.

"I didn't mean for you to get whipped."

"Why don't you just go away somewhere and die."

"Forget it, then!"

She turned and left him alone.

Caleb sulked the rest of the evening away, and the next day he went to school and did his chores and helped his father in the smithy. Before long things returned to normal. Caleb was still sore at his sister, but she didn't do anything else to pester him, and he stayed out of her way. Then, after another month had come and gone, the sickness came. Caleb himself had been the first to fall ill. He still remembered the chills and the fever, sweating in his blankets, and the awful vomiting. He was just getting past the worst of it when Emily took sick. His mother was busy night and day, applying compresses to help the fever, emptying pails full of sickness, and sitting by the beds of her children, watching every breath they took. When she too began to grow faint and weak Caleb was out of bed and moving about again. Now he helped his father tend to Emily and Mother, and word was sent to Boston for his Aunt Elizabeth to come and help out.

One day, when his sister was resting quietly, Caleb brought her a bouquet of wild flowers he had picked in the Pastures. He realized that he wasn't sore at her anymore. He even felt a little sorry for the mean things he had said and done. He didn't like seeing her so weak and ill, and he thought that if he did something nice, she might see that he cared for her after all and wanted her to get better. She was too weak to speak much, but she smiled when he showed her the flowers and put them in a glass of water by her bed.

By the time Aunt Elizabeth arrived on the stagecoach from Boston it was too late for her to help much. Emily, the day Caleb brought her the flowers, had fallen into a profound sleep from which she never awoke. His mother died the next day. Aunt Elizabeth helped arrange things for their funerals and stayed on for a few weeks, until Caleb and his father were able to begin caring for themselves. She had wanted Caleb to return to Boston with her, but Daniel Jordan did not wish to be parted from his son.

Now, as he rode through the Pine Barrens on a still morning, with his father gazing out the window, Josiah Strong dozing peacefully, the man in the tight-fitting coat concentrating on his papers, the thin gentleman staring thoughtfully into space, and the two women chatting quietly among themselves, Caleb was overwhelmed by a terrible sadness. Why, he thought once again, had God taken away Mother and Emily? But this time an answer came back: because I, Caleb Jordan, *do not deserve them*. He had been mean to his sister and disobeyed his mother and father. He remembered, too, that he had told his sister to go away and die. His mother had always said that God answers prayers, and hadn't that been a sort of prayer? Hadn't Emily done just what he had asked her to do?

Die?

Unable to contain himself, Caleb begin to cry soundlessly, his tears seeping out from his closed eyes. Then, in spite of himself, he began to make small sobbing noises.

"What's this?" his father asked.

"Hey, little man," one of the women added, "is something the matter?"

Josiah Strong, awakened by the voices of the woman and Daniel Jordan, came in. "Why these tears, soldier? We're off to a great adventure, just like Daniel Boone!"

Caleb didn't open his eyes. He didn't want to see *them* watching *him* cry. And he didn't want to tell them what the matter was. It was all too painful, and besides he was terribly ashamed of himself. He was ashamed of himself for disobeying his parents, ashamed of himself for his temper and for not being kind like Jesus commanded. And especially, he was ashamed of himself for telling his sister to die. Now she, and his mother too, were gone and it was his fault. He stifled his tears and wiped his eyes. His father put an arm around his shoulders and held him snuggly.

"Just homesickness, I'll bet," said one of the women. "You'll feel better soon, little man, don't you worry. There will be new friends where you're going."

Caleb sniffed loudly.

"Just think of all the game in those wild forests," Strong said heartily. "I'll take you hunting myself, I will."

The man in the tight-fitting coat, not liking to be disturbed, looked up from his papers and loudly clearly his throat.

"There, there," Daniel Jordan said. He patted Caleb's back. "Let's settle down now. Everything's going to be alright."

They road on, Caleb quiet now, his father's arm around his shoulders, Josiah Strong's eyes closed again, the women chatting, the man with the tight coat working on his papers, and the thin gentlemen looking earnest and preoccupied until they finally cleared the lonesome Pine Barrens. They then rode past farmers' fields and pastures until they reached their first stopping place, a tavern by the side of the road with a stables behind and a sign with a painted bull swinging on a post. The stagecoaches derived their name from the fact that they made their journeys in stages, so the horses would not grow too tired to pull at their best, and so that the drivers would not have to travel too far from home. At each stage along the route was located a tavern, with a stables, where a new team of horses would be harnessed to the coach and a new driver take over. If night were coming on, the passengers could sleep in the taverns' dormitories, and at mealtimes they could dine in the taverns' dining halls. Caleb and his traveling companions had completed the first stage of their ride to Buffalo, about fifteen miles, and they had hundreds more to go.

After the driver opened the door, Caleb and his father climbed down with the rest of the passengers. While a new team of horses was harnessed to the coach, the passengers milled about on the tavern porch. Before long the horses were harnessed and a jaunty man, low on his legs and with a spring in his step and a feather in his cap, stepped toward the porch from where he had been working with the horses.

"If you'll allow me," he said, walking by the passengers, "I'd be happy to help you into the coach now. Ladies first, of course."

The women stepped off the porch and the other passengers followed, with Caleb and his father last. When these two got to the door of the coach, the driver spoke to Caleb.

"Why so glum, my man?"

Caleb's cheeks were still stained with tears, and he wore a sad expression on his face.

"Just a little homesick, I suppose," his father said for him. "We're moving away to the Michigan country, and I suspect he's already missing the familiar people and places."

"I see," the driver said. "Well, take it from a man who's taken a turn or two around the wide world, sonny. There's always a new adventure ahead, at least as pretty as the one you left behind . . ."

Caleb didn't say anything and his father, not wanting to hold up the coach, said, "Thank you, kindly. I imagine he'll be alright once we get on our way again."

The driver stood looking at Caleb. You could almost see him thinking. "Tell you what," he finally said, "how would you like to ride up front with me, on the driver's seat? Nothing like some good fresh air to chase away the down-in-the-dumps, that's what I always say."

A faint light now shone in Caleb's eyes. His father said, "We wouldn't want to trouble you . . ."

"Trouble me? Not at all, my friend! I'd enjoy the company. What do you say, my man? Are you game?" He put a hand on Caleb's shoulder. "Come on, right this way, I'll show you how it's done."

With that he began to lead Caleb to the front of the coach, where he showed him how to climb up onto the high driver's seat. "Don't worry," he said, stepping back to Caleb's father, "I'll take good care of him."

"As long as you don't mind," Daniel Jordan said as he stepped into the coach. The driver closed the door behind him and swung himself up into the driver's seat beside Caleb.

"Alright," he said, "are we ready, my boy?"

Caleb looked ahead over the countryside before him. Forests and fields and lakes and meadows, and a high blue sky full of tall, white clouds. The four thick horses swished their tails from side to side and stomped their feet.

"Ready," Caleb replied.

"Okay then, let's get this rig going." The driver held up his whip, a thin leather ribbon on a long wooden shaft, and cracked it sharply about the horses' heads. "Let's get on," he spit out, talking to his horses now. "Come on, Molly! Come on, Andrew! You, Clyde, pull smartly now, look lively! You, Trevor, quit skulking over there! Help out, for crying out loud!" He cracked his whip again, and the horses wheeled out into the roadway, pulling hard at their harnesses.

Soon the countryside flowed by at a good pace, and Caleb felt the cool air breezing over his face. The driver introduced himself—his name was O'Hare—and he learned Caleb's name. He said that he had been to sea when a young man and gone as far away as China on a tall trading ship of the kind Caleb liked to watch at the docks in Albany. He spoke to his horses and told Caleb about them. He worked with them every day and knew each of them very well. He hardly had to use the reins, and almost never the whip, because his team responded readily to his voice commands.

O'Hare was so friendly that Caleb soon began to cheer up. O'Hare even let him hold the reins for a spell, until they came to the crest of a steep hill.

"You'd better let me take over here. These rigs ain't got no brakes, so on these steep grades we've got to run the horses flat out so as the coach don't catch up to them and bump their haunches."

With that he cracked the whip and called to his horses. "Git up, now. Let it loose. Come on, Trevor, quit lagging!"

"Hold on to your hat," he said to Caleb as the horses crested the hill at a hard gallop and charged headlong down the other side.

Caleb pressed his feet hard against the footrest to keep from being thrown from the seat, at the same time pressing his back against the coach behind him. He held his cap with one hand and with the other tightly gripped the edge of the driving seat. The chilled wind rushed over his face so hard he had to squint his eyes; the landscape became a shifting blur. But he could see every detail of the horses before him, throwing their heads and manes about as they charged forward and down.

When they reached the bottom of the hill O'Hare called to the horses again. "Whoa, now, whoa." The horses steadied their pace and slowed to a light trot.

"Well, now," he said, speaking to Caleb. "That wasn't so bad, was it?"

The fact is, Caleb had found the experience tremendously exciting, and he hoped they would soon reach another hill. "Heck no, I liked it."

"Only thing worrisome about these hills," O'Hare said,

"is there's always the chance there could be something at the bottom, and we wouldn't be able to stop in time. There could be someone lagging in the road, for example. Say, a drover with a herd of cattle, or someone bringing a flock of turkeys for market. It could even be another coach hogging the road."

"Did you ever see a wreck?" Caleb asked.

"Oh, I've seen one or two, I have. Been in a couple myself, in fact." Hearing this, Caleb wasn't so sure he wanted another hill. "But," O'Hare continued, patting Caleb on the knee, "that's nothing we're going to worry about today. We'll have our hands full with these bad roads. Old Man Winter's done his worst with them. With all these ruts and potholes, I'd be surprised if we didn't break an axle, or even tip over."

O'Hare took a deep breath of cold air and settled back with a satisfied look on his face. The coach hit a hard ridge in the road that sent a shock through the seat and almost sent O'Hare over its edge. "Whoa there," he cried out, grabbing at his hat. Caleb grabbed O'Hare by the sleeve of his coat and held it tightly until the driver had regained his balance.

"Whew," O'Hare said as he pressed his boots firmly into the footrest, "that was a close one. But don't you worry. We've got a good team of horses. Not too long ago here, one of our drivers was bumped clean out of his seat! And you know what, the horses knew the lay of the land so well, they went on and carried the passengers right to the next stop without him. There was some surprised faces, let me tell you, when the coach pulled up at the Brown Dog Tavern with no driver at the reins!"

O'Hare began to laugh, he patted Caleb boisterously on the knee, and the coach rode on until they were approaching the next stop, a clapboard building beside the road. Along the way O'Hare taught Caleb more things about the stagecoach lines and the roads they traveled, about the teamsters who hauled goods for market and the drovers who moved herds of sheep and cattle and hogs, and even whole flocks of turkeys, to towns where they could be sold and butchered for the townspeople to eat. He taught Caleb about the coaches themselves, how they were built and how they rode, and about the kinds of people that rode in them and how they spent the nights at taverns along the way.

"Here she is," O'Hare said, "the next relay." With this he reached into the deep pocket of his coat and pulled out a small tin horn. He held the horn to his lips and blew a loud salute as the coach pulled up before the tavern.

While a new team of horses was being hitched to the coach some of the passengers descended from the cab. Caleb got down from the driver's seat and went with his father into the tavern, where they were given small cakes and a cup of tea. Before they could finish eating, however, they heard the sound of the tin horn from outside, and someone called, "all aboard!" They left hurriedly and found a new driver standing by the coach. He helped the women up into the cab and the men followed. When Caleb and his father came to the door, the driver spoke to Caleb.

"I understand you like to ride up in the box, my friend," he said.

Caleb looked at his father.

"It's okay with me, as long as you mind the driver."

"Well, then," the driver said, "let's look lively and take our seats. We've got a lot of road ahead of us, and much of it's none too good."

Daniel Jordan stepped up into the coach and Caleb went to the front, where he climbed up into the driver's box the way O'Hare had taught him. The driver followed, and with a crack of his whip and a quick toot on his horn the coach pulled away from the tavern. Thus the day passed, riding the road west, stopping at the taverns along the way to change horses and drivers. At each relay the driver invited Caleb to ride on the box. The man in the tight-fitting coat got off at Schenectady, and along the way other passengers came aboard.

They rode on through the day and into the evening, until they stopped for the night at a tavern with a sign depicting a red rooster hanging in front. The thin man who had paced nervously in front of the stagecoach office in Albany was still with them, as were one of the two women, and of course Josiah Strong. They all dined together at a big table in the tavern's front hall, along with the tavern's other guests, and afterwards most of the men went into the barroom to drink whiskey and smoke cigars. Caleb and his father, however, and the thin man, a Methodist minister traveling west to take over a newly built church, went straight upstairs to the men's dormitory. There were no private bedrooms in most of the taverns along the way, and all of the men and boys slept together in one large room with several beds, with all of the women and girls in another. Caleb and his father were shown to a narrow bed by the tavern keeper, which they were to share; and the minister, whose name was Mr. Stark, was placed in the bed beside them. Caleb and his father, after saying their prayers, lay back to sleep. Reverend Stark sat on the edge of his bed, looking thoughtfully out the window into the dark night.

Before it was even light the tavern keeper appeared at the door of the dormitory with a lantern and called the guests to breakfast. In the light of the lantern, which the innkeeper had hung on a hook by the door, Caleb looked around the room. Most of the beds were full, with two men in each, all of whom were now sitting up, stretching and yawning. Caleb and his father went downstairs where, along with the other guests, they sat at the table at which they had dined the evening before. While they were finishing breakfast, a man in a thick coat with a scarf round his neck and an old straw hat on his head appeared in the dining room. "All aboard for the morning coach to Utica," he said. "We'll be leaving presently."

Caleb and his father, along with Josiah Strong, the woman who had recovered Caleb's top, Reverend Stark and four others, went out to board the coach. Once again, the driver invited Caleb to ride on the driver's box, for each driver had passed word to his replacement in the relay, and Caleb gladly accepted.

This day passed much as had the one before; and the ones that followed were much the same. Usually Caleb rode up on the driver's box, but at times he missed his father and rode in the cab with the other passengers. On a couple of the stages there were so many passengers that Daniel and Caleb Jordan both had to ride with the driver on his seat, and in one instance several passengers rode on the roof with the baggage.

The coach carried Caleb and his father and their fellow travelers ever westward. The road followed the wide and fertile valley of the Mohawk River as it wound its way between the Catskill Mountains to the south and the Adirondack Mountains to the north, cutting a pass through the Appalachian range toward the frontier lands beyond. They passed miles and miles of unbroken forest, with scattered clearings where farmsteads and dwellings had been built; there were also tidy towns; broad, cultivated fields; and stately mansions, some of them built before the Revolution. They crossed many streamsand sometimes skirted large and beautiful lakes.

On the third day there were steady spring rains, and the going grew slow on the soft and rutted roads. Many times the passengers had to get out of the coach and walk to ease the load, and more than once a rail was borrowed from a nearby fence to pry stuck wheels out of the mire. At one of the stream crossings the bridge was washed out and the driver took the coach straight through the current, which reached the bottom of the passenger cab and threatened to carry the coach along with it.

They arrived late at a tavern near the little village of Corinth. As they approached, the driver gave seven quick blasts on his horn to tell the tavern keeper that he had seven passengers for supper. Caleb and his father went in with the others to the dining room. While they were eating, Josiah Strong spoke with his father.

"Today is the eighth day of April," he said, "and we have nearly four more days before we reach Buffalo. The steamship leaves Buffalo for Detroit on the twelfth, so it looks like we're going to miss it. It takes three days in each direction, which means the *Superior* won't be back at Buffalo again until at least the eighteenth. That means we'll be stuck with a week's delay."

"Is there anything to be done about it?" Daniel Jordan asked.

"If there are enough willing passengers," Strong said,

"they'll run a night coach. That would allow us to make up the time we've lost on account of the bad roads."

"We'd be willing," Daniel Jordan said.

The lady who had been riding with them since Albany, and who had recovered Caleb's top from the floor of the coach on their first day together, was seated across the table. She had been listening to Strong speak to Caleb's father, and now she cocked her head and spoke.

"Did you say, Mr. Strong, that they will run a night coach?"

"Yes, if there are enough passengers willing to go."

"I'd very much like to go myself, if they do."

"I'm not sure that would be a good idea," Strong said, "your being a lady, and with this weather. We could run into some hard going."

"But my sister in Buffalo is ailing, and I'm extremely anxious to get there. Besides, with you and Mr. Jordan along, I'd feel quite secure."

"I'm sure it will be all right," another voice came in. It was Reverend Stark. "I'd like to come as well. I'm anxious to start my work."

After supper Josiah Strong spoke to the tavern keeper, who was also the agent for the stagecoach line, and it was agreed that a night coach would be run. Caleb and his father, Josiah Strong, Reverend Stark and the lady, whose name was Miss Telleridge, waited in the dining room while fresh horses were hitched to the coach. Then, while the tavern's other guests went upstairs to bed, they went out to continue their journey west. Before the coach departed they were joined by a stout, aging man, well-dressed, who walked with a cane and introduced himself as Judge Vanderveeden. He was traveling to the next town to sit on a Circuit Court bench, and he had to be there by morning.

The rains had subsided. Now a faint, frozen drizzle fell upon the roads. The ground grew harder, and as the night wore on, the roads themselves began to freeze. From time to time the wheels of the coach slipped, and as the roads froze further, the ruts, which had worsened with the hard rains, became sharp, unyielding ridges that sent startling shocks through the coach each time the wheels hit them. These constant jarrings made it difficult to rest; Caleb, his father, and Josiah Strong dozed fitfully, slumped on the bench that ran along the front of the coach. Along the back bench, Miss Telleridge sat quietly knitting, while Reverend Stark variously read in a thick, dark book or peered out the window into the darkness. The judge sat with eyes closed, randomly tapping his cane on the floor of the coach as they rode along.

Around two o'clock in the morning the coach hit a particularly hard bump, followed by a ripping noise and a loud thump. The passenger cab suddenly slumped to one side and then struck something with a terrific bang. Josiah Strong was thrown onto the floor, and Daniel Jordan barely managed to brace himself on the middle bench while holding his son firmly with his free hand. Miss Telleridge reached out to hold on to Reverend Stark, who braced his feet staunchly against the floor as the coach came to a lurching halt. The judge flailed about wildly with his cane; fortunately no one was struck by the stout wooden shaft.

In a moment the driver was at the door of the coach, which leaned sharply toward that side.

"I'm afraid we've lost one of the thoroughbraces," he said. He was a short, round man, with a friendly face and piercing blue eyes. His face was wet and his garments soaked.

"A thoroughbrace?" Miss Telleridge asked.

"That's the leather strap that runs between the coach's front and rear axles," the driver explained. "It's what holds up the passenger cabin. There's two of them, one on each side. We've lost the one on this side here, and the coach is sitting right on its axle."

"I see."

"We'll need to repair it, then," Josiah Strong adduced.

"Rightly said," the driver agreed, "and I could use some help."

"You've got it," Strong replied. "Mr. Jordan here is a blacksmith, by the way. I'm sure he'll be of great use."

"I'll be happy to help," Jordan said.

Caleb felt a surge of pride in his father. He knew that he

was strong and smart and could do many useful things, but it also made him feel good to see that others noticed as well.

The driver helped Miss Telleridge down from the coach, and then Caleb jumped out, followed by the men.

"The first thing we need to do," the driver said, "is to find a stout pole to replace this broke leather brace with. A good fence rail would do, but I don't know that we'll find one on this stretch. There's not a farm for miles from here."

The rain had cleared off, driven by a fresh wind that revealed a thicket of stars in the indigo sky. Off in the west a quarter moon descended toward the horizon. The road was surrounded by forest, and not far along its length the moonlight revealed a meadow. The men went up and down the road but found nothing that might serve as a temporary axle.

"Looks like we'll have to cut a tree," the driver said. He climbed onto the driver's box and lifted the seat. He pulled an ax from the box and grasped one of the lanterns which hung to either side. He came down from the coach and then and he, Josiah Strong, Daniel Jordan, and Caleb went off into the woods. Judge Vanderveeden stayed behind with Miss Telleridge.

The men soon returned to the coach carrying the trunk of a small ash tree which they had stripped of its branches before carrying it to the road. They laid it upon the roadbed and, using the ax, further shaped and sized it. Then, while Josiah Strong and Daniel Jordan held the passenger cabin up off the coach's axles, Reverend Stark helped the driver to position the pole where the thoroughbrace had been. The judge stood by and offered advice. Daniel Jordan helped the driver fix the pole to the axles with the iron axle braces, and when these two were satisfied with their work, everyone entered the coach. The driver stood at the door.

"If you folks don't mind, I think we'd best let her sit for a minute. That way we can see how she does with all the weight in the coach before we start pulling again. Meanwhile, I'll stand out here and have myself a pipe."

The driver closed the door. The men were wide awake again with their exertions, and Miss Telleridge had taken up her knitting. Josiah Strong was about to say something when he suddenly stopped, cocked his head to one side, and listened.

The others heard it too. Off in the distance, but not too far, a high-pitched, soulful cry reached their ears. Yipping and yapping, starting and stopping again . . .

"Is that a . . ." Miss Telleridge began.

"Yes," Josiah Strong answered, "it's a wolf."

Neither Miss Telleridge, nor Caleb and his father, nor Reverend Stark had ever heard the cry of a wolf. In the settled regions around Albany wolves had been hunted to extinction. But here in the western regions of New York State, where there was still much open country, wolves yet roamed, at least for a time.

"It's almost like music," Miss Telleridge said.

"I've often thought that myself," Josiah Strong agreed.

Another wolf joined in, and then another, so that their voices rose in an undulating chorus. Caleb felt a tingling in his spine. The sound of the wolves seemed familiar, though he was certain he had never heard it in his life. His father looked toward the dark night with wonder in his eyes.

"Is Mr. Partridge safe out there?" Miss Telleridge asked, worried about the driver, who still stood beside the coach smoking his pipe. "It sounds like they're not too far away."

"Oh, he's safe enough," Josiah Strong said, "unless there be some highway robbers on the road tonight. Wolves rarely go out of their way to attack people. In fact, they usually go to great lengths to avoid us. That doesn't mean I'd go wandering alone into the forest at night. Least ways, not without a good stout piece, and plenty of powder."

Reverend Stark held in his lap the book he had been reading. "One can almost detect in their howling a sort of . . . yearning," he said, "a yearning not unlike that of the human soul." He pulled back the window curtain and looked off into the night.

"My good Reverend," Judge Jones said, sounding irritated, "what silliness! That yearning is nothing more than a yearning to sink their voracious jaws around some warm flesh—including yours or mine, if they had the chance. There was a time when we had wolves in our settled regions. But our forebears, in their infinite wisdom, exerted themselves greatly to rid themselves of the vicious beasts. The wolf is a deadly predator, whose very nature is incompatible with human civilization. Indeed, we have bounties on the animal in every part of our fair state. They give twenty silver dollars for every breeding female, ten dollars for males, and five dollars for a pup. As our civilization advances westward beyond the Appalachians, and even to the farthest ends of this continent, we'll happily continue to eradicate the raving savages, until the entire country is safe for man."

"Safe for his cattle and sheep, don't you mean, Your Honor?" said Josiah Strong. "After all, attacks of the wolf upon man are exceedingly rare, are they not? And in exterminating the wolf, isn't it chiefly our herds of cattle and sheep that we are protecting?"

"That may be," said the Judge. "But doesn't the cattleman or the shepherd have a right to protect his animals? The problem with the wolf is that it knows no law. Human civilization can only exist where there is law. The wolf will ever remain untamed. Therefore it cannot exist side by side with man."

"You may be right, Your Honor," Josiah Strong said. "But I have spent a great deal of time among the Indians of the Great Lakes. And I can tell you, from experience, that the People of the Three Fires live in the forests among the wolf and have felt no need to exterminate the animal from their midst. In fact, they hold the beast in the highest reverence. For they see, in the wolf, many noble qualities which they admire."

"If cunning and viciousness are noble qualities, so be it. But what you say merely proves my point, does it not? For the Indians themselves are not civilized and live much like the wolf, moving about in the forest, hunting their prey. When they are not warring upon one another, they waste their time with heathenish rites in which they dance about and howl at the moon. They, just like the wolf, are being cast aside before the advance of civilization. Mark my words, they will continue to be dispossessed until they either learn to live like civilized human beings or are driven to extinction."

"I won't be surprised if they are driven to extinction," Josiah Strong remarked. "But I suspect we might miss them when they are gone—wolf and Indian both. They may not be civilized in the way we are, but they do have their laws, laws which they must follow as surely as we must obey our own. There are laws of nature, and in the case of the Indian, laws of the human heart. I would argue that should the time come when we have eradicated every trace of wildness from our world, when we have tamed everything to our satisfaction, we will find ourselves to be very unhappy creatures."

"Fiddlesticks," Judge Vanderveeden began to say when the door of the coach opened.

"We'll be on our way presently," the driver said. "Everything seems to be sound with the rig. It's going to be a bit bumpier, though, with the wooden pole instead of the leather strap, especially with this frozen washboard of a road. Just hold on to your seats and pray that we get through without any more breakdowns."

The passengers thanked the coachman and he closed the door. The sound of the horses' hooves on the road was heard again as the coach began its forward motion, thwacking painfully upon each hard ridge in the road. It was all the passengers could do to hold their places on their seats, enduring the constant shocks, and conversation ceased altogether. So passed the remainder of the night. Just after dawn, Caleb heard six strong blasts on the driver's horn, and the coach pulled up before the Golden Turkey Tavern.

The passengers descended and went in, where they were seated to a breakfast that consisted of meats and fowl, buckwheat cakes, and preserved fruits. After their cold night on the road Caleb and his father ate heartily, as did the others. When they had finished breakfast they were called again to the coach, whose thorougbrace had been replaced while they ate. The day was dry and sunny, somewhat warmer than the previous one, and Caleb spent most of it riding upon the driver's box. In the sun he could make out, on some of the trees, small buds glistening with the last night's rain.

Spring was coming.

Midway through the afternoon the coach approached the little village of Oneida Castle. Caleb was inside the passenger compartment with the others. The judge had been left at his destination, but Miss Telleridge and Reverend Stark still continued on with Josiah Strong, Caleb, and Daniel Jordan. At one of the stopovers three young men had boarded the coach together, men in long coats and top hats who said they were on their way to a wedding. As the afternoon was mild for the season, the leather curtains that covered the windows in foul weather had been pulled back to allow in sunshine and fresh air. This afforded the passengers a view of the greening countryside.

The road was badly rutted here, and the coachman was constrained at some places to move at a crawl. Along one of these stretches, with the coach barely moving, they approached three people, two men and a woman, by the side of the road. Caleb noticed that their skin was darker than his, their thick hair long, black, and straight. Their faces looked like those of the Indians in his picture books, but otherwise they did not resemble the hunters and warriors he admired. In place of deerskin robes and headdresses, for one thing, they wore regular clothing. And they seemed dirty, Caleb thought, their clothes torn and ragged. What's more, the way they walked was not tall and strong, as Caleb had pictured them in his mind, but slouching and weak, almost stumbling. As the coach came upon them, they held out their hands and called to the passengers. Caleb couldn't make out what they were saying.

"Why, they look drunk," Miss Telleridge said suddenly. "Who are they, and where are they from?"

"They're Mohawks," Josiah Strong replied. "The remnants of that once-flourishing people live nearby in the village of Oneida Castle. And I'm afraid you're right, they are drunk. Their people were once powerful and respected in these parts, where their villages and gardens dotted the forests all around. In the French and Indian War, an alliance with their warriors was sought by both sides, and their support was crucial to the success of the British. During the Revolution, their assistance to us Americans turned the tide in our favor. But now their lands have been taken away, and they can no longer hunt the forests. Many have died from disease. With their former way of life destroyed, some have lost their way, I'm afraid, to alcohol addiction. They are a people who are drifting without direction. Even, some say, without hope."

"God help them," Reverend Stark said.

"What are they saying?" Miss Telleridge asked. "What do they want?"

"Why, they're begging," one of the top-hatted young men said. "Listen!"

Everyone in the coach was quiet as they peered through the coach windows at the figures on the road. To Caleb, they looked sad and weary. He strained to hear their words. One of the top-hatted men spoke again.

"Why, *whiskey*, that's what they're saying. They want whiskey! My God, you'd think they'd had enough of that, by the looks of them." The man and his companions laughed heartily.

The coach lumbered on slowly, the passengers gazing silently upon the walking figures as if they were ghosts. Reaching around his shoulders and placing a hand on the side of his face, Daniel Jordan prevented Caleb from watching the Indians any longer.

"Tell me, Mr. Strong," Miss Telleridge said, "are all of the Indians like this? You know many of them, I suppose."

"Of course not," Strong answered. "The people you see here are broken. Their ancient ways, through which they had always survived, have been stripped away. The forests in which they hunted and planted their gardens have been taken over by settlers. Sadly, but understandably, many of them have given up. Now, the People of the Three Fires— the Ojibway of the Great Lakes—among whom I have chiefly spent my time, present quite a different picture. Their men are strong and agile, their women sturdy and sober-minded. They still live by the old ways, hunting and trapping, fishing in the lakes and streams. They need not beg from others. In fact, they are apt to share their provisions with any stranger who happens among them. At least that has been my experience."

With the badly rutted section of road behind them, and the coach moving along at a better pace, the drunken Indians receded away into the distance. Josiah Strong took one last look back at them and then turned again to Miss Telleridge.

"Settlers are coming into the Michigan country now, just as they came before to the Ohio Country, and just as they have come into western New York. I fear that as our people flood into Michigan to take the forests from the Indians, the People of the Three Fires will be weakened, as have these unfortunate souls. Perhaps even destroyed . . ."

"I see." Miss Telleridge herself turned to glance at the distant figures on the road behind them. All was quiet again in the coach, punctuated only by the occasional laughter of the three wedding guests.

The coach rode on through the day, stopping at relays for changes of drivers and horses, until nightfall, when Caleb and his father and Josiah Strong settled into a tavern to dine and sleep. The wedding guests had left them during the afternoon, and Reverend Stark had reached the town where he was to take up his duties ministering at a newly built church. Only Miss Telleridge, of their original traveling companions, remained.

The next two days passed uneventfully while the coach descended over the broad watershed of Lake Ontario towards Buffalo at the edge of Lake Erie. When the coach pulled up to the tavern at that port town, the Jordans said their goodbyes to Miss Telleridge, who had accepted Josiah Strong's offer to escort her to the home of her sister.

"He's as sweet on her as a bear on a honeycomb," Daniel Jordan said to his son. Caleb laughed as they entered the tavern, followed by the coachman and another man pulling their large trunk behind him.

Chapter 10

A Journey at Sea

DANIEL AND CALEB JORDAN had been wise to take the overnight coach, for they arrived in Buffalo the very day before the steamship was to sail. They had their supper in the tavern and then walked about the little seaside town until after dark. Buffalo, New York, which by 1900 was to become one of the largest cities in America, was at the time of our story the home of a mere two thousand souls. Streets had been laid out along a perfect grid, but there were many more vacant lots than buildings. During the War of 1812 the British and their allies among the First Peoples had burned the entire place to the ground. They left only one building standing, the home of a poor widow who had pleaded with the British commander to spare her home.

Now the town was rebuilding, and its inhabitants were filled with excitement. In every shop Caleb and his father entered, and at the tavern, there was talk of the great things that would come to Buffalo when Governor Clinton's "ditch"—which is what the people called the Erie Canal—was completed. It had been decided that the canal's terminus (that is, its end) was to be at Buffalo. This would mean that huge shipments of farm produce from the faraway west, grains and meats to feed the people of the large cities of the East Coast, after being ferried across Lake Erie on merchant ships, would be arriving at Buffalo's wharfs. There they would be loaded onto canal boats heading east. Packaging plants, ship-yards, mills, stevedore companies, shipping lines, banks: the citizens of little Buffalo were certain that all of these things would come to their town with the canal, bringing jobs and prosperity.

Caleb and his father walked down to the wharf and looked out over the vastness of Lake Erie. It was as big as an ocean, or so it seemed. As far as they could see there was nothing but water, all the way to the distant horizon. Caleb had spent many hours watching the ships loading and unloading at Albany's docks, or sailing off into the wide Hudson River, but he had never seen so much water in all his life. Small waves blew across the lake's surface, and near the shore boats rocked in the current. Further out, standing offshore, was the steamboat *Superior*, the ship that Caleb and his father were to board the next morning for the Michigan territory. Though the light was growing dim, they could make out the big paddle wheels that jutted from the ship's middle on both sides, a tall smokestack, and two masts silhouetted against the sky. A few lights sparkled from inside the ship's cabins.

In the morning the Jordans, along with Josiah Strong, made their way down to the wharf again. They were accompanied by a cartman they had hired to haul their baggage. There was a crowd at the harbor, a few dozen people who all waited, like them, to board the *Superior*, which now sat at the dock. Though the day was brisk it was sunny, and Caleb could now examine the ship more carefully than he had been able to do the evening before. Sunlight glinted off its metal fittings, and its bright white smokestack stood out against the clear, blue sky. The ship's hull was made of wood and was about as long, Caleb calculated, as his family's church in Albany, but not half so wide. The slender vessel, with its two high masts and elegantly up-curved prow, was built much like the ships Caleb was used to seeing at the docks of his home town. The main difference was that tall smokestack behind the aft mast, along with the big paddle wheel boxes jutting out from the ship's middle. Unlike the sailing ships that carried trading goods to and from Albany, the *Superior* was powered by steam, steam created by heating water in the ship's big metal boiler. That steam was routed through pipes to the paddle wheels, making them turn and propelling the ship through the water. Steamships were a new invention in Caleb Jordan's time, and the *Superior* was only the second such ship to ply the waters of Lake Erie. Though the vessel was designed to travel chiefly by steam power, when the winds were favorable the captain could also unfurl square-rigged sails for additional speed.

Among the people waiting to board the steamer were a few matronly women in flouncy dresses, a couple of men in military uniforms, others in broadcoats, young couples with small children (who reminded Caleb of his own family when his mother and Emily were still alive), and a man dressed like a preacher. They all stood amid piles of crates and trunks and duffel bags and suitcases. Before long men in work clothes began to circulate among the passengers, marking and hauling away the baggage. They loaded it onto the *Superior*, and then the passengers were allowed to board the ship up a slanted gangway.

The fancy-dressed folks were called by name and shown to their cabins by the ship's mates. Josiah Strong was among them. Next all of the plain-dressed people, including Caleb and his father, were led below the deck to an area of the ship called "steerage." Here they were all crowded together, with no rooms of their own, and nothing to sit or lie down upon other than their own baggage. Caleb and his father found their things amid the pile of luggage that had been carried down by the ship's mates, and they gathered it together near one side of the room. They then said hello to their neighbors and climbed back up the steep, narrow steps to the ship's deck.

The last of the ship's passengers were now on board. The ship had pulled away from the dock and was beginning to maneuver its way through Buffalo's harbor and into Lake Erie. Many of the other passengers had also come up to the deck to see the land fade away as the ship steamed out to sea. There were choppy waves on the water, and they slapped against the hull of the ship. The big paddle wheels turned, and the smokestack belched out dense black clouds that floated over the stern as the ship picked up speed.

Caleb and his father encountered Josiah Strong near the prow. A crowd had gathered there to watch one of the ship's mates fire a small cannon; this was how the ship said good-bye to the people of Buffalo as it left port. Holding the burning brand with which he would light the artillery piece, the mate turned to tell the women passengers to hold their ears. These did as he suggested, while the men stood proudly with their hands at their sides, not wishing to appear afraid of anything so small as the blast of a cannon. Now the mate touched the brand to the fuse, the cannon exploded with a terrific bang, and everyone on the deck gave up a loud cheer. This they heard echoed from people at the docks, some of whom waved to the ship's passengers.

The passengers began to circulate freely now. Many went below deck to escape the cold wind that whisked across the waters of the lake, for only weeks before the harbor had been encrusted with ice. Caleb amused himself examining the cannon, and then he leaned over the rail to get a better look at the paddle wheel as it chugged through the choppy waters. While he was doing this, Josiah Strong approached his father and engaged him in conversation.

"Caleb," he heard his father call, "don't lean so far over that rail! You'll end up in the lake as sure as I'm standing here. You'd be frozen solid before we could get you out. Besides, come over here. I've got some news for you."

Caleb reluctantly pulled himself away from the rail and came over to where his father stood with Josiah Strong. He looked up at them both, wondering what news his father might be talking about.

"Mr. Strong has arranged for us to make the passage afore-ship, with a private cabin of our own," his father said. "I told him that we would be fine with all the other plain people, but . . ."

"There's no point in that," Strong put in. "The governor told me to make sure you were well taken care of. Besides, we've come this far together, and I think it only right that we share the rest of the journey. Meals are much better in the cabin class, and you'll be more comfortable. You'll sleep better, too."

"If you're sure it won't be any trouble," Caleb's father said.

"No trouble at all, like I told you. How about you, my friend," Strong said, looking down at Caleb, "what do you think about it?"

Caleb thought it was grand, he said. He was growing to like Josiah Strong more every day.

"I suppose we should bring our things up to the cabin," Daniel Jordan said.

"No need for that," Strong replied, "the ship's mates will take care of it. They'll be putting out dinner soon. I'll show you your quarters, and then we can eat."

Caleb followed his father and Josiah Strong back below deck, but this time they went toward the front of the ship, instead of toward the stern where the steerage passengers were crowded together. They walked down a short, narrow hallway, opened a door, and entered a small room. It was furnished like a parlor. Several men sat about the room puffing on pipes. "This is the smoking room," Strong told them.

Passing through the smoking room and out a door on its opposite end, they came to a dining room occupied by three stout tables running its entire length; ship's crew rushed about setting tables for the coming meal. Our travelers crossed the room and passed through another doorway into a further hallway. Along this hallway were doors to private cabins. Strong showed Caleb and his father theirs. There were two narrow bunks, with a slender space between them.

"I'm right over here," Strong said, "across the hall. And now, to dinner!"

Caleb and his father followed Strong back to the dining room and took seats at one of the tables. Other passengers were entering and taking seats as well. It was just before one o'clock. In those days, most people ate their largest meal right in the middle of the day, and they called it dinner. Ship's mates were placing dishes on the tables. Fish and fowl, meats and vegetables, beans of various kinds, and lots of good, brown bread were laid out. Soon passengers had occupied most of the tables in the room.

At one precisely the ship's captain, Captain Rogers, entered the room and approached one of the tables. He stood behind his chair and welcomed everyone aboard the ship. He told them that their passage to Detroit would take three days, more or less, and he told them also when the *Superior* would touch port at Erie, Pennsylvania, and at Cleveland and Sandusky, Ohio, along the way. "We've just passed Point Abino"—the captain cleared his throat loudly—"and are well underway. Conditions are clear, and I think we can expect an uneventful passage." He said that he would do everything possible to ensure his passengers' comfort and safety during the voyage, and he urged them to come to him if they experienced any difficulties during the trip. Finally he asked everyone to bow their heads, pronounced a blessing over the meal, and seated himself.

Not far from where Caleb sat with his father and Josiah Strong, a woman in a long white dress suddenly spoke to the man beside her. "Point Abino," she said in an anxious near-whisper, "that's where it all started!"

The man beside her, who appeared to be her husband, patted her hand.

"What a horrid night!" she exclaimed.

"Madam, were you on the *Walk in the Water*?," another passenger, who sat nearby, asked.

"Yes, I'm afraid we were," the man who appeared to be the lady's husband said soberly.

"I read the accounts in the newspapers," the other passenger said. "It must have been absolutely terrifying for all of you."

"Naturally," the husband replied.

"Fortunately," the woman who had first spoken said, "we had Captain Rogers—this very same man—at the helm. He saved us all with his cool-headedness."

"That's what I have heard," Josiah Strong now remarked, joining their conversation. "I understand that the ship we ride on today carries that fated vessel's very same engine."

"Yes," the woman's husband said, "they were indeed able to save the engine. It and the boiler were virtually undamaged, I hear. But that was all they were able to salvage from the wreckage."

"It was at this very place on the lake," his wife took up again now, a little breathlessly, "that the wind began to blow such a gale. Captain Rogers struggled to get us behind the Point, but the wind came on so strong that he couldn't make any headway. It was so dark, and the rain came down in pouring streams! To make matters worse, the boat had begun to leak quite badly . . ."

The lady's husband patted her hand again. "The captain finally put about," he said, taking up the tale, "and made for Buffalo again. About eight o'clock in the evening, I believe it was. The sailing master, a Mr. Miller, wanted to run the ship up into the river and anchor, but the captain feared she might strike the pier in the darkness. If that were to happen, the captain said, no power on earth would be able to save a soul on board."

"Such a prudent man, Captain Rogers," the woman said. "He brought us within a few miles of the pier, but the night was so thick with rain and fog, we couldn't even make out the lighthouse. They dropped the anchors, one with a chain and two with hempen cables. But still the ship plunged wildly against her moorings. You should have seen it! Meanwhile the leak grew worse by the hour, and all the power of the engine was applied to the pumps . . ."

The husband looked around the table at his auditeurs. "Unfortunately," he sighed, "the *Walk-in-the-Water's* pumps weren't adequate to the task. The water just kept gaining on us, and it was my opinion that, unless we could somehow get to shore, the ship was going to capsize and founder."

"The suspense was terrible," the woman said. "We could hear the boat dragging at its anchors, and water was starting to seep in under the doorways of the cabins. It was the impression of the greater number of those on board that none of us would live to see the morning."

"Now, now," the husband said, turning to his wife. "You'll get yourself upset all over again." He took her hand and gently squeezed it.

"But it's true," she said. She scanned the eyes of her listeners around the table. "As I said before, had it not been for Captain Rogers, we all surely would have perished!"

The woman then took up her knife and fork and began to eat her dinner, as did her husband. But those who had been listening to their tale had ceased eating and stared up at them, waiting for their story to continue. As these two seemed oblivious to the others' stares, Josiah Strong finally said, after loudly clearing his throat, "I'm sure we are all curious to hear how your adventure ended that stormy night. That is, if you don't mind telling it."

The other passengers nodded their agreement.

The husband put down his fork and wiped his mouth with his napkin. "If you wish," he said soberly. He glanced at his wife before turning again to the others. "As my wife just told you, the Captain anchored the ship as near to shore as he thought prudent. He wanted to wait until daylight, when he would be able to see where he was going, before bringing her into the docks. The problem was, as I already mentioned, the pumps were not adequate to expel the water that was seeping rapidly into the ship's hold, and we were in danger of sinking. The Captain knew—from the sound of the breakers, I imagine—that we were very near to the shore. As the boat was taking on more water with each passing minute, he finally decided that our only hope was to cut the anchor lines and allow the boat to be pushed onto the coast by the current."

Josiah Strong spoke. "But wasn't he afraid the ship might crash into the piers, or break up against the rocks?"

"Indeed," the man said. "But it was either that or sit about doing nothing, waiting to sink to the bottom of the lake."

"I had taken the children into the cabin," the woman came in again. "We were utterly exhausted, naturally, with our anxious waiting. My husband stayed on deck with most of the other men. How the ship's timbers creaked throughout that awful night! Then, about four o'clock in the morning, word was sent down that we should all come up to the deck. Once everyone was assembled there, the Captain explained that the *Walk-in-the-Water* was to be allowed to run against the shore. He told us, quite honestly, that it was altogether likely that none of us would survive the ordeal. We were shocked, of course! But we could see that there was no other choice, as the water was now ankle-deep in our cabins, and steadily rising."

The woman gazed down at her dinner for a moment, and then she continued.

"I have never known such anxious moments in my entire life. We passengers stood staring at one another, all with the most worried expressions—except," she added after a pause, "for a certain Mr. Thurston. I think I shall never forget him. When we were told to come on deck and prepare for the worst, I remember him saying, perfectly calmly, that he had absolute faith in the good Captain Rogers. He said that the captain had promised to land him in Cleveland, and that he had every confidence that he would do so. Then he proceeded to lie himself down on a settee in the smoking room, as calmly as you please, and fell soundly asleep!"

Here some of those listening to the story laughed, including the woman's husband, who now took the relay of the story.

"Yes," he said, "good old Mr. Thurston. The rest of the passengers, however, stood on the deck as the anchor lines were cut. The storm still raged terribly, and we could feel the ship drifting beneath us. Then, after a short interval, we could hear the waves breaking against the shore. It was only minutes after that that the ship ran aground . . ."

"I won't forget the sound of that hideous crash if I live to be one hundred!" his wife exclaimed, "—the sound of crockery shattering, the awful crunch of the ship's timbers breaking apart! Nor have I forgotten the frigid, bone-chilling waves that washed over the deck, drenching us all. Each time the ship was lifted by the swells, we were doused with the freezing water, until the vessel finally came to rest against the lake's sandy bottom."

"Happily," the husband now said, "all were safe, though we were not completely out of danger. The *Walk-in-the-Water* was resting in water up to her gunwales, and the surf crashed wildly around us, threatening to break the hull apart. But it was nearly dawn, and at daylight one of the sailors managed to row one of the ship's yawls through the breakers—wild as they were!—and tie a hawser to a tree. By holding onto this hawser, the mates were able to safely maneuver the yawl back and forth to shore, disembarking the ship's passengers a few at a time."

"Safely," the woman put in, "if not dryly . . ."

"Ah, yes," the husband said with a small laugh, "you would have to remind me!"

"When it came our turn to go ashore," the woman explained, "the Captain helped me down into the boat quite easily. However, when Lawrence proceeded to jump, a swell came up, the yawl suddenly lurched, and he ended up in the water, soaked to the bone . . ."

"A very—chilling—experience," her husband said. "But it was a minor inconvenience, considering how close we had all come to losing our lives."

"Very true," the lady agreed. "Fortunately, as it happened, we struck shore not more than a mile from the Buffalo lighthouse. The lightkeeper had kept a vigil throughout that stormy night, fearing there might be wrecks. He had a great fire blazing, and the people of the town all came down with blankets and victuals and did all they could to make us comfortable. Finally they took us to the Landon House hotel, where we all stayed until arrangements could be made to resume our various journeys."

"Did you ever make it to Detroit?" Josiah Strong asked.

"Oh yes," the man said, "though not without difficulty. But that is another story, and we've captured your attention long enough already, I'm sure." He now began to eat his dinner in earnest, as did those who had been listening to he and his wife's tale.

Caleb ate quickly. As soon as he was finished he ran up to the deck—with his father's permission, of course—to make sure that the weather was still clear, the ship not in any trouble. But when he emerged into open air all was blue skies, with a few bright clouds, seabirds and gulls, and the ship's paddles walking steadily through the waves, moving Caleb and his fellow passengers ever westward.

How did the remainder of Caleb's sea journey pass? There were days spent on deck watching the waves and sky and birds, or exploring every inch of the ship's quarters; nights sleeping in the rolling cabin; and stories of adventure told over the dining table. In those days, before the invention of television, radio and the Internet, people entertained one another with stories about their lives, about interesting things they had heard from others, and about the long ago.

At dinner on the second day Caleb and his father found themselves seated near a Dr. Seavers. He was a fine looking gentleman in a fine looking suit, with graying hair and thick sideburns, and an habitual expression that bespoke both curiosity and compassion. Josiah Strong asked him why he was traveling west. He explained that he had a sister who had emigrated with her family to the small outpost at Detroit, and that he was going there to visit them."I am also interested," the Doctor continued, "in looking into the condition of the Indians in that country, both as a medical man and as a man of science."

"In that I can help you, if you wish," Strong said. "I have the acquaintance of many of them."

"I would be obliged."

"Have you yet had the opportunity to know many of the country's original inhabitants?" Strong asked.

"My home is in Genosea," the Doctor said, "in western New York. That town is not far from Beard's Town, where many of the Seneca tribe have taken refuge. Over the years I have come to know many of the Seneca people, as my medical practice has called me from time to time to their community. Of late I have made the special acquaintance of a fascinating old woman who, though born of a white family, is now every bit as much Seneca as any born into their tribe."

"How is that?" asked the woman who had told the story of the wreck of the *Walk-in-the-Water* on the first day of the voyage.

"This lady," the Doctor replied, "a Mary Jemison by name

(or *Dehewamis*, as she is known among the Seneca), was captured from her home by a Shawnee raiding party when she was just a girl, and she has lived among the Indians ever since. I found her story so fascinating that I have persuaded her to relate it to me. I am writing it all down, and I intend to publish it in a small book."

"You don't say," the woman's husband said, his eyes alight with curiosity. "Please, tell us more."

"Certainly," the Doctor said after wiping his mouth and laying his napkin aside. "This took place, I should first make plain, in the days before the Revolution. Mary Jemison's family owned a farm, at that time, in the valley of the Susquehanna River, not far west of Philadelphia. Now mind, in those days, during the French and Indian War, that country was only sparsely settled, and those who had established farmsteads were in constant danger of attack. The Indians were greatly incensed about white settlers moving into their hunting territories, and the French, who claimed all that country for their own, were the Indians' allies."

"I suppose after the defeat of General Braddock's forces at Fort Pitt," Josiah Strong put in, "American settlers of that region had little protection from such attacks."

"That's precisely the size of it," the Doctor said, "—as my friend Mary's story will illustrate. It all started one spring morning, you see, when she and her family were going about their normal chores on the farm. Mary was inside the house with her mother and sisters, shucking corn, when suddenly they heard gunshots outside. Looking out the window Mary saw, first, one of the neighbors, who had been staying with them, lying dead on the ground. She then saw that a band of seven Shawnee Indians and four Frenchmen were raiding the farm. Mary watched the raiders take captive her father, who had been helving an ax. Then they entered the house and captured the women and the children."

The woman who had told the story of the shipwreck of the *Walk-in-the-Water* gasped loudly, and her husband took her by the hand.

"After gathering up all the food they could find," the

Doctor continued, "the raiders led Mary and her family off into the woods. They marched them quickly along the trail, lashing the children with a whip if they didn't move quickly enough . . ."

"How savage!" one of the women at the table exclaimed breathlessly.

"I'm afraid that's not the worst of it," said the Doctor. "Are you sure I should continue? I don't want to upset any of you ladies."

"I think we're quite capable of hearing the truth," the woman of the shipwreck said, "as awful as it might be." The other women nodded their assent.

"Well, then," the Doctor continued, "if you're certain . . ." He looked around the table, expecting an objection, but when none came he went on. "The second night on the trail, one of the Shawnee Indians came to Mary and replaced her shoes with Indian moccasins. He also gave moccasins to a young boy, one of Mary's neighbors, who had been captured at the farm. Now, in the ways of the Shawnee, this meant that these two would be kept—or adopted—by the Indians. Mary's mother, seeing that neither she nor any of the others had been given moccasins, came near to Mary and spoke to her privately. She said she feared they would soon be parted forever, and she told her never to forget her name, her English language, or her prayers. And the mother's intuition proved to be spot on, I'm afraid, because shortly after that conversation, Mary and the young boy—his name was Davy, I believe—were taken away from the others and guarded by one of the Indian braves. And in the morning, when these two resumed their journey with the Shawnees, Mary's mother, father and the rest of her family were gone."

One of the women gasped again.

"That's right," the Doctor said, "they had been killed. That second night, in fact, when the raiders made camp, Mary saw the Indians drying and preparing the scalps they had cut from the heads of her own family. She could even recognize each of her relatives from the color of their hair."

"How appalling!" one of the women said.

"My God," the shipwreck woman's husband put in, "appalling is too weak a word!"

"Fortunately," the Doctor went on, "that is the worst of it. About a week later Mary and the boy were taken to Fort Duquesne. Though they were forced to march through the snow with little food or water, they were not otherwise mistreated."

Josiah Strong turned to Caleb and explained. "Fort Duquesne, that's where the town of Pittsburgh is today," he said. "Back in those days, though, it was just a French outpost in the wilderness."

"That's correct," the Doctor seconded. "Now, once at Fort Duquesne, the little boy was turned over to the French. But Mary was given to two Indian women of the Seneca tribe. These women, Shining Star and Squirrel Woman by name, were sisters, and they took Mary with them to their village."

"Were they going to kill her?" one of the women asked anxiously.

"No, not at all," the Doctor replied. "You see, many of our Indian tribes share a peculiar custom. When one of their family dies—often a brave killed in battle—they will adopt a child to replace the lost family member. And it happened to be the case that these two sisters, Shining Star and Squirrel Woman, had a brother who had been killed in battle the year before. Mary, of course, was to be his replacement. So, when they all reached the Seneca village, the sisters first bathed her in the river, as was their custom when adopting a new member into the tribe. They then took away her American clothes and gave her a new suit of buckskin clothing, such as the Seneca Indians wore at that time . . .

"After Mary donned the buckskin, the sisters brought her to a wigwam in which many women of the village had gathered. All of these women had recently lost someone near and dear to them. And as Mary sat among them, they began to grieve and wail, along with Shining Star and Squirrel Woman, as if once again mourning the passing of their own beloved relatives. After some time, however, having expressed their grief in this manner, their faces took on expressions of happiness. They rose up and showered Mary with affectionate gestures, as if she were their departed relation returned from the land of the dead. From this time forward, Shining Star and Squirrel Woman treated Mary as if she were their own true sister, replacing the brother they had lost in the warfare of the previous season."

"Interesting," the husband of the shipwreck woman said. "I wonder if this custom is widespread among the Indians."

"It most definitely is," Josiah Strong put in. "I can tell you that it was a common custom among all of the Ohio Indians, as well as those living to the north of there, with whom I have had considerable dealings."

"Pray tell us," one of the other women said to the Doctor, "how did this . . . Mary . . . make out among the Indians?"

"If I might skip over certain . . . childhood adventures," said the Doctor, "in her seventeenth year Mary Jemison married a young brave of the Delaware band, with whom she had a son. She named this son Thomas, after her departed father. She later traveled with her new family to the seat of the Seneca people, near where she now lives. Her first husband had taken ill and died, and by and by she married one of the Seneca chiefs. These two had six children together. He is gone now, and Mary herself is quite old, but she has many grandchildren."

"Has she never yearned to return to the society of white people?" the shipwreck woman's husband asked.

"She tells me," said the Doctor, "that there were times when she considered returning to the society of whites. But she knew that her half-breed children would never be accepted by white society, and this decided her against any such notions. She continued among the Seneca, sharing their way of living, and no doubt will do so until she dies."

Those at the table grew quiet for a while, until someone else began to tell of some other adventure. Caleb's father slept soundly in their cabin that night, because he had grown used to the sound of the big paddle wheels walking through the water and the rolling of the ship. But Caleb did nothing but toss and turn, for whenever he closed his eyes he pictured little Mary Jemison being taken captive by Indians. He thought of her neighbor, the boy Davy, and he wondered what had become of him.

The next day the *Superior* stopped at Erie, a small Pennsylvania settlement on the southern shore of the lake of the same name. They took on some passengers there and dropped off several others. They then continued westward, and the ship reached Cleveland late in the day. There, once again, they boarded and disembarked passengers before continuing on their way toward Detroit.

In the afternoon of the following day they approached their last stop before they would reach Detroit, the little frontier settlement of Sandusky, Ohio. Caleb was on the deck, watching one of the ship's mates, a Mr. Wilson by name, go about his chores. Mr. Wilson, a free black man, had found Caleb snooping around the ship's boiler the day before. Caleb feared he would be in trouble, but instead of scolding him Mr. Wilson showed him where they put in the firewood—many cords every day—that boiled the water that made the steam that made the ship's paddles turn. Caleb liked watching the searing fire through the hatch when it was opened, and Mr. Wilson allowed him to remain there awhile.

Now Mr. Wilson was beginning to prepare the ship to dock at Sandusky and other passengers, including Caleb's father and Josiah Strong, were coming to the deck to watch the ship make landfall. The *Superior* had just entered Put-In-Bay. There the land enveloped the well-protected harbor in a wide semi-circle.

Mr. Wilson had come near to where Caleb was standing with his father and Josiah Strong, and Daniel Jordan spoke to him.

"Sir, could you please tell me, if you know, where it was that Commodore Perry defeated the British fleet?"

"I can tell you for certain," Mr. Wilson said, "because I was right there in the middle of it."

Commodore Perry was an American navy commander who fought against the British navy on Lake Erie during the War of 1812. Here at Sandusky, Commodore Perry captured

Britain's entire Great Lakes fleet of six ships. If he had failed to defeat the British on Lake Erie, the British would have been able to attack New York and Ohio, and those parts of the United States may have ended up being part of Canada today.

"You were with Perry at the Battle of Put-in-Bay, you say?" remarked one of the other men, many of whom, along with several women, had now gathered round.

"I most certainly was," Wilson replied, and he then turned to look out over the water. He pointed ahead, to the right of where the steamship was now heading. "Right out there," he said, "that's where the main action happened."

"Which of Commodore Perry's ships were you on, if I might ask?" one of the women said.

"I was on the *Niagara*."

"You don't say, with Commodore Perry himself?" another of the bystanders remarked. They all drew closer to Mr. Wilson now, that they might not miss a word of his account.

"Absolutely," the mate said. Glancing at Caleb, he could see that he was confused, and he spoke to him directly. "The *Niagara* didn't start out being the Commodore's ship, but the Commodore ended up on it before the battle was over."

"Tell us about it!" one of the men said.

"I'd be happy to," Wilson replied, "but I can only take a minute, because we've got to get this ship ashore." He moved to the rail and gestured out toward the Lake. "The way it happened," he began, "the British fleet was stationed over there, on the other side of the Lake, over in Canada. Now, what was it they were doing over there, you might ask? Well, they were building more ships, so they could mount a big attack on our forces around this lake. But since Commodore Perry's fleet was here at Put-in-Bay, old Barclay—he was the commander of the British fleet—couldn't send any ships down the Lake for supplies. Perry had him blocked in, you see, and pretty soon Barclay and his men were running out of provisions. They had no food, no hardware for building ships, nothing. Finally old Barclay decided he would just sail over here and try and wipe us out."

"How many ships did you have?" Caleb asked.

"We had nine," Wilson said. "There was Commodore Perry's brig, the *Lawrence*. Then there was the *Niagara*—that was another brig. The rest were smaller gunboats . . ."

Several men nodded together.

"I'll never forget that morning," Wilson took up again. "It wasn't much after dawn the lookout spotted Barclay's fleet coming across the Lake. There were six ships in all, two big brigs and four smaller gunboats. Commodore Perry got all fired up. Yes sir, he was ready for battle! He ordered extra rations for the men so we could last out the day. He also ordered for sawdust to be spread on the decks, what for to soak up all the blood and such . . ."

Caleb winced at the thought of American sailors bleeding from wounds inflicted by the heavy cannons of the British ships.

"We sailed out of the Bay in our battle line," Wilson went on, "with Commodore Perry up front on the *Lawrence*. Now, it couldn't have been more than half an hour before the Commodore's ship closed with the British line and started to have it out with them. From where I was, back on the *Niagara* with Captain Elliot, we could see that the *Lawrence* was taking an awful pounding, all alone up there against three British ships. Some of the men wanted to sail ahead and help out, but Perry had ordered Captain Elliot to stay in line. And the Captain wasn't about to disobey the Commodore's orders."

"My God, man!" one of the men exclaimed, "hang the orders! When his friends were in a predicament like that, Elliott should have sailed ahead and helped out."

"That's what some say," Wilson responded, "but I could also see Captain Elliot's point of view. He had his orders, and he was obeying them. And I can tell you, from personal experience, the Commodore didn't take lightly to anybody disobeying his orders. In any case, before long the *Lawrence* was beat up so bad Commodore Perry had to abandon ship. He climbed down in one of the ship's boats with a few sailors and rowed straight toward where we were waiting in the *Niagara*. Never mind that all this time the British cannons were booming, their marksmen taking pot shots at him. When Perry finally reached our ship, he ordered Captain Elliott to go back down the line in one of the ship's boats and bring up the rest of the fleet. The Commodore himself took over command of the *Niagara*, and after giving us sailors a few shouts of encouragement, he steered us straight toward the British fleet!

"Those Brits were mighty surprised, let me tell you. After the pounding the *Lawrence* took, I guess anyone would have expected the Commodore to give up the fight. But instead, good old Perry put the *Niagara* right in the middle of their ships and, without so much as a how d'ya do, opened up with broadsides in both directions."

The passengers who surrounded Mr. Wilson, grown tense and animated now, vocally cheered on their American fleet.

"Pretty soon all the top British officers were dead or wounded," Wilson went on gravely. "Some of their lieutenants stepped in to take command, but they got their ships so tangled up they couldn't maneuver properly. Couldn't even defend themselves. And on top of the shellacking we were giving them from the *Niagara*, our other ships had come up to the line, and they were also starting to let loose.

"It didn't take those Brits long to see that the fight was up. They had no choice but to lower their flag and surrender."

"Here, here!" those listening to Mr. Wilson cheered in patriotism.

"There was an awful lot of misery on those ships," Wilson said, shaking his head, "I can tell you that. Theirs, and ours too, with all the dead and wounded. But if you'll excuse me now, I've got to get back to my duties . . ."

With that Wilson moved away to continue preparing the ship to dock at Sandusky. The vessel was steaming its way through Put-in-Bay, heading toward the docks, and all was calm and quiet. But in Caleb's mind the terrible explosions of naval bombardments echoed. He could almost see the masts crashing down, the sailors loading and firing the big cannons or rushing about the ship hoisting and lowering sails. Their clothes were torn and tattered, many were wounded, and others lay dead or dying on the decks.

Chapter 11
Into the Michigan Territory

AFTER disembarking some passengers at Sandusky, and taking on a few others and some freight, the *Superior* made its way back through Put-in-Bay and out into Lake Erie. Her passengers were near the end of their sea journey, for Detroit lay just across the Lake to the north.

In those days, not long after the Revolution—and not long after General Wayne had defeated the First Peoples of the Ohio Country; and General Harrison had chased Tecumseh and his warriors into Canada—Detroit was the farthest limit of American civilization on the North American continent. It was situated, as it is today, in the southeastern corner of the Michigan territory. Beyond it, stretching far and away into the north and west, the remainder of Michigan, and all of America, was a land of scattered Indian villages amid untamed wilderness.

For two hundred years Frenchmen from Canada, then the British and now Americans, had come to the Michigan woods to trade with Michigan's First People—the Ojibway—for furs. But aside from a few trading posts scattered far and wide, and a couple of forts, the Michigan territory bore few traces of the Europeans' presence. All was unbroken forest, intercut with streams and rivers and surrounded by the mighty Great Lakes. There were no towns beyond Detroit, only the small and scattered camps of the People of the Three Fires. Nor were there any roads. The fur traders who traveled through the Michigan country walked—or rode on horseback—along the same paths the Ojibway had long used, or traveled over lakes and rivers in birch bark canoes they had learned to build from the First Peoples. A man could travel for many days through that territory without seeing another human soul.

This was the land to which Caleb Jordan and his father had now come. As the steamship *Superior* approached the mouth of the Detroit River, four miles wide, its noisy paddle wheels broke the silence of the surrounding forests. The steamer entered the river after making its way around the islands that lay about its delta. On the right bank lay Canada, on the left the Michigan Territory. Most of the passengers had come to the deck. When the ship passed Fort Malden on the Canadian bank, Mr. Wilson pointed out that it was from here that the British fleet under Commander Barclay had embarked to engage Commodore Perry's fleet at Put-in-Bay. From the battlements at each corner of the fort the Union Jack, the British flag, flapped briskly in the wind. Off the ship's starboard stern an Indian canoe tracked the vessel's progress.

Soon the wharves at the foot of Detroit came into view. The town stretched back up the hillside from the river for a few hundred yards. From where Caleb stood on the *Superior's* deck a church's steeple could be seen, and behind the town, the watchtowers of Fort Detroit.

The ship docked, with mates rushing about fastening lines, and the passengers disembarked. Josiah Strong hired a cart. He showed Caleb and his father to a tavern where they would stay for a couple of days before commencing their journey into deep Michigan country.

The cartman carried the Jordans' things into the tavern. Josiah Strong followed with Caleb and his father. He paid the cartman and then approached the counter that stood across the far end of the foyer. He told the tavern keeper about Caleb and his father, and he told him that the United States government would be paying for their stay. "I've got some business to attend to now," Strong said when he returned to Caleb and his father. "I'll be back this evening. Then we'll see about getting you up to the fort at Saginaw. You'll be staying there at first, until they can get you a cabin built."

The Jordans bid Strong goodbye and the tavern keeper showed them to the room where they would be sleeping. Afterwards they went out to see the sights of Detroit.

It was a bright, cold, and sunny day. The streets of the little town, still covered in snow from the frosty northern winter, were crowded with an assortment of people such as Caleb had never seen. There were army officers looking proud in their uniforms, and fur traders in buckskin clothing whose scraggly beards and flowing hair bore witness to the long winter months they had spent in the forests trading with the Ojibway people for furs. There were also the First Peoples themselves, come to Detroit to sell the pelts they had taken during their winter trapping season. Dressed in buckskin or broadcloth clothing, sometimes wrapped in a blanket or adorned with feathered headdresses, they strode along the streets singly or in groups.

Caleb stared in wide-eyed wonder. It was as if his toy figures had come to life!

And how many languages Caleb heard spoken! First there was English with every imaginable accent, from American to Canadian to British, Scots and Irish. There were also many French speakers, for France had once owned the site of Detroit and many French families still lived in the town. Finally there were the languages of the First Peoples, which sounded even stranger to Caleb's ears than the guttural and nasal syllables of the French Canadians.

Amid this swarm of people, enveloped in a symphony of languages, Caleb and his father wandered the streets of the town. Climbing toward the battlements of the fort, they passed the jail and the Catholic church whose tall steeple they had seen from aboard the ship. The main street led to huge gates, for a high palisade fence enclosed the town. Detroit had been attacked by the British and their First Peoples allies during the War of 1812, and the townspeople still did not feel safe. Lastly Caleb and Daniel Jordan made their way down to the river to watch the ships sitting at the docks, or moving off into the current carrying their cargoes.

As they made their way back to the tavern Caleb and

Daniel Jordan witnessed an unusual site. Gruff soldiers escorted groups of First Peoples along the streets. Some of the Indians went quietly, but others complained angrily. Caleb and his father followed one such group along the main street until they watched the soldiers see the First Peoples out of the town's gate. It was growing dark; Caleb and his father went back to the tavern. When they arrived there, Daniel Jordan asked the tavern keeper about what they had witnessed.

"Ain't no Indians allowed in the town after dark," the tavern keeper said. "The problem is, we can't trust 'em. Who can say when they'll take to the warpath again? They can only stay overnight if they're put up at a private home, where somebody can make sure they keep out of trouble."

The Jordans went up to their room, where they left their heavy coats, and then they returned downstairs to eat in the tavern's dining parlor. There was a blazing fire in a stone hearth along one wall, from which the room received most of its light. Opposite that, traders and soldiers stood drinking whiskey and beer at a bar. Crowded into the center of the room were rough wooden tables of thick oak with heavy chairs. About half of these were occupied. Daniel and Caleb Jordan entered the room and took a seat at one of them.

A woman approached them and took their orders for supper. While they were waiting for their food, Caleb heard two men talking in subdued tones at the next table. He cocked his head slightly so that he might see them. They were rough looking men, bundled in tattered clothing that was none too clean. They drank beer, and several empty glasses sat scattered across their table. Caleb's father noticed him looking at the men and gave him a look that Caleb knew meant to stop staring. Caleb turned his head, but his curiosity was only increased, and he listened intently to see if he could hear what the men were talking about.

"A wolf's a wolf, as far as I'm concerned," one of them said. "What's the difference if it's a Michigan wolf or a Ohio wolf? They're giving a bounty of five good American dollars for every grown wolf killed, and three dollars for pups. All we got to do is deliver the hides to Cleveland. It's simple as that."

"Are you sure they ain't some way they can know we didn't get the wolfs in Ohio? Cause we just got out of jail for stealing that cow and I don't want to get back in there just yet if I can help it. I suppose if the Ohio folks are giving a bounty to capture wolfs, it's for wolfs that's in Ohio, not wolfs that's in Michigan."

"Numbskull! How are they going to know if it's a Michigan wolf or a Ohio wolf? What, do you think they got their territory painted across their furs or something? A wolf's a wolf. Listen, the way I see it, the pickings is better up here. All them woods out there, hardly touched by man. Except the Indians, but they don't count for men, cause they're nothing but animals!" The man began to laugh but choked on his beer and had to cough loudly to clear his throat. When he finished coughing he continued. "Now listen, Homer, don't be some kind of dern chicken. Ain't nothing going to happen to us. Those woods out there are full of wolfs at five dollars a pop. We don't have to tell them people at Cleveland where they come from. If anybody asks any questions, just let me do the talking."

Caleb's father noticed that he was eavesdropping and so he began to speak to him about their journey, about the people they had seen around the town that day, and about the odd objects that hung from the walls of the tavern's dining room. There were animals' heads, old pots and pans, pieces of crockery, and derelict farm tools.

Before long the serving woman came with their food and they began to eat. While they were eating there was a commotion at the bar, and both Caleb and his father looked up to see what was happening. A group of men, many of them soldiers, stood in a circle. They lifted their beer glasses as they raised a toast to a man who stood in their midst. The man they celebrated was dressed in a working man's clothing, and his thinning hair reached to his shoulders. On closer inspection it could be seen that one of his legs was missing below the knee; a wooden post was now its substitute.

"Hear, hear, everyone," one of the soldiers announced

loudly as he raised his glass. "Let's hear it for Mr. Dougherty. He was with General Harrison at the battle of Tippecanoe!"

The men at the bar separated so that the one-legged man, Mr. Dougherty, could be seen by the rest of the dining room's occupants. They raised another cheer. Mr. Dougherty, for his part, looked abashed at the attention he was receiving. He smiled weakly, lifted his glass uncertainly, and joined the toast.

There were further bravos and cheers from many of the diners, and then someone called out, "Tell us about it, sir, if you'd be so kind."

Mr. Dougherty turned with difficulty. "It ain't exactly no easy thing to tell," he croaked out hoarsely.

"That's all right, we've got all the time in the world," the man who had called out said. "Won't you sit down, make yourself comfortable?"

The man stood up, pulled away a chair from his table, and offered it to Mr. Dougherty. With some encouragement from the soldiers at the bar Dougherty made the few steps to the man's table, which was not far from where Caleb sat with his father. The old soldier's wooden leg sharply rapped the floorboards with every step.

Dougherty dropped into the chair, allowing his wooden leg to stretch straight out before him. His face glowed red in the light from the fireplace, and he emitted a sigh as he spoke. "It was a close fought thing, I can tell you that much."

"You weren't with Captain Spencer's Yellow Jackets, were you?" someone called out.

"Oh, no, not I," Dougherty said. "Regular Indiana militia, I was. We was called out by General Harrison to go and see about those Indians; you know, that group that was threatening to go on the warpath. Tecumseh was roaming the country, trying to muster up as many allies as he could. He wanted to fight us settlers, drive us clear out of Indiana Territory! He and his brother, who they called the Prophet, had this big village they called Prophet Town. They was gathering up all their braves there, just waiting till they was strong enough to slaughter us."

"Bah!," one of the men Caleb had heard talking about wolves said. "Filthy Indians!"

"Now, back then," Dougherty went on, "there weren't many of us settlers down that way. And what there was of us pretty much stuck near the rivers, along the Wabash and Ohio. The rest of it was just woods and Indians, as far as you could travel. Except you wouldn't want to travel in that Indian country, seeing how they were so fired up to take our scalps . . ."

"Trash!" the wolf man put in.

"I was still unmarried then," Dougherty now said, looking slowly around at his listeners, "just helping out on my Daddy's farm. So, when General Harrison called for militiamen to fight the Indians, I went in and volunteered."

"What time of year was it?" one of the bystanders asked.

"It was early autumn time," old Dougherty replied. "The leaves was just changing when we rendy-vooed with General Harrison at Maria's Creek. I can still see it like it was yesterday. The General stood before us and told us that Tecumseh and his brother was up to no good at Prophet Town. He said that if we wanted to settle that territory without losing our scalps, we was going to have to go up there and teach them Indians a lesson."

Caleb heard men mumbling and murmuring around him, but he could not make out what they were saying.

"After we marched about two weeks," Dougherty took up again, "we stopped and put up a stockade fort we called Fort Harrison. The woods around there was full of Indians, you see, and a band of them had attacked some of our scouts. After that we couldn't go out in the woods to hunt, so the General put us on half rations. We like to starve, until they finally brought a boat up the Wabash with more supplies.

"Once we'd gotten a little food in us, and the men was back in shape, the General ordered us to march up to Prophet Town. We were one thousand men strong. Now, as we come near, the Prophet, they called him, sent one of his braves out under the white flag of truce. The brave said the Prophet wanted a ceasefire. He said the Prophet wanted to talk to

General Harrison the next day, and that maybe the two leaders could work things out between them."

"Bah!" the man of the wolves said again.

Dougherty glanced briefly in the man's direction before continuing. "Well, the General agreed to the ceasefire," he said, "but he wasn't rightly sure if he could trust them Indians. So that night he put sentries all around the camp to keep watch. As for the rest of us soldiers, he had us sleep in our full uniforms—and with our weapons at the ready."

The dining room grew very quiet. Everyone strained so as not to miss a single one of Dougherty's words.

"Old Harrison knew what he was about, too," Dougherty said, almost whispering now, "because before the sun was even up them Indians was on us. First we heard the war whoops, then the shots. By the time I got out of my sleeping roll they was in our camp. Captain Spencer's Yellow Jackets took the worst of it. Our militia company was right down the line from their position, and I could see how fierce it was over there. Some of the braves broke through our lines then, and if it hadn't been for Ensign Tipton's men, they would have overrun the whole camp.

"It went on like that—the fiercest fighting you ever saw—for more than two hours! Them charging in at us, us charging back at them. Rifles, muskets, bayonets and war-knives. Finally, about the time the sun was coming up, the Indians ran out of ammunition and started to fade off. They hadn't been able to take our camp, but they did us some horrible damage. More than fifty men were killed . . . and plenty more wounded."

"Didn't you destroy Prophet Town?" someone asked.

"Oh, yeah," Dougherty said, "we rightly did. We marched up there, after the battle, and we found the place plum deserted. All the Indians had left except for one old woman. We left her with an old chief we found on the battleground, and General Harrison ordered everything burned to the ground. Yep, we burned all their winter food stores, and everything to cook with, so they wouldn't be able to feed themselves. That way, the General figured, they'd have to leave the Territory and quit pestering us."

"How'd you wind up in these parts?" one of the soldiers at the bar asked.

"Oh, that," Dougherty said, glancing over at the man. "Well, as fate would have it, I guess you could say, come the next year there was more Indian trouble. We got in that little fight with the British—War of 1812, I think they call it. This time Tecumseh and his warriors were allied with the English. As you surely know, they captured this very town of Detroit. And just like before, General Harrison was ordered to come up here and clear them out. He put out the call for the militia again and, just like before, I answered it.

"We militiamen assembled in quick order and followed the General up here into Michigan Territory. We had some pretty rough skirmishes, but we managed to chase Tecumseh's warriors and the British right over into Canada. We followed 'em, fought 'em on the Thames River, and had a great victory. The British were beat so bad they didn't even think about trying to take Detroit again. And Tecumseh, the Indians' best leader, was killed. As for myself, I would have made out all right, except one of the braves' musket balls cracked up my knee so bad it couldn't be fixed. That's why I walk around on this post."

Old Dougherty lifted his peg leg off the floor so that everyone could see it.

"As you can imagine," he went on, "I was laid up here for some while with my bad leg. I took a liking to a little gal who was helping nurse me, and I guess one thing led to another, like they say. After I healed up, the little lady and me got married, took a homestead, and set up a little farm. It's right down along the river there." Dougherty pointed out the windows of the tavern.

Everyone was quiet in the room now for a moment, until the man of the wolves spoke in a voice that was both harsh and sloppy.

"It's like I always say, you can't trust a Indian no further than you can throw him."

At that point an imposing figure rose out of the shadows

in a far corner of the room. Everyone's eyes turned toward the man as he advanced toward the table where the man of the wolves sat. He was an Ojibway, dressed in buckskin trousers and a cotton shirt, with an eagle feather stuck in long black hair that was tied behind his head. As he stood before the men who had spoken of wolves, his features were highlighted by the reddish glow of the fire.

"You say that the Indian cannot be trusted," he said. "But who can trust the white man? Were we Indians not told that the land across the mountains was ours to hold forever? But your people broke that promise and settled in the Ohio Country. And when General Wayne made us sign the Treaty of Greenville, were we not told that we would keep all the lands beyond Ohio to the west? But General Harrison took away even more of our hunting territories, all the way to the Wabash! Now, because Tecumseh and his brother fought for the promises you yourselves made, you call him treacherous? And you say that the *Indian* cannot be trusted. Bah!"

At this the man who had spoken of wolves pushed back his chair and rose to confront the Ojibway.

"I say you lie," he growled, squinting up at the Ojibway man, who was nearly a foot taller than him. The Ojibway made no response, but gazed steadily into the other man's eyes.

"I say you are a liar," the man said again, "and you're going to have to take back your stinking Indian lies."

The Ojibway man glanced around the room, but no one moved nor made a sound. As he shifted his eyes back to the man of the wolves, he saw him remove a knife from a sheath he kept on his belt and begin to raise it. So quickly that it was just a blur to those who watched, the Ojibway wrested the knife from the man's hand and, in one swift movement, grazed it across the man's cheek and tossed it onto the ground.

The man of the wolves brought his hand to his face, feeling the bloody wound there. The Ojibway had not injured him badly, just enough to make a point. The man of the wolves made a movement toward the knife but the Ojibway stepped on his hand and pinned it to the ground.

The man of the wolves' companion rose from his chair now and was about to hit the Ojibway man over the head with a bottle. But before he could accomplish this, striding suddenly from the dining room's doorway Josiah Strong leapt upon him. He wrested the bottle from the man and threw it to the floor; the man staggered back and away. His companion spoke angrily, addressing the Ojibway warrior.

"I'll have the law on you for this, you dirty Indian," he said. "You ain't even supposed to be in town after nightfall."

"He's with me," Strong said. "He stays in town as my guest."

"And who are you?" The man screwed up his face strangely.

"I work for Governor Cass, and let me suggest that you and your friend get out of town before I have the law on you."

The man looked with pleading eyes around the room, and especially at the soldiers who stood at the bar, hoping that someone might come to his defense. But all in the room remained mute, and so grumbling, "someone's going to pay for this," the man straightened himself up, helped his companion from the floor, and they both left the tavern.

Josiah Strong brought the Ojibway man over to the table where Caleb sat with his father. "This is Standing Bear," he said. "I asked him to meet us here. May we sit with you awhile?"

"Of course," Danial Jordan said.

"I've been making inquiries about how to get you to the fort at Saginaw Bay," Strong said. "I was going to have you take the schooner, but the spring ice floes from Lake Huron have blocked the channel in the Saint Mary's River. It won't be clear for at least a couple of weeks. Standing Bear here can guide you to Saginaw over trails, if you don't mind. He knows the woods well, and he'll take good care of you."

Both Caleb and his father fixed their gaze on Standing Bear. Caleb's father was trying to determine if he was the kind of man who could be trusted to guide him and his son through one hundred miles of wilderness. Caleb, for his part, was astonished to be sitting at the same table with a real Indian. Josiah Strong must have noticed their stares, for he spoke up.

"You needn't worry about Standing Bear," he said. "I've known this man since he was a boy, and he is completely trustworthy. The reason I threatened to have the law on those two ruffians is because I knew that if they were involved in a quarrel with my friend here, it was not his fault."

Standing Bear neither spoke nor made any perceptible gesture.

Daniel looked in Standing Bear's eyes. "If you're a friend of Mr. Strong's," he said, "you're fine by me. When do we leave?"

"I see no reason why you can't start tomorrow," Strong said. "I know Standing Bear is ready, and I have already procured a packhorse for your things. You can pick it up at the fort." He then turned to Standing Bear. "Standing Bear, can you be here at first light tomorrow?"

Standing Bear nodded.

"Okay then," Strong said, "it's all set. I'll say my goodbyes now, because I'll be off again tomorrow on important business for the Governor. If you should need to contact me about anything, the commander at the Saginaw fort will know how to find me. He also has supplies for you, as well as your wages. Meanwhile, God speed, and I'm sure we will be seeing one another again." Strong rose from the table, as did Standing Bear.

Daniel Jordan also rose and shook Josiah Strong's hand; Caleb did as his father had done, and Strong and Standing Bear walked steadily out of the dining room together.

The next day at dawn Caleb and his father found Standing Bear waiting for them on the street in front of the tavern. They walked together to the fort on the rise behind the town, where Daniel Jordan spoke to the officer in charge. They were taken to the fort's stable, where a big bay horse, loaded with leather packs, stood waiting. Daniel signed a paper for the horse; and then he and Caleb and Standing Bear led the horse back to the tavern, where Daniel and Caleb brought their things down from their room and loaded them onto the horse's back.

When they had firmly lashed and tightened all of the Jordans' belongings on the bay, they proceeded toward the town's gates. When they arrived there, the soldier on guard opened the tall wooden door in the palisade, and Caleb and his companions led the horse through.

The road continued on for a little space beyond the gates. Toward the river Caleb could see the farmsteads of the old French settlers who huddled near the fort at Detroit. All around, in the open spaces, the sun gleamed off the remains of winter snows that still covered the ground. Before they had walked a mile they were in the woods. The road had ended now, and there were no longer farms, or any sign of human life around them, but only the primeval forest, towering beech and maple trees and also pine and fir, and the narrow footpath along which Caleb followed Standing Bear. His father led the big bay horse behind.

They walked along the trail throughout the day. In the morning their feet crunched on the light snow cover, but the footing grew slushy as the day warmed above freezing. The bay horse occasionally snorted, sending a big cloud of steam out its nostrils each time. Around noon they stopped to rest awhile, and to eat some of the food they had brought along for the journey.

When the sun began to sink through the trees Standing Bear stopped. He spoke to Daniel Jordan, telling him that they would make camp for the night. He led them off the trail to a nearby clearing and then he, and Daniel and Caleb, spread into the forest to collect wood for a fire.

The next two days passed much the same way, walking the old Ojibway trail deep through the Michigan woods toward Saginaw Bay, stopping at night to make camp. They passed few others on the trail: a couple of groups of Ojibway people, a fur trader traveling on his own, and a detachment of soldiers on their way to Detroit from the Saginaw fort. At each encounter they spoke with these trail companions, asking about the trail ahead. When they met Ojibway groups

Standing Bear spoke with them in their own language, and neither Caleb nor his father understood what they said to one another. Standing Bear did not feel the need to enlighten them after his friends moved on.

On their third day out from Detroit, when they were still some distance from the fort at Saginaw, they awoke to heavy snowfall. They collected their things and resumed their journey. Throughout the morning the flakes grew thicker and fell all the while faster. By the time they stopped at midday to rest and eat, the white stuff was piling up on the trail. They could barely see through the swirl of frozen crystals that filled the forest.

It was through the muffled silence of snow that, late in the afternoon, they heard gunshots off the trail. Standing Bear turned around and, without saying a word, gestured to Daniel Jordan that he was leaving the trail to investigate. He stepped off into the forest while Daniel and Caleb, and the big bay horse, waited behind.

Caleb and his father stood still and listened. For some time they heard nothing. Then there was another gunshot. They waited. Nothing. An hour went by, but Standing Bear did not return from the woods.

Daniel Jordan spoke to Caleb.

"Son," he said, "I had better go and look for Standing Bear."

"What happened?" Caleb asked.

"I don't know. But I'm afraid that something might be wrong with him. It's been near an hour now, and it will soon be dark. It's time for us to make camp. Maybe he shot a buck or something. He might need help hauling it back here, or skinning it.

"I need you to stay here with the horse, you hear?" Daniel continued. "And don't you move from this trail no matter what. I'll go looking for Standing Bear, and then I'll come right back to this spot."

For reasons he couldn't explain, Caleb felt uneasy. "What if you don't come back?" he asked.

"Of course I'm coming back. You just stay put like I told

you."

"But what if you get lost? What if we get separated?"

"Listen," Daniel said, and he took his son by the shoulders, "haven't I told you before? If we ever get separated, I'll come find you no matter where you are, or where I am. And no matter how long it takes. Don't you remember?"

"Yes," Caleb agreed, though he still felt uneasy.

"Well, then, just do like I'm telling you, and stay put until I get back."

Daniel Jordan pulled his rifle from its holster on the horse's pack and walked off into the woods in the direction Standing Bear had taken. Holding the big bay's lead, Caleb watched his father disappear into the snow.

He stood like this, holding the horse's lead and waiting for his father, for some time. But as daylight drained from the forest, he was startled by the sound of yet another gunshot. This increased his uneasiness, which intensified further when his father failed to return even after it had grown dark. The snow grew thicker and piled up on the trail. Caleb called out into the forest for his father, then for Standing Bear, and then for his father again, but no response echoed from the darkened woods. He was glad at least that he had the horse for company. But when he looked into the placid eyes of the big bay, it seemed dumbly unaware of his anxiety.

Finally Caleb could no longer stand waiting. He felt certain that something was wrong. He tied the bay's lead to the trunk of a slender tree and went off into the woods in the direction his father and Standing Bear had taken. As he strode along, he called out to them continually.

Caleb did not know that neither Standing Bear nor his father would be able to answer his calls. For Standing Bear lay dead, and his father unconscious in the snowy woods.

When Standing Bear had gone off into the woods to investigate the first gunshots, he had expected to find friendly Ojibway hunters. For this reason, he had not been on his guard. But the men who had fired their rifles in the forest were not friendly. Nor were they good men. They were, in fact, the two wolf-bounty hunters Standing Bear had fought with at the tavern in Detroit.

When these two, who called themselves Ralph and Roger, heard Standing Bear calling out an Ojibway greeting as he approached them in the forest, they had taken cover.

"Indian!" Ralph, who was the mean one, said. "Let's see what he's up to."

It was Ralph and Roger who had fired the gunshots that Caleb, his father, and Standing Bear heard as they walked along the trail. They had fired at a black she-wolf that had come trotting through the woods, not far from the blind they had built to conceal themselves. Ralph's first shot, though it hit the animal, had not hit her cleanly. The she-wolf, alerted to their presence, galloped off and away, and she eluded the second bullet sent by Roger. They were beginning to track the animal's blood drippings in the snow when they heard Standing Bear calling in the woods. They doubled back and concealed themselves once again in the wolf blind.

When Standing Bear approached, Ralph recognized him. "Look who it is," he whispered to Roger. "It's that stinking Indian from the tavern." He lifted his rifle's muzzle.

"You ain't going to shoot him, are you?" Roger said.

"The only good Indian is a dead Indian," Ralph replied. "Besides, what do think he'd do to us if he found us out here? He'd scalp us sure as day."

Ralph cocked the rifle. Standing Bear heard the dull click but not in time. Ralph pulled the trigger, and this time his aim was sure. Standing Bear fell back onto the snowy ground.

Ralph and Roger were stripping Standing Bear of his valuables—a fine hunting knife, his rifle and a few coins—when they heard Daniel Jordan calling out through the woods. They went back to the wolf blind to hide; from there they watched Jordan find Standing Bear's body in the snow. Daniel bent over him and checked for any sign of life, but he could neither feel his pulse nor sense any breath coming from his gaping mouth. He stood up and peered through the forest, but he saw no one. He decided to go back for the packhorse so that he could bring his dead guide's body to the fort at Saginaw.

Ralph, when he saw Daniel begin to walk back toward the trail, spoke to Roger.

"We've got to stop him," he said. "He'll go and snitch, and the law will be on our tail sure as day. Come on! Shssshh!"

Ralph crawled quietly out of the blind and Roger followed. Moving stealthily through the snow, the two men made a wide arc around Jordan and hid behind a thick maple tree. Here they waited. When Daniel walked by, Ralph leapt from behind the tree and struck Jordan's head cleanly and hard with the butt of his rifle. Daniel Jordan fell unconscious in the snow.

"That ought to give us time to clear out of here. Let's get!"

The two criminals trotted off into the woods in the direction of their wolf blind.

Now Caleb Jordan strode through the dark forest looking for his father and Standing Bear. He continued to call out to them. But no one heard him except the wolf-bounty hunters, and they were in too great a hurry to bother with the shouts of a boy. Caleb passed not far from where his father lay, but the thickly falling snow had already covered him with a thin layer of whiteness. Standing Bear's body, further on, was now completely buried.

It was so dark that Caleb could barely see where he was going. Only the faint glow from a nearly full moon veiled by snow clouds allowed him to distinguish the trees from the sky. Having no luck finding his father and Standing Bear, he decided to go back to the trail, hoping they had returned there. But everything beneath his feet was only snow, and the trunks of the trees all looked the same against the dull sky, and he could not find his way back to where he had left the big bay horse standing on the trail, snorting steam from its nostrils. He wandered in ever widening circles, sometimes calling out for his father or Standing Bear, at other times remaining quiet so that he could concentrate on where he was going.

An hour went by, and then another. It became more and more difficult to walk in the deepening snow, and Caleb began to grow tired. In his fatigue he began to step wildly, without direction. He felt more hopeless every minute until, without warning, his footing gave way beneath him. He found himself sliding madly down a bank, landing with a thump against the trunk of a tree at the bottom of the ravine into which he had fallen.

He lay there covered with snow, exhausted and shivering with cold. He listened. Somewhere, nearby, he heard something—a small, whining noise. It came from the direction of the steep bank he had fallen over.

With some difficulty he got himself up and trudged through the deep snow at the bottom of the ravine. When he reached the bank he stopped and listened. This is where the whining noise seemed to come from. At the place where it was loudest he began to dig away the snow. Eventually he tunneled through to the opening of a small cave in the side of the ravine's wall.

He pulled a packet of matches from the pocket of his trousers and lit one. He then thrust it into the opening of the cave so that he could see what was inside.

Among the shadows of the hollow place a pair of small blue eyes glowed in the light of the match. Caleb crept partly into the opening and held the match closer. There on the floor of the cave lay a wolf pup, not more than a few weeks old. It was furry and fuzzy, and also quite helpless looking.

This must be a wolf den, Caleb thought. But if it was, where was the mother wolf? And shouldn't there be other puppies, the brothers and sisters of this little one?

A chill of fear gripped Caleb with the thought that the mother wolf might soon return and find him in her den. But the pup was whining louder and trying to crawl, in its unsteady way, toward Caleb. "I'll just stay a moment," he thought to himself. "It's warm in here and dry. Besides, this little guy looks like he needs some company."

Caleb curled himself into the den, which was not tall enough for him to stand in, and took the wolf pup into his lap. When he stroked its fur it stopped its sad whining and instead began to yelp in a contented way. It curled itself up in Caleb's lap and Caleb felt its warmth. The wolf pup too must have felt the warmth of Caleb's body, because it soon quit yelping and fell asleep. Caleb, overcome with the fatigue of a long and stressful day, began to grow drowsy himself. He told himself that he must leave the den before the mother wolf returned; that he mustn't fall asleep, no matter what. But it was awfully cold outside the den, and in spite of his intentions he found himself slumping against the den's earthen wall and closing his eyes.

The next Caleb knew bright sunlight showed through the mouth of the den. He lay curled just as he had been the night before. The wolf pup playfully climbed over his arms, tugging at his clothes with its tiny teeth.

He got himself onto his hands and knees and crawled to the opening. He stuck his head outside cautiously, wondering whether the mother wolf might be somewhere near.

But nothing moved in the chill air except a couple of crows that whooshed loudly from a tree branch when they saw Caleb's head emerge from the den. Everywhere the forest was piled high with snow. The branches of the trees, the underlying brush, and the land itself all were covered.

The first thing on Caleb's mind was to find his father. He crawled back into the den and took the wolf pup in his hands.

"I have to leave now," he said. "I'll come back and check on you later."

The wolf pup yelped in a very high voice, and when Caleb put it down and crawled out of the den he heard it begin to whine behind him. But he did not look back as he stood up and moved away, for he was determined to find his father and Standing Bear.

The snow had drifted high into the ravine overnight, and it was difficult for Caleb to make his way out. Even once on level ground, he crunched through the crusty surface up to his waste with every step. But the morning air was clear and crisp, and Caleb could at least now see through the trunks of the trees, instead of wandering aimlessly as he had done the night before. He explored the area in widening circles, calling out to his father and sometimes to Standing Bear also, but no one returned his cries. As he wandered further and further away from the ravine, he tried to remember the way back so that he could again find the wolf den.

He grew hungry during the day and found it increasingly difficult to make his way through the snow. At least he could take handfuls of the frozen wetness to quench his thirst. As the hours went by, with no sign of either his father or Standing Bear, he grew discouraged. Nor had he been able to locate the trail again, or the big bay horse. He was completely lost and alone, deep in the wilds of the Michigan woods.

At midafternoon, scanning over the ground in front of him, he noticed something odd-looking. It was a funny patch of snow where the surface was humped up and ruffled in a strange way. He went over to it and prodded at it with his foot. There was something solid under the surface. He broke a small branch from a tree and poked the irregular mound, and then he began to scrape away the snow.

First there emerged the tips of bristled black hairs, and then the body, stiff and lifeless, of a wolf. The snow was blood-stained where it lay. This was the she-wolf that the bounty hunters had shot the day before.

The she-wolf was not the first of her pack that Ralph and Roger had killed in these woods. First they had heard them howling at night, and then they caught the faintest glimpse of one of them—a young male—rushing through the trees at a great distance. They had set traps throughout the area, and then they set up their blind and waited.

On their second day in the blind they had trying calling to the wolves. They howled and waited, for they knew there was a good chance that the wolves, who will fight to keep other wolves out of their territories, would come to investigate. Then they howled and waited and howled and waited again.

At the end of the day the wolves began to howl in response, and the bounty hunters answered their calls. They prepared their rifles and fell silent. The wolves approached through the forest. Warily, sniffing the air, they feinted and dodged among the trees.

There were four of them, and they belonged to the same pack. A wolf pack acts together as a team. There are usually six or eight wolves in a pack. The leader of the pack is called the alpha male, and the dominant female is called the alpha female. Each spring the alpha male and alpha female produce one litter of pups. The other members of the pack, aunts and uncles and brothers and sisters, help to raise them. They bring food to the mother wolf while she is nursing her pups, help to keep predators away from the den, and they babysit when the pups are old enough to play outside. The wolves that approached Roger and Ralph, the wolf-bounty hunters, belonged to the same pack as the pup Caleb found in the ravine.

Ralph and Roger remained dead silent. The wolves, in their curiosity, approached the blind more closely. They were upwind of the hunters and did not detect their presence with their keen sense of smell. But when they were fifty yards away, a rustling in the blind made them wary. They began to step uncertainly, weaving sideways and taking small steps backwards. Ralph and Roger fired. Two of the wolves staggered and fell upon the snowy ground. The other two dashed away through the forest.

In this way Ralph and Roger hunted the wolves, moving their blind each day. They also caught two of them in their traps. By the time Standing Bear happened upon them in the forest they had killed every wolf from the den at the ravine except for the mother, for she had stayed at the den to nurse the pups. When the other wolves did not return to the den, the mother wolf went out to find them. She saw the bounty hunters through the forest trees, though they did not see her. Fearful of these two-legged creatures, she resolved to move her pups to another den, some distance away, that she had used the year before. She was in the midst of carrying the pups to this other den when, on her return for the last pup, she too had been shot by Ralph.

Caleb knelt in the snow to feel the broad ribs of the she-wolf. He felt that something should be done with her, a proper burial, for to leave such a beautiful creature lying like refuse in the snow seemed wrong. But he had no tools, the ground was frozen solid, and he knew he must keep moving to find his father. With a sad look backwards, he walked on.

As the afternoon wound down Caleb had still not found the trail, nor any trace of his father or Standing Bear. He grew increasingly worried that he might not be able to find his way out of these thick woods, and that he might die from hunger or cold. He also began to fear that something horrible had happened to his father and Standing Bear. There had been gunshots, and he could not understand why his father had not come for him. Why, he wondered, had he not heard his father calling to him in the forest, as he had been calling for his father, unless some terrible thing had happened? He felt more strongly than ever that he must find him, help him. But he could see that the day would soon be over, and he realized sadly that there was no point in wandering aimlessly in the dark. He would have to begin again in the morning. He began to make his way back to the wolf den, for it would be warmer there. He also looked forward to the company of the pup. He guessed, correctly, that the mother wolf must not be alive, for she had not returned to the den the previous night. He considered the possibility, also correct, that the black she-wolf he had found in the woods was the pup's mother.

On his way back to the den he came across a clearing in the woods in which some sort of camp had been made. At the center of the clearing was a bare place where the still warm embers of a fire had kept the snow from accumulating. There was a lean-to structure to one side of the clearing made of brush and covered with pine and fir branches. On the opposite side of the clearing were five wolf pelts, bristled with frost, stretched out on frames also made of branches. This was the camp where Ralph and Roger had slept, and where they had begun to prepare the hides of the wolves they had killed. They had planned to sell the pelts and bring the ears to the authorities in Ohio for the bounty payments. But in their haste to leave the forest after shooting Standing Bear, they were forced to leave them behind.

Caleb went to the pelts, brushed the frost off of one of them, and felt the texture of the tough, outer guard hairs. The furs were large. One was as tall as Caleb himself, and he thought it would make a good, warm blanket. So, using a knife he carried on his belt, he cut the pelt down from its frame and wrapped it around him. In this way, wrapped in wolf fur, he found his way back to the ravine and went into the den.

The pup whined with cold and hunger, and Caleb wished he had something to feed it. He also wished he had something to eat himself. He went back out of the den and called loudly for his father. Then he called for Standing Bear. "Tomorrow," he thought to himself, "I must find the trail, I must! I probably got myself all turned around, wandering in these woods. In the morning I will search in the other direction." Exhausted with his wanderings, he crawled back into the den, wrapped the wolf fur securely around him, and lay against the den's wall of earth. He took up the wolf pup and cradled it in his arms. It nuzzled into the furry wolf pelt, the scent of which it recognized as one of its uncles, and after several minutes its whinings grew fainter. Then Caleb was asleep.

Chapter 12

A Fortunate Meeting

IN THE MORNING Caleb was awakened by the sound of human voices outside the den. How excited he was—it must be his father! But then he listened more closely. These voices spoke in sounds he could not understand. It sounded like the language Standing Bear had spoken when they met with other Ojibway people on the trail. Perhaps, Caleb thought, Standing Bear had come with others to find him. He clutched the pup, which was softly whimpering, in one hand, and with the wolf skin wrapped around his shoulders, got onto his knees and began to crawl through the short tunnel that led out of the den.

Outside the den were waiting Singing Loon, the father of the Ojibway girl Morning Star, and her uncle Talks Too Much. Morning Star's family had left their sugarbush the week before, and they were now making there way toward Thomas Campau's trading post on Saginaw Bay. They were traveling along the Chippewa River in two birch bark canoes. The canoes were loaded with packs of deer hides and animal furs they planned to trade with Thomas Campau for American goods like woven blankets, steel axes, cooking pots, and stout hunting rifles.

The night before they had pulled up their canoes on the riverbank and made camp. Before dawn, Singing Loon and Talks Too Much went into the woods to hunt for meat. They had killed a deer and were carrying it back toward the river, following the course of the ravine where the wolf den was located. They saw the hole in the snowy bank and heard the soft whining and occasional yelping of the pup. They stopped, took hold of their rifles, and began to speak in the Ojibway language.

"I wonder if the mother is in there," Talks Too Much said.

"Be careful," Singing Loon said, "she won't like us getting too close to her den."

"Yes," Talks Too Much replied, "but a wolf skin will bring five good dollars from Thomas Campau."

As Singing Loon and Talks Too Much spoke together like this, Caleb, still wrapped from head to toe in the wolf skin, and carrying the wolf pup under his breast, thrust his free hand out of the mouth of the den. Talks Too Much raised his rifle, but Singing Loon reached up and pushed the barrel aside.

"Wait," he said, "that's no wolf!"

The two men stepped back and watched Caleb emerge from the snowy bank, carrying the wolf pup. His wolf pelt blanket glistened with a frosty dusting that fell around him as he moved through the narrow opening. Singing Loon and Talks Too Much stood in amazement when Caleb pulled back the fur and raised his face toward them.

"Why, it's a boy!" Talks Too Much said.

"Or a vision!" said Singing Loon.

Caleb struggled to right himself in the still-deep snow. He finally stood on shaky legs.

"Are you friends of Standing Bear?" he asked.

Singing Loon and Talks Too Much stood silent, still bewildered at having found a boy—or was it a vision?—alone in these deep woods. Neither one of them could understand the English language.

"It speaks," Talks Too Much said to Singing Loon.

"What can it mean?" said Singing Loon.

Caleb tried to speak to the men again. "Do you know where my father is? Do you know Standing Bear?"

The men, still not sure whether they were speaking to a real boy or to some kind of vision, gestured to Caleb that they could not understand him.

Caleb, using gestures himself, tried to make the men

understand that he had become separated from his father, that he was lost in these woods, and that he had found the wolf pup alone in its den. Singing Loon and Talks Too Much could not understand much of what he was trying to say, but they understood that he had wandered the woods in search of someone bigger than himself, because Caleb raised both hands high to show his father. Talks Too Much beckoned Caleb to follow him and Singing Loon. Singing Loon tried to take the wolf pup from Caleb so that he might return it to the den.

"She must be moving her den," he said to Talks Too Much. "She will come back for this one. We can make a blind, and hunt her when she returns."

Caleb refused to let go of the pup. Singing Loon, still thinking that Caleb might just be a vision sent from Spirit, did not force the pup away from him, but let Caleb carry it with him as he followed the two Ojibway men toward the river.

When these three—the two men carrying the deer they had hunted between them, Caleb following behind holding the wolf pup—neared the Ojibway family's camp near the river, Caleb saw smoke rising through the forest. When they entered the camp, Morning Star came running over to greet her father and uncle. Her eyes widened with surprise when she saw Caleb behind them.

"What? Who?" she said in the Ojibway language.

"He came from a wolf den," Singing Loon said. "We think he has lost his people."

"Or . . ." Talks Too Much began, but he was reluctant to say what he was thinking—*he is a vision sent from the Spirit world.*

"From a wolf den?" Morning Star was puzzled.

"We could not understand him well," Talks Too Much said. "He speaks only English."

Morning Star walked over to Caleb and stood before him.

"Hello," she said. Morning Star was very clever, and she had learned a little English when she visited the Americans' trading posts with her family.

"Hello," Caleb returned.

She wanted to know where he had come from, and why

he was in these woods, but she did not know all the English words for these things. So she asked with her eyes and hands if she could hold the wolf pup. Caleb paused a moment, but seeing her pleading eyes, he put the pup into her arms. She cradled it and laughed, and she smiled at Caleb and he smiled too. She noticed that Caleb was shivering, and she led him toward the fire and invited him to crouch beside it and warm himself.

While they sat beside the fire like this, Singing Loon and Talks Too Much went to the river bank to tell Braided Waters, Morning Star's mother, and Grandmother what had happened. Morning Star, using the English words she knew, and many gestures, learned the following things from Caleb: that he had come from far away on a big ship; that he was traveling in the woods from Detroit on his way north with his father, who was a blacksmith, and an Ojibway man named Standing Bear; that he had heard gunshots off the trail; that in a sudden spring blizzard Caleb lost his father and Standing Bear; that he found a camp where wolf hides were being dried; that he found a dead she-wolf in the snow; and that he had taken refuge in a wolf den hollowed into a steep ravine in the woods.

When Singing Loon and Talks Too Much returned from the river, Braided Waters and Grandmother walked alongside them, speaking in worried murmurs. Morning Star rose from the fire and placed the wolf pup in Caleb's arms. Running to her family, she told them in a rush of Ojibway words Caleb could not understand everything she had learned of his experiences.

"We should try to find the men who traveled with the boy," Braided Waters said. "Do you suppose they are lost out there still?"

"We saw no sign of them while we were hunting," Talks Too Much said.

"But we were looking for deer, not human beings," Singing Loon said.

"If they were traveling north," Talks Too Much said, "they must have been going to the fort at Saginaw. Morning Star says the boy's father is a worker of iron. He must be the one the government promised to send to help us Ojibway take up the white man's road. The Ojibway man must have been his guide. I bet they have gone back on the trail toward the fort."

"I do not believe it," Braided Waters said. "Morning Star says the boy lost his father in the blizzard. That was only two days ago. The father would not leave his boy in these woods without searching for more than two days!"

"You speak rightly," Singing Loon said. "Either they are searching for the boy or something has happened to them. Morning Star said there were gunshots. Talks Too Much and I will go back into the forest and search for the boy's people."

"We will dress the deer you have killed and prepare a good meal for your return," Grandmother said. "Be careful."

At that Talks Too Much and Singing Loon went off again into the forest. Braided Waters had a worried look on her face. She and Grandmother followed Morning Star over to the campfire, where Caleb still crouched warming himself. Braided Waters went to him. She brushed hair back from his forehead and touched his cheek. "Two days in the woods," she said, "you must be starved." She told Morning Star to bring water for him to drink. Then she went to her stores and prepared a meal for him, dried venison meat and cranberries and some corn hominy with maple sugar. She tried to take the pup away from Caleb so that he could eat more freely, but Caleb would not release his grasp. She handed him his plate and stepped away.

Morning Star approached him then, and she smiled and gestured with her arms, and Caleb let her hold the pup and he began to eat. To Caleb, who had never in his life gone for more than one evening without food (when he misbehaved and had been sent to bed without supper), food had never tasted so delicious, and he ate ravenously. While he ate, Morning Star made him understand that her father and uncle had gone to search for his father and Standing Bear. Sitting there at the warm fire, through which he could see Morning Star holding the wolf pup, he believed that everything would soon be alright.

Caleb spent the day with Morning Star, playing with the wolf pup, going to look at the river, and making a big snowman. Braided Waters gave him two more large meals, which he ate with almost as much relish as the first. During one of these, Braided Waters and Grandmother stood apart from where Caleb and Morning Star sat near the fire and conferred quietly among themselves. They spoke about the wolf pup.

"It looks like it is barely weaned," Grandmother said.

"Yes," Braided Waters agreed, "and it needs food."

"It is too young to live on its own. It needs its mother."

"Singing Loon wanted to put it back in the den, but the boy would not let it go."

"I'm afraid he'll have to give it up," Grandmother said. "Though it is possible to raise a wolf pup—as our people have done—his father's people will surely not want it. They only want to kill the wolves and drive them out, just as they wish to do with us."

Braided Waters looked at Caleb thoughtfully. "I hope Singing Loon and Talks Too Much find his father," she said. She then called Morning Star away and told her that the wolf pup needed food. By closely watching the animals of the forest, the Ojibway people learned much about their habits. Braided Waters knew that when wolf pups were not old enough to eat solid food on their own, mother wolves sometimes chewed their food for them. She now gave Morning Star a couple of handfuls of corn hominy and told her to chew it until it was very soft, spit it out, and feed it to the pup. Morning Star went back to Caleb. She shared some of the corn with him and the two fed the hungry pup. It gulped down the mushy corn as fast as it could swallow.

Singing Loon and Talks Too Much arrived back at the camp at the end of the afternoon. Unfortunately, neither Caleb's father nor Standing Bear was with them. At the sight of them coming into the clearing by themselves, Caleb's heart sank. They went to where Braided Waters and Grandmother were preparing supper and spoke to them in serious tones.

"We found the Ojibway," Singing Loon said. "He was lying dead in the snow, left to be eaten by the crows!"

The spring temperatures had begun to warm again. The high-piled snow of the blizzard had receded, so Standing Bear's body was only half-covered when Singing Loon and Talks Too Much searched through that area of the forest.

"He was shot," Talks Too Much said. "Nearby there was a hunting blind. Not far away there was a camp. It looked like they were hunting wolf. It's no wonder the pack was moving the den."

"Did you know the man?" Grandmother asked.

"I think I may have seen him once, many years ago," Singing Loon said, "when I traveled to Detroit."

"What about the boy's father?" Braided Waters asked. "Any sign of him?"

Talks Too Much held out an object. "We found this, not far from the Ojibway man."

Caleb stared hard at the object that Talks Too Much held in his hand. It was his father's beaverskin hat, limp and wet from lying in the melting snow. He rushed to where Singing Loon and Talks Too Much spoke with Braided Waters and Grandmother.

"That's my father's hat!" he exclaimed. Caleb grasped the hat from the hand of Talks Too Much. He sunk his fingers into its furry crown. Talks Too Much could not understand Caleb's words. But he could see, by Caleb's attachment to the object, that the hat must have belonged to his father. Along one edge of the hat, the fur was stained with blood.

"It must have been the father's," Braided Waters said. "See how he clings to it."

"It is certainly so," Grandmother agreed.

"You saw no sign of the man?" Braided Waters asked Singing Loon and Talks Too Much.

"None," Talks Too Much said.

"How very strange," said Braided Waters.

After the wolf hunter Ralph struck Daniel Jordan in the head with the butt of his rifle, Daniel Jordan lay unconscious throughout the night, the snow piling high around him. When he came to the next morning his head felt light, almost like it was floating away, and he was unsteady on his feet; he had suffered a concussion from the rifle blow. In his grogginess he failed to retrieve his hat, which lay buried in the snow. Through the dull aching in his woozy brain, Daniel Jordan could think of only one thing: he had to find Caleb. He remembered coming into the woods the day before and searching for Standing Bear, who had gone off to investigate the gunshots they heard. He remembered finding Standing Bear dead on the ground. He also remembered walking toward to the trail, where he had left Caleb, so that he could bring the packhorse to carry the body of their guide to the fort at Saginaw.

After that, all was a blur.

Daniel Jordan now staggered off in what he guessed was the direction of the trail. He plowed through the thick snow as best he could. But his brain was not right, and all was now covered in the same whiteness, and he could not really remember in which direction he should walk. He wandered aimlessly, in ever increasing circles, all the time calling out for Caleb. But Caleb, who had wandered in another direction, was miles away from where his father now searched for him.

In mid-afternoon Daniel Jordan finally came across the trail, but there was no sign of either Caleb or the horse. He walked up and down the narrow path, wandering far in both directions, and when the sun began to set he was forced to end his searching for the day. He made a fire, using the tin of matches he carried in the pocket of his coat. Sitting on an old log, he tried to figure out what might have become of his son. He hoped that Caleb, after he failed to return, had mounted the horse and ridden back along the trail toward Detroit. He remembered that there were three forks along the way, and he hoped that Caleb would choose the right direction. He decided that, the next morning, he would travel south along the trail himself. He hoped either to catch his son on the trail, or to find him when he reached Detroit, safe and sound.

He thought of Caleb's mother and contemplated what she would do. Then he said a prayer to his God and fell asleep.

Daniel's head ached steadily when he awoke in the

morning, and his legs were wobbly, but he nonetheless began to move southward along the trail. He hoped that, when he came to forks, he would remember rightly which way to go.

Caleb stood by the Chippewa River with Singing Loon, Talks Too Much, Braided Waters and Grandmother, holding his father's beaverskin hat. Neither he nor his new Ojibway friends knew that his father was alive and well. Because of Standing Bear, killed by a gunshot wound, and because of the blood-stained hat, the Ojibway were not hopeful about the fate of Daniel Jordan. They spoke among themselves, using their Ojibway language that Caleb could not understand.

"It doesn't look good," Grandmother said.

"Why would a man leave such a good hat," Talks Too Much said, "made with good beaver fur?"

"It's very strange," said Singing Loon.

"I can't think why somebody would kill the Ojibway man," Grandmother said. "Maybe it was the same ones who were hunting the wolves."

"That hat has blood on it. The white man was injured on the head."

"Maybe he was shot, too," Talks Too Much said.

"It could be that whoever shot him took the body some-place and buried it."

Everyone was quiet now. Caleb stared at them with great intensity, still clutching his father's hat in his hands. "Where is my father?" he asked.

They stared back at him. No one understood what he was saying.

Morning Star approached. She carried Wind-in-Grass on her back in his baby board. She had heard the voices of Singing Loon and Talks Too Much, and had come to see what they had found in the woods. Her mother turned to her.

"Singing Loon and Talks Too Much found the hat of this boy's father," she said.

Morning Star saw the beaverskin hat in Caleb's hands, its brown fur lustrous and wet. Caleb turned toward Morning Star.

"Where is my father?" he said again.

Morning Star went to him. She knew that Caleb spoke of his father, but she was not certain of the meaning of "Where is." She touched the beaverskin hat and held it with her hands. She saw the tears in Caleb's eyes. She spoke to him in Ojibway and gestured with the hat. Caleb returned her gestures and spoke in more English words, some she understood, and some that she did not. Finally she turned to her family.

"He wants to know where his father is," she said. "His father liked the hat a great deal, for it was a gift from a friend."

Morning Star's family exchanged solemn glances.

"Something bad has happened to him," Talks Too Much said with confidence. "No man would leave such a fine hat lying in the woods, not unless he were not well."

"Have you searched well, little brother?" Braided Waters asked him.

"As well as we could in one day," Talks Too Much said.

"Who knows where he could be," said Singing Loon.

"It doesn't look good," Grandmother said again.

Braided Waters spoke to Morning Star. "I'm afraid the boy's father was probably killed with the Ojibway man. But don't tell the boy that. Say instead that we don't know where his father is."

Morning Star told Caleb, with her words and gestures, that they had not found his father.

"But you've got to find him!" Caleb blurted out. "He's my father!"

The family stared at him. They understood his distress, although they did not know the meaning of his words. Morning Star took Caleb's arm and led him to where the family's campfire burned. Nearby the family's dogs played with the wolf pup. She tried to interest him in joining their play, but all he could think about was his lost father. He had already lost his mother and sister. Forever. He was bursting with frustration, because no one seemed to be able to help him. Morning Star could see how he felt, and she soon gave up her efforts to amuse him. Instead she sat quietly beside him while he stared into the fire, his eyes intense and fierce.

As he watched the flames lick the cold air, Caleb's mind relaxed a little. He remembered what his father had told him before he went off into the woods to search for Standing Bear. If they were ever to be separated, his father said, he would come to find him, no matter where he was or how long it took. Remembering this made Caleb's pain easier to bear. But still he was glum, and he remained ever silent as he stared into the fire. Not far off Morning Star's family continued their conversation.

"What shall we do with the boy?" Singing Loon said.

"We can't leave him here alone," said Braided Waters.

"Of course not," said Grandmother.

"We will take him with us to Campau's trading post," Singing Loon said. "Campau will know what to do."

With their silence, the others agreed.

Chapter 13

A Northward Journey

CALEB spent that night with the Ojibway family. They slept in a temporary lodge constructed of sapling trunks and cedar boughs, with a glowing fire in the middle. The men and Caleb slept on one side and the women and baby and Morning Star on the other. The adults slept nearest the lodge's entrance, the children in the middle nearest the fire, and Grandmother in the rear. They piled cedar boughs on the ground and covered these with deer and bear skins. Overall the sleeping arrangements were not too uncomfortable for Caleb, who slept with the wolf pup curled in his arms. When dawn came the Ojibway family roused themselves. Braided Waters and Grandmother began to make breakfast, and Singing Loon and Talks Too Much began to load the canoes so that they might continue their journey downriver.

While they ate Braided Waters saw how glum Caleb looked, and that he was not eating, but just absently stroked the fuzzy fur of the wolf pup. She asked Morning Star to tell him that they would take him with them to a white man's trading post, and that the trader would be able to help find his father.

With this news Caleb felt a little better, and he ate a little.

When they had finished eating the adults spoke among themselves. Braided Waters gave instructions to Morning Star and she began to collect the cooking utensils. After the camp was completely struck, they all began to move toward the canoes. Singing Loon turned toward Caleb and stared hard at the wolf pup. Caleb clutched the pup against his breast, fearing that Singing Loon would make him leave it behind. Caleb clutched harder still, and Braided Waters spoke quietly to Singing Loon. Finally Singing Loon turned and the Ojibway family began to settle into the canoes.

Caleb was reluctant to follow them. There was a chance that his father was still back in those woods, and Caleb thought it best to continue to search for him. But Braided Waters came to him and put an arm around his shoulders. Though she spoke to him in words he did not understand, she somehow convinced him that it would be best to come with her family. The woods were vast, she had said, and Caleb's father probably no longer where he had been three days before. Caleb was but a boy and small, she said, and the woods were full of many dangers.

By the comforting tones of her voice, and the arm around his shoulders, she made him to know that she was his friend. She would help him find his father, or do anything else needed to make sure he did not come to harm. Of that Caleb somehow felt certain. So he climbed into one canoe with Morning Star and Talks Too Much, and Braided Waters and Singing Loon and Grandmother climbed into the other. Braided Waters held Wind-in-Grass in a sling across her middle. Caleb positioned himself in the back of Talks to Much's canoe among the deerhide bundles. From the front of the boat, Talks Too Much raised a paddle and through gestures asked Caleb if he knew how to row. Caleb nodded his assent, Talks Too Much handed the paddle to Morning Star, and she passed it back to her new friend. Talks Too Much and Singing Loon pushed off their canoes from the bank. Then, with Caleb helping, they paddled out into the middle of the narrow river and the canoes began to move quickly downstream.

Just before the fall of evening they brought their canoes ashore at a place where Caleb saw two substantial log buildings through trees that there overhung the riverbank. After they got out of the boats and began to walk toward the buildings, Caleb noticed that there were Ojibway lodges scattered around the edges of the clearing in which the log buildings sat. As he and Morningstar's family passed these, their inhabitants, other Ojibway people, greeted them. Some of the other Ojibway seemed to know Morning Star's family and always they asked many questions. Caleb knew these questions were about him. He could see that they were surprised to see an American boy among their Ojibway friends.

When Caleb and Morning Star's family arrived at the larger of the two log buildings, they climbed some steps to a porch and went into the place. They were in a large, open room, with a blazing fire in one corner and a counter along the other side. There were many deerhide bundles, much like the ones Caleb's new friends had carried in their canoes, piled about. Sorting through these was a burly man with reddish hair and a bushy beard.

"Well, if it ain't Singing Loon," the man said in the Ojibway language, barely looking up at them. "Come to do your trading, I reckon."

"Yes. We have some furs, bear oil, and a good number of deer skins."

"Why don't you bring it all in," the trader, whose name was Thomas Campau, said. He did not bother to turn away from his work.

Singing Loon loudly cleared his throat. "There is something else we have brought along as well."

Trader Campau continued with his sorting. He was waiting for Singing Loon to finish, but Singing Loon remained silent.

Finally the trader straightened himself with a groan. His groan had two meanings. One was that he was getting older, which made it difficult for him to straighten up. The other was that he didn't like to be interrupted in his work. "Well," he said impatiently, "what is it?"

Reaching back to where Caleb stood behind him, Singing Loon took him gently by the arm. He pulled him forward so that Trader Campau could see him.

"We found him near the river, one day's canoe from here," Singing Loon said. "He was hiding in a wolf den. He has lost his father. We found this hat."

Singing Loon reached back again and Braided Waters

handed him Caleb's father's hat. Singing Loon gave the hat to Trader Campau.

Trader Campau examined the hat and looked at Caleb, who held the wolf pup in his arms, and spoke now in English.

"This is your father's hat, son?"

"Yes sir."

"What's your name?"

"Caleb Jordan."

"These folks say you've lost your father. Is that right?"

"Yes, sir."

"What's his name?"

"Daniel Jordan."

"You must be new in these parts."

"Yes sir. We've come from Albany, so my pa can blacksmith for the Indians."

"I see."

"Josiah Strong brought us."

"I understand. And where did you last see your father?"

"We were coming up from Detroit," Caleb said, a little excitedly now. "We had an Indian guide named Standing Bear. He went into the woods, and then we heard a gunshot. Then my pa went off to find Standing Bear and told me to stay put. It started to snow, real hard, and after a spell I got nervous and went off to find him. But I never did."

"That looks like a wolf pup you've got there," Campau said.

"Yes, sir."

"I reckon you ought to stay here while I get in touch with the fort and tell them what happened. They can see about finding your pa." Trader Campau and Singing Loon then spoke together. Because they spoke in the Ojibway language, Caleb could not understand what they said:

"This hat," Campau said to Singing Loon, "it's bloody."

"Yes," Talks Too Much said, stepping forward. "That's how we found it. Also we found the guide, the man the boy called Standing Bear. He was shot dead. Nearby there was a wolf hunters' camp."

"It don't look good," Trader Campau said. "But I'll see

what I can do for the boy. You all go ahead and bring your trade goods in."

Caleb's new friends began to leave the trading post, and Caleb began to follow.

"No," the trader said, "you stay here with me. I'll have Mrs. Campau fix you up a nice hot supper and show you where you can sleep tonight."

Campau put a strong arm on Caleb's shoulder and held him steady. Morning Star's family stood in the doorway.

"What about my pup?" Caleb asked. "That Indian lady was helping me to feed him."

"Don't you worry about that," the trader said. "We'll take care of everything."

Caleb's eyes sought out those of Braided Waters, who looked at him reassuringly. Then he sought the eyes of Morning Star. She smiled and said with her little English that they would soon return. The Ojibway family stepped out onto the porch and closed the door behind them.

When they had left, Trader Campau called back into the house, and soon Mrs. Campau appeared. She was an Ojibway woman with deep, dark eyes. Her long, black hair was woven into careful braids. She wore a gingham dress much like Caleb's mother used to wear.

"We'll be keeping this boy over for the night," Thomas Campau said to her in English. "Singing Loon's family found him in the woods. He lost his father while they were on their way to the fort to blacksmith for your people. Can you see about fixing him some supper?"

Mrs. Campau, who spoke English perfectly, told Caleb to come with her. He followed her out of the room to a kitchen in the back of the log house. She sat him at the table and worked at a stove until she had prepared a plate of venison with corn hominy and bread. She also mashed up some corn for the wolf puppy, added a little milk from a jug, and put it in a dish on the floor; both Caleb and the pup ate until they were satisfied. Mrs. Campau spoke to Caleb about his father and asked about his family. He told her how his mother and sister had died from the terrible sickness, and how he and his father had traveled across Lake Erie to the Michigan country so that they might work as blacksmiths for the Ojibway people. Seeing that he was very worried about his father, Mrs. Campau tried to comfort him.

"The soldiers at the fort will search the woods," she said. "They will surely find him. Who knows, maybe he has already gone back to Detroit."

Caleb, who had taken the puppy up in his arms again, said, "Can I go with them—the soldiers?"

"That will be up to the Captain. For tonight you will stay with us. Tomorrow my husband will take you to the fort."

Mrs. Campau took Caleb up some stairs and showed him to a room off a short hallway. It wasn't a bedroom, but some kind of storeroom, with wooden crates and burlap sacks stacked all around.

"I'll make you up a bed," Mrs. Campau said. "If you want, you can take your puppy outside and play."

Caleb thanked Mrs. Campau. He carried the wolf pup down the stairs and through the front room and out into the yard in front of the log house. He saw smoke rising from the lodges of the Ojibway families camped all around the clearing. There were dogs running and Ojibway children playing and women cooking over fires outside the lodges. Before long he saw his friends coming toward the log house from the river. They carried on their backs the deerhide bundles with skins and furs that they would trade with Trader Campau. Only Morning Star did not carry a bundle, for she carried Wind-in-Grass on her back in his baby board.

When they all reached the log house Morning Star stopped to play with Caleb and his puppy, and when her family went back to the river for more bundles she was allowed to stay. Some of the other Ojibway children came over and spoke with Morning Star in her language, and Caleb let them play with the puppy; and they touched Caleb's blond hair and his light-colored face because they were not used to seeing a boy who was not Ojibway like them.

When Singing Loon had done his trading with Trader Campau, his family came out of the log house. Mrs. Campau was with them, and she spoke to Morning Star's mother. They then came over to where Caleb and the other children were playing. Braided Waters spoke to Morning Star, and Caleb knew that she was telling her that it was time to go. Morning Star spoke to Caleb as best she could with her English words. All Caleb could understand was that Morning Star and her family were going away somewhere in their canoes. Mrs. Campau, who could speak English as well as the Ojibway language, helped to explain.

"In the morning Morning Star and her family will be leaving here. They are traveling far to the north, and they will not return. She said that she is your friend and she hopes that one day she will see you again."

Caleb felt a sudden pang. Although he had just gotten to know Morning Star and her family, he liked them all, and he did not like the idea that he would never see them again. Unfortunately, he didn't know how to express such complicated feelings. So he remained silent as Morning Star handed the wolf pup to him and, with a backward glance, walked off toward the river with her family.

Caleb remained outdoors, sharing his pup with the Ojibway children, until darkness fell and Mrs. Campau came to the door of the log house and beckoned him to come inside. She took him upstairs and showed him the pallet she had made for him to sleep on, some woven mats and a couple of blankets. She left him with an oil lamp, and also she gave him some toy soldiers and a couple of books she had found among Trader Campau's things. He passed the evening looking at the books and playing with the soldiers, and fooling around with his puppy, until finally he grew drowsy and lay down with the pup on the pallet to go to sleep.

He must have drifted off, for the next thing he knew he was hearing the voices of Trader and Mrs. Campau in the hallway. They had come upstairs to go to bed. It was well past midnight, for Trader Campau had done much trading during the day, and he had stayed up late to work on his accounts.

"It doesn't look good about the boy's father," Campau said. "Odds are he's dead out there somewhere. That's an awful nice beaver hat, and a man just doesn't walk off and leave a hat like that lying in the woods. What's more, that hat had blood on it, and the man's guide was shot clean dead!"

Caleb stiffened. He couldn't believe what he was hearing! He had been worried about his father, but one thing he hadn't considered was that he might have been killed. He just couldn't be dead! He was the only person Caleb had left in the whole world . . .

"Shhh," Mrs. Campau said, "the boy might hear you."

"Naw," Campau said, "he'll be sound asleep in there, what with journeying all day. It's nearly three of the morning."

"Still . . ." Mrs. Campau said. She spoke in a hushed voice.

Caleb rose up from his pallet. He went to the door and put his ear to it. He heard Trader Campau and his wife stepping down the hallway toward their bedroom. Mrs. Campau spoke now.

"The boy's mother and sister died in a big sickness. Where will he go?"

"He'll probably end up in an orphanage," Campau said.

"At least he has his puppy."

"Hmmph," Campau grunted, "that's not going to last long. You can't raise a wolf. Heck, every state in the Union has a bounty on the beasts, trying to kill them out! They'll take it away from him at the fort tomorrow, probably drown it in a pail . . ."

The door to the Campau's bedroom closed and Caleb could hear no more. But he had already heard more than enough! His father dead? How could that be! Hadn't Daniel Jordan told Caleb that if they were ever separated he would come to find him, come to find him no matter where he was?

Caleb was frightened. He felt that the only friend he had left in the world was the wolf pup. Perhaps Morning Star also, but she had gone. Now Trader Campau said that they would take away the pup. It that were to happen, he would be completely alone, with no parents and left in an orphanage!

And how could they kill the little puppy? he said to himself. It wasn't hurting anyone.

He felt desperately agitated. At first he wanted to run down the hallway and tell Trader Campau that everything he had said was wrong and a lie. His father *wasn't* dead, he wanted to scream in Campau's face. The men at the Fort *wouldn't* take away the pup and drown it in a pail. But after he thought for a moment, he knew that yelling at Trader Campau would only make things worse. The trader seemed a nice man, and Mrs. Campau had treated him kindly.

He went to the window of the small room and looked out into the dark night. Smoke rose from the fires of the Ojibway families camped around the trading post. He wondered if one of those fires belonged to Morning Star and her family. He had only known them for a few days, but they felt like friends to him: almost family, even. Singing Loon was so stern and steady, Talks Too Much was funny, old Grandmother was quiet and wise, and Braided Waters was a lot like his own mother had been, kind and good. And Morning Star, well, even if she was a girl, was fun to play with. He began to wish that he were going away with them in their canoes instead of staying behind at the trading post. They wouldn't kill his puppy, or put him in an orphanage! Trader and Mrs. Campau had been kind to take him in, but he began to feel as though he were in a prison.

He put on his shoes and coat and picked up the wolf pup. Then he opened the door to his small room, tiptoed down the hallway to the stairs and went silently down the steps to the front room of the house. Unbolting the door as quietly as he could, he opened it and slipped out into the night.

He had decided to ask Morning Star's family to help him, and walking among the lodges in the clearing, he hoped to find them somewhere. As he wandered among the small, temporary dwellings, the sky began to lighten in the east, for dawn was not far off. Finally, not far from the river, he found them. They were already up and about, for they had a long journey ahead and Singing Loon wanted to get an early start. They were loading their things into the canoes, preparing to be on their way.

It was Talks Too Much who first spotted Caleb. He spoke aloud to the others, and they looked up to see him standing there holding the wolf pup. Morning Star put down the things she was carrying and ran to him. He began to ramble excitedly.

"Please tell your family to take me with you," he said. "Trader Campau said my father is dead! They want to put me in an orphanage and drown my pup in a pail of water. Please, ask them, please!"

Morning Star couldn't understand everything Caleb was saying. But by encouraging him to say more, using words she knew and also gestures and facial expressions, she was able to learn why he had come. She went to her family and told them that Caleb wanted to join them on their journey to the north.

"He does not know our ways," Singing Loon said. "How will he live among our people?"

"In the old days," Grandmother objected, "when our warriors took up the hatchet against the Americans, many a child was captured and brought among us. They were adopted into our grieving families to ease the pain for those we had lost. He too can learn our ways."

"What you say is true," Singing Loon said. "But those days are gone. We have buried the hatchet and agreed to live in peace with the Americans. If the boy comes with us they will say that we stole him, and much trouble will come."

"He seems to be a smart little fellow," Talks Too Much said. "He hasn't been any bother."

They all looked to where Caleb stood ten paces away. Even in the dim early light they could see the tears glistening on his face. Morning Star wished that her family would take Caleb along with them, for in him she saw a new companion, just as her brother had been before he died. She was just as fascinated with the wolf puppy as Caleb, and she also remembered the dream she had during her vision quest, when she saw her brother in the eyes of a wolf. But she did not mention these things. Among the Ojibway, when serious matters were being discussed, it was the custom for children to keep their silence while the adults decided the matter. Now Grandmother, as if she knew Morning Star's heart, spoke.

"Morning Star had a vision," Grandmother said. "She saw her brother in the skin of a wolf. Now this boy has come to us from the den of the pathfinder. Perhaps the Master of Life has sent him to ease our souls for the loss of Fleeting Elk."

"Who can know the ways of Kitchi Manitou?" Singing Loon said.

"He looks so sad," said Braided Waters. "If he goes with the whites, who will care for him? He has no family."

"You say he has no family," Singing Loon said. "Yes, we believe the father was killed. But what if we are wrong, and the father lives?"

"Then the father will come to find the boy," Braided Waters said. "What man will leave his son for lost?"

Singing Loon looked off toward the river, where his family's canoes sat half loaded on the bank. He thought of his own son, Fleeting Elk, who had been lost to sickness the previous autumn. He knew that what his wife said was true. If there were any way for him to find his son, to bring him back to the land of the living, he would not hesitate to undertake any journey, no mattter how far. But since Fleeting Elk was now in a place no living man could go, all Singing Loon could do was care for those who remained. He looked at Caleb, shivering in the cold morning, and somehow knew he must take him along.

"He can come," he said simply, and returned to the work of loading the canoes. Morning Star ran to tell Caleb the news, and Caleb began to help with the work. When the canoes were both loaded they all climbed in. Caleb helped Talks Too Much row as he had done the day before, and they moved briskly down the river toward Saginaw Bay. When they reached the bay, they paddled through the mists of its northern shore toward Lake Huron. After they entered the great lake, they pointed their prows northward, staying close to shore to avoid the ice floes that still traversed the lake's depths.

The day had broken strong and clear, and the two canoes made their way steadily northward along Lake Huron's western shore. In the first canoe Singing Loon rowed in front, with Grandmother in the middle and Braided Waters rowing in the back. In the second, Talks Too Much sat in front, with Caleb rowing in back and Morning Star in the middle. She had Wind-in-Grass on her back in his baby board, and she held the wolf puppy in her arms. In each of the canoes rode one of the family's two dogs.

They paddled along the lakeshore this way, occasionally passing the encampments of other Ojibway families along the banks. Once they stopped to take a meal and share the fire of one of those families. Caleb liked rowing the canoe. From where he sat he could see the broad lake spread out beyond him on one side, the tall Michigan forests on the other, and directly before him Wind-in-Grass strapped onto Morning Star's back in his babyboard.

When evening came they pulled the canoes ashore and made a temporary camp. They made a fire and ate food from their stores of dried venison and corn, all seasoned with plenty of the maple sugar the family had collected at the sugarbush. In the morning they boarded the canoes and resumed their journey.

Eleven days passed this way, canoeing along the lakeshore, camping at night, occasionally coming across another family camped on the bank. Sometimes they would stop and speak with these others, ask them questions about the journey ahead. Most often they would just holler a greeting over the waves and keep paddling.

With the burgeoning spring the lake was now largely free of ice, and on the twelfth day Singing Loon pointed the prow of his canoe straight into the offing, Talks Too Much followed, and Caleb's new family paddled out through the tall waves of Lake Huron. It took the better part of the day for them to reach the mouth of the Saint Mary's River on the other side. When they did, they hauled up on the river's bank and made camp. They stoked a fire and cooked fish that Talks Too Much and Singing Loon speared in the river. While the adults sat about, smoking tobacco pipes and talking of their journey, Caleb and Morning Star played with the wolf pup.

The next day they paddled upriver towards the trading

post at Sault Sainte Marie (which was pronounced "Soo Saint Marie"), where they hoped to find news of Braided Waters' clan relations. Before reaching the trading post they had to bring the canoes ashore, for they had reached the rapids which occupied a long stretch of the Saint Mary's River where it emptied out of Lake Superior.

They journeyed through the woods on foot until they came near the trading post. When they saw the log buildings through the trees, Singing Loon signaled for them to stop.

"Someone should stay here with the boy," he said in his language. "If the white men see him with us, they will ask many questions."

"Why should they ask questions?" Braided Waters said. "The boy wants to come with us. He has no family of his own."

"That is true," Singing Loon said, "but they will not believe an Indian. They will say that we stole him."

"I will stay here with the boy," Grandmother said.

"Me too," said Morning Star, who held the wolf puppy.

Singing Loon and Braided Waters and Talks Too Much then walked off toward the trading post, and Morning Star and Caleb sat down on the trunk of a fallen tree. Grandmother told stories of the old days, and the dogs nudged the wolf puppy along on the ground between them.

When the others came back, Singing Loon and Talks Too Much were both leading horses. They had hired them, with money they had received from trading furs with Trader Campau, from an Ojibway man camped at the post. They all then went back to where they had left the canoes and loaded their things onto the backs of the horses. While they were working, Braided Waters spoke to Morning Star in the Ojibway language. Morning Star came to Caleb and explained what she had been told, doing the best she could with the words she knew and gestures. Caleb came to understand that Braided Waters' relations, with whom they were going to, had traveled far to the west. They were now at a summer village on the Copper Peninsula, which juts into Lake Superior from its southern shore. Morning Star's family was going to carry their canoes to the shores of Lake Superior, with their things loaded onto the horses, and then travel along the shores of the great lake to find Braided Waters' clan relations.

After Caleb helped load the cargo onto the horses he helped Talks Too Much carry one of the canoes. Singing Loon and Braided Waters carried the other, and Grandmother led the horses in tandem. Morning Star continued to carry Wind-in-Grass on her back and the wolf puppy in her arms. After a hard day's walking they reached the shore of Lake Superior, the largest freshwater lake in the world. They stood on its pebbly shore and looked out over vast, blue waters that disappeared into a distant horizon. Then they unloaded the horses and made a fire, over which Braided Waters and Grandmother began to cook supper. Talks Too Much mounted one of the horses, a pretty little paint and, taking the other by its lead, rode off to the trading post to return them both. The others made camp there by the lake. Late that night Talks Too Much returned on foot. He was breathless, for he had run much of the way.

In the morning they set out on the great lake, paddling westward. They stayed close to shore as they had done on Lake Huron. As they journeyed, they passed not merely small family groups along the shore of the lake, but also larger congregations. The Ojibway had begun to gather in their summer villages, where they would vist with their relatives and friends. They would hold feasts, plant gardens, work the lake's waters for fish and mussels, and share stories of their adventures at the winter hunting camps.

Caleb and his friends journeyed along the shores of Lake Superior for almost two weeks. They stopped at night at the villages they passed, where they swapped stories, shared the warmth of fires, and left gifts of sculpted maple sugar. When they reached the Copper Peninsula, where deposits of copper could be dug up from the earth, they rowed nearly to its point, until they came to the village where they found Braided Waters' clan relations. There was great joy when Braided Waters greeted relatives she had not seen for many years. Her mother and father were there, and also aunts and uncles, her brothers and sisters and many cousins.

That night they held a feast, with fish caught from the lake, game hunted in the woods, and much singing and dancing. Caleb stayed a little apart from the others. He knew that he was different, and he could not understand the words the people spoke or the songs they sang. He sat at the edge of the firelight, watching the others laughing and singing, and held the wolf puppy in his lap.

He felt a deep pang at the thought of losing his father. That reminded him of his mother and of his sister Emily, whom he had also lost, and he began to feel very sad. But Morning Star came to him with special treats of food, and she sat with him awhile and stroked the puppy's fur, and her company made him feel better. When she went off, Caleb told himself that his father must not be dead, but that he would one day come to find him, just as he had always promised he would. Later Morning Star brought her cousins to where Caleb sat, and Caleb let them hold the wolf pup. Some of these, like the children at the trading post, wanted to touch his hair, for they had never seen a boy whose hair shone like gold.

The next day, soon after everyone awoke, Braided Waters and Morning Star came to Caleb. Braided Waters carried a suit of clothes such as the Ojibway wear and a pair of new deerskin moccasins. With Morning Star's help, Braided Waters told Caleb that he must come with them, and that something very big was about to happen. Caleb could not understand what this something was, but he followed them to the banks of a stream that ran into the lake. Braided Waters made him undress down to his underwear, against his objections, and they scrubbed him in the stream. When they were done, they helped him put on the Ojibway clothes that Braided Waters had brought.

When they returned with him to the village, all of Braided Waters's clan relations were waiting. When they saw Caleb in his new clothes they smiled and greeted him warmly. While he stood near a huge bonfire they sang and danced around him, and gave him presents, and then they held a great feast that lasted almost all the day. When they were done, Morning

Star explained to him that he was now part of their tribe, for through the day's ceremony he had been adopted. She smiled a broad smile and taught him the new name he had been given. That name was Mahengun-wangawi, and it meant *Wolftamer*.

For he had been found in the den of a wolf.

Chapter 14

A Father's Promise

IT TOOK DANIEL JORDAN over a week to reach Detroit. He was tired and exhausted and had no food. At times his head hurt so badly that it made everything around him spin, and he had to stop and rest. When he finally straggled into the town he went directly to the fort. Once at its gates he nearly collapsed into the arms of the sentries. They helped him inside and he spoke to the captain there. He told him that he had lost his son in the woods.

"I had hoped that he would return here," Jordan said weakly.

"We've seen no sign of the boy," the captain said. "But we'll put out word. We'll send to the tavern. Maybe he returned there. We'll also send to the fort at Saginaw and mount a search party. Do you remember where you were when you lost one another?"

Jordan could only say that they were still some distance from the Saginaw fort. He told the captain that Standing Bear had been killed, and how he himself had been attacked from behind.

"I see," the captain said.

Then, because Daniel Jordan was utterly spent, and his head hurt badly, they put him in a bed and called for a doctor. A kind woman came into the room and fed him soup with a spoon. A little later the doctor came and treated the wound in his head where the wolf-bounty hunter had struck him, and he gave him some medicine which made him fall asleep.

When Daniel awoke, Josiah Strong was sitting beside his

bed.

"I hear you've lost your boy," Strong said.

"We were separated on the trail," Jordan replied.

"Maybe Caleb went on with the horse to the fort at Saginaw."

"But he would have arrived by now, wouldn't he?" Jordan said. "Surely the captain there would have sent word."

"You never know. Maybe they're all out looking for you. Maybe Caleb was found by some other travelers on the trail. They could be bringing him here as we speak."

"I've got to get up," Jordan suddenly stammered, "—got to find Caleb." He pulled himself from the bed, but he was still woozy from the medicine the doctor had given him, and from many days without food, and he faltered on his feet.

"Not so fast," Strong said as he leapt up and lowered Daniel Jordan back onto the bed. "The doctor says you need a few days' rest. That's a nasty wound you've got."

"But I've got to find my boy . . ." Jordan began but, as he let out a painful groan, his head dropped back onto the bed. For a moment it looked as though he would pass out. Then he opened his eyes a slit, peering at Josiah Strong with a silent pleading.

"Listen to me," Strong said, "I'll presently be leaving here with three Ojibway friends. They know the woods from here to Saginaw like you know the back of your hand. We're going to search for Caleb. If he's in those woods, I assure you we'll find him. I've been told that the captain has sent word up to Fort Saginaw, and they'll surely send out their own search party. I'll report back to you within a couple of weeks. Meanwhile, the best thing for you to do is to heal up and regain your strength."

Strong grasped Daniel Jordan's arm and squeezed it firmly.

"Have faith," he said.

Jordan wanted to thank him, but waves of exhaustion spread over his brain and he could not speak. He closed his eyes and dropped into a very deep sleep.

Daniel Jordan spent almost three weeks at Fort Detroit. By the second week he spent most of the day out of bed, but he was still wobbly on his legs. When Josiah Strong returned, at the end of that week, he had regained the better part of his strength.

"We didn't find Caleb, I'm afraid," Strong said. "But the man who runs the trading post up that way—Campau's his name—saw him. Caleb spent a night there, in fact. He was brought in by an Ojibway man named Singing Loon and his family. Unfortunately, in the morning he was gone. It looks like he ran off."

"Ran off?" Jordan said. "Where could he have gone?"

"No one seems to know. Some of the Ojibway who were camped around the post said they saw him with the family that brought him in. Maybe he went off with them."

"We've got to find them," Jordan said.

"That's not going to be easy. Singing Loon's family generally stays around Saginaw Bay during the summer. But a couple of the Ojibway who were there seemed to believe they were heading north. Nobody knows where they might be now. They could be way up along Lake Superior, or closer to the straits at Mackinac. Some of the Ojibway travel clear out past the Grand Portage, up Minnesota way, or even into Canada. That's hundreds and hundreds of miles. And most of it's pure wilderness, with no roads, just Indian trails."

"Just the same, I've got to find my son."

"Of course you do," Strong said gravely, and the two men fell silent.

"I'll have to ask you to release me from my promise to blacksmith for the Indians," Daniel Jordan said after a moment, "at least for now."

"Of course," Strong said. "What do you plan to do?"

"I'm going to set to searching for Caleb. As soon as I can get a horse and some provisions, I'll be off."

"Perhaps I can help," Strong said. He took a purse from his buckskin jacket and opened it. "Please take this, to help with your provisions." He handed Jordan several gold coins.

Jordan thanked him and said that he would repay him

when he could. He told Josiah Strong that he must prepare for his journey, and Strong asked Jordan to come to see him before he left Detroit.

Daniel Jordan spent the next several days buying provisions. He purchased a good horse, a hunting rifle and ammunition, a bed roll, cooking tools, corn meal, beans, and beef jerky. He loaded his things into saddle bags and rode to the place where Josiah Strong was staying. Strong asked if he might take a cup of tea, but Jordan was in a great hurry and said that he could not linger. Strong told him that he had sent word out among his Ojibway friends. He learned that Singing Loon's family had stopped at Sault Sainte Marie, but that Caleb had not been with them.

Strong asked Daniel Jordan to wait at the door. He then went into a closet and brought out a large leather sack which he handed him.

"Here," Strong said, "I got these for you. They may come in handy."

Jordan opened the bag. Inside was a set of blacksmithing tools."You're likely to find work at the trading posts and Ojibway villages," Strong said. "They're always in need of a good smith to mend their pots and pans, their rifles and axes. That way you can earn your keep while you're traveling. I know you lost your tools with the horse on the trail."

Jordan remarked that they were a fine set of tools and thanked Strong for his many kindnesses. He went out into the street, fastened the bag of tools to his horse, mounted, and rode toward the gates of the town.

After passing through the gates he rode northward on the same trail he and Caleb had followed with Standing Bear. He frequently called out Caleb's name, in case he were nearby, wandering in the woods. Perhaps he had not gone with the Ojibway family when he ran off from Mr. Campau's trading post, Jordan thought, but instead tried to find his way back to Detroit. From time to time he said a quiet prayer, "Please Lord, help me find my son!"

He rode on toward Fort Saginaw, stopping at night to build a fire and make camp. The trees of the forest, which were nought but bare branches when he rode this way with Caleb and Standing Bear three weeks earlier, now sported reddish buds opening into small green leaves. The snow had melted from the wet ground, and the smaller plants of the forest floor (mayapple and yarrow, nettle and ironweed) had begun to send their shoots skyward.

After four days travel Daniel Jordan reached Fort Saginaw. He spoke to the captain there, but the search parties he had sent out had not found any trace of Caleb. He then went to Trader Campau's trading post, but he received no more news of Caleb then what Josiah Strong had already told him. He inquired of the Ojibway families who were camped around the post, but few of them spoke English, and those who did knew nothing of Caleb's whereabouts.

"All I can figure is that he went off with Singing Loon's family, the ones who brought him in," Trader Campau said. "From what I remember them saying, they were heading north, up to the Sault."

Jordan did not know what *the Sault* was.

"That's Sault Sainte Marie," Campau said. "The first part is pronounced like the name *Sue.* It's up where Lake Superior runs into the Saint Mary's River. There's a fort there and a big trading post. Lots of the Ojibway gather there this time of year."

"How can I get there?" Jordan asked.

"There's only one way," Campau replied, "and that's by boat. It's clear across Lake Huron."

"But I have no boat."

"I see." Campau rubbed his chin and thought for a moment. "In that case, you can either ride back to Detroit and wait for the schooner, or you could see if any of these Indians are heading that way. They might be willing to take you along, for a reasonable fee, of course."

Daniel Jordan was anxious to find Caleb and did not want to backtrack to Detroit. He said that he would rather go with the Indians if any were going and would take him. Trader Campau said that he would inquire with the Ojibway families camped around the post and let him know. He called his wife and asked her to lay out dinner for Jordan, and she led him to the kitchen and gave him good, hot food.

When he had eaten he thanked her, and Trader Campau came in. He said that he had found an Ojibway family who was rowing to the Sault the next day and that they agreed to take Jordan along. Daniel Jordan thanked him. Then Jordan said that he had noticed that one of the legs of Mrs. Campau's iron stove had come free. Two bricks, stacked one upon the other, supported that corner of the stove. He asked if he might mend it in gratitude for the Campaus' kindnesses, both to his son and to himself. Trader Campau said that he would be obliged for the favor and he and Daniel, along with a couple of Ojibway men Campau recruited from around the post, carried the heavy iron stove out into the yard. Jordan first dug a pit, in which he stoked a fire which soon grew very hot. He found a hard stone near the river which he used as an anvil, and he mended the broken stove-leg with the blacksmithing tools Josiah Strong had given him.

When he finished with the stove the day was dying. After Jordan and Trader Campau, with the help of a few of the Ojibway men who were nearby, carried the heavy stove back into the kitchen, Mrs. Campau prepared supper. She then showed Daniel Jordan upstairs to the same room his son had slept in, where she now made up a pallet where Daniel could sleep. He was very tired from his journey and he was soon asleep.

In the morning Trader Campau took Daniel Jordan to the Ojibway family who had agreed to take him across Lake Huron to Sault Sainte Marie. Campau paid him a fair price for the horse he had bought in Detroit, for Jordan would not be able to take the animal across the lake in the Ojibway canoes. Together they loaded his things with the family's belongings; Jordan then got into one of the vessels; and they pushed off into the river and paddled out toward Saginaw Bay.

Chapter 15

Among the Ojibway

AFTER THE CEREMONY in which Caleb was adopted into Morning Star's tribe, he settled into life among the Ojibway. His adoptive family treated him just as if he were their own, and he soon felt comfortable among them. Singing Loon and Talks Too Much began to tutor him in the daily activities of the Ojibway men. Every morning they brought him along when they went to hunt in the forests, or paddled out into the lake to capture sturgeon, bass, and lake trout.

Caleb learned that when the Ojibway killed an animal, especially a large one, they offered thanks both to the Master of Life and to the spirit of the animal itself. The Ojibway believed that every animal species had its own special spirit, which they called its Owner. When they were able to find and kill an animal to feed themselves and their families, they felt that this was a gift for which they should give proper thanks.

One day Caleb was out hunting with Talks Too Much when a big black bear came lumbering over a rise. Talks Too Much raised his rifle and fired. The bear ripped through the brush with a terrible cry, for fifty yards or more, and then crumpled onto the ground in a furry heap. Talks Too Much and Caleb rushed toward the beast. When they were still twenty paces away, Talks Too Much held his arm out to stop Caleb. He was afraid the bear might still be alive. He quietly stepped another ten paces and fired his hunting rifle again. The bullet landed with a sharp thud in the thick fur behind the bear's skull, and the bear did not move again. Talks Too Much gestured to Caleb, and they went up to the fallen animal.

Before dressing the bear, Talks Too Much knelt beside it and began to speak. Caleb could only understand an occasional word, for his knowledge of the Ojibway language was still weak. But were he able to understand it all, this is what he would have heard:

"Thank you, noble one. I am sorry to have to end your life. But being a man, I must eat, and I must bring meat for my family. Please do not hold it against me. Do not be angry."

Talks Too Much dressed the bear, and with Caleb's help they dragged it back to the village. That evening a feast was held so that everyone could share in the meat. The head of the bear was placed on a little ledge in the wigwam of Caleb's family, and Talks Too Much burned tobacco before it so that the spirit of the bear might enjoy its aroma and not be angry with him for taking its life.

In this way, little by little, Caleb learned the ways of the Ojibway. Singing Loon gave him a good hunting rifle, and soon Caleb was bringing down game himself: mainly deer, but also wild turkey and sometimes elk. Now, when they fished in the lake, Singing Loon and Talks Too Much did not need to show Caleb everything he must do. He worked with them easily, for he had learned how to spear fish and place nets, and when to help haul them in and how. He was also learning the Ojibway words for things, like *namewag*, which meant sturgeon, or *jiimaan*, which meant canoe.

When he was not hunting or fishing with Singing Loon and Talks Too Much, Caleb played with the other boys of the summer village. Like boys everywhere, they loved to play games of running and jumping and also games with balls. They held contests to see who could run the fastest or swim the furthest, and sometimes they wrestled or held mock battles. Caleb was not the best at these games, but he was not the worst. The Ojibway boys at first made him prove himself. Sometimes they teased him, calling him "white face" and "straw hair." But they soon came to respect him, because he never gave up. Nor did he cry when they annoyed him. Later they grew to like him because he was always friendly and kind, as his mother and father had taught him to be.

Caleb saw how the women of the summer village, Grandmother and Braided Waters and the others, spent their days while the men went out to hunt and fish. They cared for the children, gathered wood for their cooking fires, made and mended clothing, and tended rich gardens of corn, beans, and squash. Sometimes they went into the forests to search for wild foods like stinging nettles, leaves for making tea, or roots that could be used to heal wounds and sicknesses. Caleb saw how Morning Star helped her mother in all of these tasks, for she was learning to be an Ojibway woman.

Sometimes in the evenings there were feasting and dancing. At other times Caleb's new family sat around the cooking fire telling stories of the day's hunt, or long-remembered tales of the Ojibway people.

One evening Grandmother told the tale of Turtle Island:

"It was long ago," she began, "in the Time Before Time. Kitchi Manitou, the Master of Life, had created the earth and filled it with the Original People. For a time everything was fine. The people showed respect for Spirit and for one another, and everyone got along. But then, after a while, the people forgot the good traditions that had been handed down and became filled with greed and self-centeredness. They fought with each other over hunting territories, fishing rights and garden plots. Before long life was miserable for everyone, with one bloody battle after another.

"Well," Grandmother went on, looking around the circle of her audience, "Kitchi Manitou, who can see all things and was watching the behavior of the Original People, was pretty upset. He didn't like seeing his children, whom he had created, behaving no better than wild beasts. It grieved him sorely, and he finally decided there was nothing for it but to wipe them out, before they had a chance to bring more shame upon themselves with their wickedness.

"So, what Kitchi Manitou did was he made a big flood, one that covered the entire earth. The waters rose and rose until there was no place left to hide. Not even the tallest trees, or even mountains, offered refuge from the waters that Kitchi Manitou sent to purify the earth. Of all the Original People only Nanabush, by clinging to a floating log, was able to survive.

"Nanabush allowed some of the animals and birds to share his log, such as Muskrat and Mink, or Turtle and Loon, and these too survived the flood.

"Finally, when the swirling waters settled down a bit, Nanabush said to the others that he had a plan to restore the earth again. He would swim to the bottom of the waters and retrieve some soil. With this they could begin to build a new world. And without hesitating one second further, he leapt from the log and disappeared under the surface.

"Nanabush was gone for so long that the others feared he had drowned. And when he finally emerged, near the log, he was so winded he couldn't speak for several minutes. 'Too deep,' he said when he had caught his breath. 'Never . . . make it.' With that he collapsed upon the log in exhaustion.

"Loon then volunteered to try. 'I spend my days diving in the lakes for my supper,' he piped up. 'I'm sure I can get to the bottom and back.'"

"The others stood back while Loon leapt into the water and disappeared below the surface. Minutes and minutes went by, far longer than the time Nanabush had been gone. And when Longneck—which is the nickname the others had for Loon—finally came back to the surface, some distance from the log, he was barely conscious. So weak was he, in fact, that Mink had to swim over and help him back to the log.

"Several others volunteered to swim to the bottom for earth, Otter, for example, and also Snake. But none fared any better than had Nanabush and Loon.

"All of the creatures who were gathered there on the flotsam now felt completed dejected, for it seemed there was no hope of finding a solution to their dilemma. But after a moment of sad silence, a small voice piped up from one side of the log. It was Wa'zhushk—Muskrat. 'I'd be willing to give it a try,' she said."

"The others couldn't help but laugh, for if larger, stronger animals like Otter had not been able to reach the bottom, and even Nanabush, how could little Muskrat make it? But

Nanabush admonished them, saying that only the Master of Life—Kitchi Manitou—was capable of judging its creations. The others grew silent, and without further ado Muskrat slipped quietly off the log and disappeared below.

"Muskrat was gone far longer than any of the others, and Mink remarked cattily that she would surely never be seen again. But no sooner had these words left Mink's mouth than someone spotted a patch of brown fur bobbing in the current nearby. It was indeed Muskrat. Nanabush scrambled to pull her body to safety; unfortunately, it was limp and lifeless.

"'Just as we thought,' Loon piped up, 'she drowned before she could get to the bottom.'

"The animals began to sing a death song while Nanabush laid Muskrat's body out on the log. But as he did this, stretching her arms along her sides, he couldn't help notice that one of her hands was clenched firmly upon itself. And prying open the fingers, what did he find in the palm of Muskrat's hand but a patch of dark, moist soil! The others turned in amazement. It seemed that little Muskrat had somehow managed to reach the bottom after all, where she had retrieved this small patch of earth. Now Turtle spoke up.

"'I have an idea," he said. "What if I float in the water, and one of you places that wee bit of earth on my back? In that way, with Kitchi Manitou's help, we can begin again to make the earth.'"

"Turtle then shoved off from the log and floated in the water, and Nanabush placed the patch of soil on his back. At that moment Kitchi Manitou, pleased to see his children cooperating and helping one another again, instead of bickering and fighting, began to make the winds blow from all of the Four Directions. They blew wildly upon the piece of earth, and it began to expand until it was large enough for the animals—who were filled with joy that the earth was being rebuilt again—to dance upon and sing. The earth grew heavier and heavier, but still Turtle remained strong, and before long Turtle Island grew into what today we call North America.

"You should always remember," Grandmother now said, turning especially to the children as she finished her tale, "to follow the good ways of your ancestors, obey your parents, and cooperate and help one another."

Sometimes, when they weren't busy helping with work, Caleb and Morning Star played together with the wolf puppy. They would run with him along the shores of the lake, or play tug-of-war with a piece of old cloth. Caleb and Morning Star had agree that Caleb would speak only Ojibway when they were together, and Morning Star only English. This way, correcting and helping each other, they each learned to speak in the way of the other.

When Singing Loon was satisfied that Caleb could take care of himself in the woods, he began to allow him to hunt on his own. Caleb practiced the things that Singing Loon and Talks Too Much had taught him, such as how to track animals by their footprints, how to stalk them without making even the slightest sound, or how to remain downwind of them so they would not smell you as you approached them. When Caleb went out to hunt, his wolf puppy followed along. He did not need to teach the pup to remain quiet when they stalked their quarry, for the wolf was a hunter by nature. It seemed to Caleb that the wolf could almost read his mind. When they made their way through the forest together, he hardly had to say a thing to make it do as he wanted. Sometimes Caleb followed the wolf, for its hunting instincts were strong, and this way they stalked their prey together.

The puppy grew quickly, and by the time of the summer solstice he stood at the height of Caleb's hips. He was mostly brownish-gray, with white on its legs and chest, and long ears that stood straight up on its head. He slept outside the wigwam with the family's other two dogs, and he liked to tussle with them. At first the dogs had easily put the wolf puppy in its place. But even now, when the pup was far from fully grown, the dogs began to feel its strength and were reluctant to pick a fight. As the puppy grew, the other boys of the village greatly admired Caleb. They wondered what special medicine he must possess to tame a wolf.

The summer came and passed with hunting in the forest and fishing in the lake. In the long twilight evenings of the north, Caleb ran with the other boys of the village or sat by his adopted family's fire. He continued to practice speaking his new language with Morning Star, and by summer's end he could understand most of the things that were said around the fires in the evenings.

Sometimes Caleb sat apart, staring into the flames, and thought about his own family. First and foremost, he still wondered what had happened to his father. Was he dead, as Trader Campau had said, or was he still alive? Would he ever see him again, or was he gone forever, like his mother and sister? The memory of the mother and sister would then fill his mind, and he would start to wonder where they were as well.

He still felt sharp pangs of grief when he recalled the horrible things he had said to Emily, and now it was too late to ask her forgiveness. At times his sadness would be such that he almost ceased to be aware of the others around the fire. The wolf pup, lying at his feet, would look up at him and whine; but it would receive no answer. If Morning Star came to him with a funny story, or to ask him questions, as she often did, he would barely notice her presence. Feeling ignored and unhappy, she would go away.

One evening when he was like this, late in summer, Braided Waters came around the fire to where he sat and stood over him. He did not notice her at first, but finally he looked up into her face.

"Come with me," she said in the language of the Ojibway. "We will talk."

Caleb stood up, and Braided Waters walked away from the family's fire toward the lake. Caleb followed. All that remained of the day was a weak, silvery light. When Braided Waters and Caleb came near the shore, they walked along together over the pebbly beach.

"What do you think about," Braided Waters said, "when you sit so quietly? You stare into the fire as if you are in world of your own."

Caleb wanted to speak, to tell her all of the painful things he felt inside. But he was afraid to, for he feared that she would think he was foolish.

"You know," Braided Waters said, "if you keep hard things inside for too long, they will eat their way out, whether you like it or not."

Caleb still was silent, for he did not know how to put words on the things he felt. They walked awhile, and then Braided Waters spoke again.

"Is it your father you think about? I know you must miss him."

"Yes," Caleb said. "Trader Campau said he was dead, but I don't believe it."

"If he is alive," said Braided Waters, "surely he will come for you, will he not?"

"But he won't know where I am."

"I think he will find you, if he is still living. Perhaps we can find a way to send word to Detroit, to see if there is any news of him. Would that make you feel better?"

"Yes."

"It is very far away, but I will see if it can be done."

"Thank you," Caleb said.

They stopped walking and turned back toward where the others sat around the fires. They could hear the distant voices and the small, choppy waves of the lake slapping against the shore. Caleb stared out across the vast waters, and Braided Waters watched him.

"So it's just your father, and what has become of him, that you think about so deeply," she asked, "staring into the fire, unaware of all that goes on around you?"

Caleb shrugged his shoulders.

"Look at me," Braided Waters said. She took him by the shoulders and turned him toward her. "For every hurt there is a cause, and for every grief there is a cure. You are afraid to speak, because you are afraid that the grief you feel can never be cured. But to speak of it is a beginning. The Master of Life can do all things, even for a boy like you."

Braided Waters looked deep into Caleb's eyes. And because she was a mother, she saw Caleb's mother's image their. And because she was a sister, she also saw his sister Emily there.

"Tell me about your mother and your sister," she said.

Caleb was more than a little amazed, because she had seemed to read his mind. He realized that she must care for him almost as much as his own mother had. A tear appeared in his eye, and he told Braided Waters about how she had died in the big sickness that had come to Albany. He told her also how he had lost his sister, and of the terrible things he had said to her in anger before she died. He wanted to cry. But he held in his tears, for the Ojibway, like his own people, thought it good that a man not show his tears. He did not want Braided Waters to think him weak.

Tears came to Braided Waters's eyes, though, because she remembered her own son Fleeting Elk, who had also died in a terrible sickness. She thought of Morning Star, and how badly she missed her brother after he was gone. But she spoke steadily, as she held Caleb again by his shoulders.

"I know how you feel about your sister," she said. "We must remember that our words can be like weapons. They can wound just as surely, and just as painfully. But it was not your words that took your sister's life. Only Kichi Manitou knows our true purpose here, on this earth, and only He knows when our time is done.

"Your grief is a good thing, because it shows that you have a heart. It also shows that you have learned. You have learned what a good thing it is to have a sister, to have relations who love us. And you have learned that we must control our tongues, so that we do not hurt those we love. These are valuable lessons. You are a good and a smart boy to have learned them. Come, we will return."

They began to walk toward the family's fire.

"Among our people," Braided Waters said, after they had walked several paces, "it is customary for a boy your age to seek a vision."

"I know," Caleb said. He had heard the other boys speak of vision quests, and Morning Star once told him of how she had fasted for four days in the forest.

"I think it is time for you," Braided Waters said.

"I am willing to try."

After Caleb's conversation with Braided Waters his spirit began to feel lighter. Though he still missed his father and still grieved over his mother and sister, especially about the way he had treated his sister before she died, he found these hurts easier to bear. He was not so apt to sit staring in a world of his own while the others told tales and laughed around the fire. Braided Waters had not yet said anything about sending word to Detroit. But he believed in her, and he felt certain that she would try to obtain news of his father.

When the month of September came, which the Ojibway call the Ricing Moon, everyone in the village moved inland to a marsh choked with thick stands of wild rice. They set up their wigwams along its edges, for they would live among the wetlands for many weeks. After making prayers to Kitchi Manitou, the Underneath Beings and the Thunderers, they set about harvesting the grain, which grew on stalks that stood as much as ten feet high. Since the grain grew in water, it was necessary to harvest it from canoes. Caleb poled one of these canoes through the grain beds while Braided Waters and Morning Star used beating sticks to gently knock the ripe grain kernels from the tall stalks and into the craft.

After the grains were harvested in this way, the women of the village still had a great deal of work to do. The kernels had to be dried, so they would not rot from moisture, and then winnowed, to separate the chaff, which cannot be eaten, from the nutritious seed. Next the men "danced" the rice, stomping on it to remove the rough hulls from the tasty grains. Finally, after a big feast was held, the remaining rice was stored away; these stores would help the people live through the long northern winter that was soon to come upon them.

After the rice harvest the cranberries began to ripen. Now the women and children of the village spent their days in the cranberry bogs, wet places where the cranberry bushes grew, harvesting the tart red fruits. The berries could be cooked into other foods, or dried and mixed with deer meat to make pemmican. Pemmican was a sort of jerky that could be carried on the hunt and would not spoil.

One evening Morning Star led Caleb through the forest to

the cranberry bogs, for she wanted him to see them. She still remembered how much fun she used to have picking cranberries with her brother, Fleeting Elk. She led Caleb out into the bog, which was soft and spongy underfoot. She jumped up and down, which made the ground under them pitch and roll, for in the bog the soil floated on water underneath. Caleb began to jump also and the ground wobbled even more. They laughed because the wolf, who had accompanied them, did not understand. It yelped excitedly while it leapt back and forth, trying to keep its balance.

The wolf was not quite five months old now. It was yet much smaller than an adult wolf, skinny and a little awkward. Still the village dogs had ceased to pick on him, for he was no longer an easy target. His teeth were long and sharp, and the clamping power of his jaws was a great deal stronger than that of any domestic canine. When the wolf approached them, all but the largest and boldest now rolled onto the ground and exposed their bellies. In this way they admitted that they were weaker.

The wolf's growing strength had been the subject of a conversation just days before between Singing Loon and Braided Waters.

"The wolf will soon need to go," Singing Loon had said. "By the time of the Freezing Over Moon he will be too big to handle. He will not be safe among the children."

"Yes, I know," said Braided Waters. "but it is good that we allowed Mahengun-wangawi to bring him to the summer village. He was so alone, and the puppy was his only friend. What will we do now with the wolf?"

"We will stop feeding it and drive it from the village. It will have to find new friends among the pathfinders."

"I hope Mahengun-wangawi will not be too unhappy."

"No one escapes unhappiness in this world."

While Caleb and Morning Star were on their way back to the village from the cranberry bogs, the wolf beside them, an encounter took place which would in time ease the worries of Morning Star's parents. They had come to an opening in the forest where a wide meadow led up to the crest of a low hill. The wolf stiffened. Its ears stood straight up and it began to make a low, whining sound. Caleb and Morning Star followed its gaze to the top of the rise. There, against the darkening sky, stood another wolf. All alone, it stared down at them, shifting on its feet as though prepared to flee. It was a she-wolf, older than Caleb's wolf but still young. Caleb's wolf whined and made a few leaping motions toward the wolf on the rise. He turned to Caleb and Morning Star and emitted a sharp, quick yelp. The she-wolf began to whine and yip, and Caleb's wolf yipped also. He sat on his haunches and began to howl.

The she-wolf joined in and the two wolves howled together for a minute or more. Then, suddenly, Caleb's wolf broke and ran half-way up the hill toward her. She trotted back and forth across the top of the rise. She was reluctant to come any closer to Caleb and Morning Star, for she feared human beings. Caleb's wolf turned again to Caleb and yipped at him. Then it turned and ran to the crest of the hill. He and the she-wolf sniffed one another. They touched their noses together. The she-wolf disappeared over the rise, and Caleb's wolf followed her.

Caleb and Morning Star ran up the hill to see where the wolves had gone, but the land on the other side of the rise sloped down into thick woods. They could not see the wolves, though they heard their keening and yelping. Caleb called to his wolf but it did not come. He stood and waited, and after a minute called some more, and finally the wolf emerged from the edge of the forest. It ran toward Caleb and Morning Star. Then it stopped, turned, and looked toward the woods.

The she-wolf was there, almost invisible in the shadows of the trees. She whined toward Caleb's wolf and let out a loud yelp, but she would not come into the open while Caleb and Morning Star were there. Caleb's wolf doubled back toward the woods. He leapt and yelped, but the she-wolf would not follow. Caleb called again to him. Finally the wolf ran up the slope. He followed Caleb and Morning Star back over the rise and home to the village.

When the cranberry harvest was done, the people of the village packed their things and moved to the mouth of a large stream that emptied into the lake. This is where they now set up camp, so the men could trap the salmon and trout that came into the streams to spawn every autumn. The broad-leaved trees had all gone gold and red, and the air was brisk with cold. While the men trapped fish, the women worked hard drying them; in this way they would add the smoked fillets to their winter food stores. All day long the drying fires were going and the sweet, oily smell of fish hung over the camp.

It was now that Caleb went into the woods to seek a vision.

He had learned about the spirit beings of the Ojibway people from the stories told around the camp fires: the Thunderers and the Owners of the Animals, the many manitous, and the Great Manitou, the Master of Life. Grandmother had taught him special spirit songs, and Talks Too Much and Singing Loon had told him how every man must seek a vision to guide his life. Without help from Spirit, they said, he would have great difficulty supporting his family as a hunter, and doing all the other things an Ojibway man must do to live.

On the appointed day, Caleb and Talks Too Much struck out into the forest. They walked the better part of a day before finding a place that felt right, a clearing in the forest far removed from the busy-ness and noise of the fishing camp. Talks Too Much showed Caleb how to make a circle on the ground with stones he collected from the earth around him. This is where he would seek his vision. Talks Too Much left the water they had brought and returned to the camp. As he had been instructed, Caleb sat in the middle of the circle of stones. He began to sing the spirit songs that Grandmother, Braided Waters, and Talks Too Much had taught him.

Thus Caleb spent the day. From time to time he stopped singing and sipped a little water. He did not eat, for he must fast until he should receive a vision from Spirit. That night he slept on the ground within his circle of rocks, wrapped in a bear skin. At dawn he awoke and watched the daylight slowly fill the forest. He did not go to explore through the woods, however, as he might have liked to do. He had been told by Talks Too Much to stay within the circle until he should receive a vision, or until he could stand it no longer. He sipped some water and, remembering why he was there, began to sing spirit songs.

Sometimes he ceased singing and just sat and listened to the sounds of the forest. Here and there a bird would call. At times he heard an animal crunch across the dry leaves that lay on the forest floor. Once a large flock of geese flapped noisily overhead on their way south for the winter. His stomach began to trouble him somewhat, for he had gone an entire day and night without eating. He got onto his knees. Placing his forehead on the ground before him, he called to Kitchi Manitou:

"Master of Life," he said, "please come to me with a vision, or send a spirit being. Please, make it soon! I am very hungry, and I don't know how much longer I can stand it!"

Speaking to Kitchi Manitou this way came naturally to Caleb. Although the ways of the Ojibway differed from the Christian religion, with its Bible and church, his mother had taught him to pray when he was a small child, and he was accustomed to speaking to God.

He prayed several times more to Kitchi Manitou that day, and he sang his spirit songs with great energy. But still a vision did not come. To relieve his restlessness he got on his feet and danced in place, as he had learned to do from the Ojibway. He sang his spirit songs while he danced, but also old songs his mother had taught him, or even songs he made up on the spot.

When he tired he would sit again and try not to notice the way his stomach tugged at him. He would think of his father, wondering where he was, or think of his mother and Emily and how they used to live together in Albany, New York. Midway through the afternoon he hung his head down and for loneliness and hunger began to cry. But the sun streaming through the falling leaves brought him around again, and by the time darkness approached he sat calmly, quietly singing his songs to Spirit. When the woods grew dark he kept on singing, and finally he dropped off to sleep.

When he awoke it was the dead of night. Somewhere close by he heard the hoot of an owl, and also wolves howling in the distance. He pulled the bear skin close around him. He tried to be very quiet, so that if there were wolves or cougars nearby they would not know that he was there.

The next day passed much the same way, with singing and beseeching and dancing in place in his circle of stones. His stomach had now ceased to gnaw at him. Instead he felt very light and intensely attuned to everything around him. Every small detail of the leaves on the ground, or the bark of the trees, stood out more clearly than he had ever seen. Every scent of the forest was very distinct, and he could make out even the tiniest sounds: insects crawling, or twigs falling to the forest floor. At the coming of darkness he did not go to sleep but sat far into the night singing songs of Spirit.

The next he knew it was dawn, and there before him, staring directly into his eyes, stood a buck deer with a big, branching rack!

He started and began to back away; but much to his amazement, the deer seemed to speak to him.

"Don't be afraid," the deer said. "I am here to help you. Rise to your feet and follow me."

The deer took off running through the forest. Caleb jumped up and followed. The deer leapt along with great quickness, but somehow Caleb was able to run like the wind and had no trouble keeping up. Finally, coming to a small clearing, the deer leapt straight into a big hole in the forest floor. Caleb stretched out his arms and dove in after him.

Only an instant later it seemed to Caleb that he was flying. As he glided along he could see the earth below, mountains and a swiftly running stream, with vast cloud shadows moving over the land. After flying like this for several minutes he plunged suddenly and radically downward, went straight through the trunk of a tree, and emerged from a large cavity at the base of the tree onto the ground.

He began to walk, seeking something familiar. When he

reached the stream that he had seen from the air he followed along its bank. A large turtle came floating by and he leapt upon its back, letting it carry him downstream. In this way he followed the stream for some time. After a while he began to hear the voices of people ahead. They were singing together. When the stream reached a lake, Caleb climbed off the back of the turtle and onto the beach.

There across the sandy beach that bordered the lake were many, many people. Among them were the Ojibway people among whom Caleb now lived. Singing Loon was there and Braided Waters, Talks Too Much, Grandmother and Morning Star, and also the boys and girls Caleb had played with along the shores of Lake Superior. As he walked further along the beach in the direction of the gathering he saw that many other people were there also, except these were not Indians but people he had known when he lived in Albany. His schoolteacher was there and the men he used to watch load the big sailing ships at the docks, the drovers whom he and Thomas helped drive their cattle to the Pastures, all the tradespeople and merchants of the town, and the many townspeople he would meet at the market when he would help his mother pick up her stores and supplies.

All of the people, Indians and white, sang together and danced on the sandy beach, gathered around huge bonfires that had been lit up and down the shoreline. They ate fish they had culled from the lake and cooked on tall smoking racks, along with big ears of corn roasted in the fires; they had beans and squashes and also venison meat, and all was dressed with maple syrup brought from the sugarbushes of the many Ojibway families gathered there.

As Caleb reached this convocation, someone stepped out of the crowd. It was Joshua Strong, wearing a big beaver skin cap and gesturing to him to join the celebration. Caleb ran to meet him, glad to see a friendly face and eager for news of his father. But when he reached the edge of the crowd, Strong had vanished. Caleb wandered through the crowd, looking for him, but after a moment or two he encountered Morning Star. Morning Star smiled at him and took him by the hand,

and he completely forgot about finding Joshua Strong.

Without words Morning Star led him through the crowd to one of the biggest fires. When she and Caleb reached it, Caleb gasped. For there, sitting around the fire on stout logs were not only Braided Waters and Singing Loon, and Grandmother and Talks Too Much—but also Caleb's own mother and sister! They chatted quietly with Morning Star's family and shared their food. Filled with amazement, Caleb made to run toward them but Morning Star, placing a hand on his arm, held him back. She gestured to a place beyond the crowd, out toward the shore of the lake. Looking to where she pointed he saw his father, in buckskin clothes and leading a horse, wandering along the sand, searching. He seemed not to be aware of the many people gathered so nearby.

Caleb began to run toward his father, and now Morning Star did not try to stop him but ran with him instead. They wended their way through the many people until they broke free of the throng. They ran swiftly toward Caleb's father, who walked away from them. But the harder they ran, the further he faded into the distance.

That is when the wolves appeared.

They came running down the beach, from the direction in which Daniel Jordan and his horse had disappeared, straight toward Morning Star and Caleb. When they reached them they rallied, leaping and yelping and crashing forcefully up against them to show their joy. Morning Star and Caleb also leapt with the wolves, and Caleb found himself yelping also, and at times the beginnings of a howl escaped him. The wolves ran toward the forest now and Caleb and Morning Star ran with them. They ran through the trees, weaving and dodging and treading low, and whenever they reached a meadow they ran more freely. They drank in the streams and stopped on a hilltop to join in a chorus of braided howling.

Running with the wolves, Caleb felt happy and strong. He felt almost that he was a wolf himself. Morning Star was beside him, and somehow he knew that he would never really be alone. He felt bright inside and contented.

The next he knew he lay within the circle of rocks he had

made with Talks Too Much. The wolves were gone. He was alone but did not feel lonely. Though he still had not eaten he felt strong with the food he had seen at the gathering on the beach. He remembered seeing Daniel Jordan wandering, wandering and searching, and knew in his heart that his father would find him, somehow.

Chapter 16

Mackinac

IT TOOK THREE WEEKS for Daniel Jordan to reach Sault
Sainte Marie with the Ojibway family who allowed him to
ride along in their canoe. Just as Morning Star's family had
done, they followed closely along the shores of Lake Huron,
stopping at the end of the day to camp on the land, until
they reached the Straits of Mackinac. Sometimes they stayed
ashore for a second day to hunt game in the forest and rest
around a fire. Once at the Straits, they launched across the
Lake where it is narrow and found their way into the mouth
of the Saint Mary's River on the opposite shore.

After Daniel Jordan and his guides traveled up the river and portaged the canoe around the rapids, they reached
the trading post at Sault Sainte Marie. Jordan went immediately into the log building that stood there and spoke with
some men he found, Americans like himself and also French
Canadians, but none of them knew the whereabouts of his
son. Trader Campau had told the Ojibway family with whom
Jordan traveled that he was searching for the family of Singing Loon; and when they arrived at Sault Sainte Marie they
inquired of other Ojibway families they met whether they
knew where Singing Loon's family might be found. Unluck-
ily, none of the Ojibway families gathered around the trading post at Sault Sainte Marie had been there when Singing
Loon's family came into the post, and none knew where they
had gone.

Daniel Jordan then spoke with the trader, a man named
Stockton.

"Do you have any idea where Singing Loon and his family may have gone?" he asked.

"They could be just about anywhere," Trader Stockton said, "—anywhere along the shores of the lakes, that is. They always gather along the lakeshores in the summertime, to hold their feasts and what not."

"Is that all you know?" Jordan asked, more eagerly now. "Didn't you see the family of Singing Loon here? Did you see a young American boy with them?"

Of course Trader Stockton had not seen Caleb, for Morning Star's family left him in the woods when they approached the trading post, for fear that the Americans would accuse them of kidnapping him. Nor, for that matter, had Trader Stockton seen or spoken to Singing Loon and his family, for they had not gone into the store. They had only come to talk to other Ojibway families gathered at the post, so that they might learn where they might find Braided Waters's relations.

"I'm sorry for your plight," the trader said to Jordan, "but I never saw this Singing Loon, and I haven't seen any American boys traveling with Indians."

"I must find my son," Jordan said. "Can you give me any advice? Where do you think they might have gone?"

"I can't say," said Stockton. "I'm afraid you'll have to search until you find them. I wish you the best of luck in that. Like I told you, they'll be leaving their winter camps and starting to move to the lakeshores this time of year. Quite a few Ojibway will be gathered around Fort Mackinac to trade furs. You might start that way. Maybe they've heard something at the fort."

Jordan asked Stockton if he might sell him a horse to replace the one he had sold to Trader Campau.

"I reckon I can get you one," Stockton said, "but it will take several days time."

"Can't it be done any faster?"

"I'll see what I can do," Stockton said. "Horses don't grow on trees, you know."

Daniel Jordan was disappointed that he could not leave immediately to begin his search, but he would need a horse.

It would take much longer on foot and, besides, how would he carry the heavy tools the Ojibway family had helped him bring to Sault Sainte Marie in their canoe?

"Okay," he said to Trader Stockton, "I will wait."

"You can check back with me in three days time," Stockton said, and Jordan left the trading post.

Daniel Jordan camped in the woods near the post while he waited for Trader Stockton to find a horse. Several Ojibway families were also camped there, while others were coming and going; and though Jordan could not speak their language nor they his, he greeted them as best and courteously as he could using gestures and facial expressions. Some nodded silently, but others were gruff and unfriendly, because there was still much resentment among the Ojibway people about the way the American government was taking away their lands. After some of them learned from Trader Stockton that Daniel Jordan was a blacksmith, he grew considerably in their estimation. They came to him with broken gunstocks, pots, and hatchets and asked him, with their best gestures and some English words, if he might repair the damaged items. Using other gestures and words, they showed him things they would trade for his work: animal skins, dried venison meat, and cakes of dried maple sugar. They helped him to make a hot fire in a pit and, using an old piece of discarded iron as an anvil and the blacksmithing tools Joshua Strong had brought him in Saginaw, Daniel Jordan was able to mend the Indians' metal implements.

By the time he learned that Trader Stockton had found a horse for him, Jordan had made several friends among the Ojibway at the trading post. He had also learned many important Ojibway words, like *ishkode*, for fire, or *jiibaakwewakik*, for cooking pot.

The mare that Stockton sold to Daniel Jordan was strong and sturdy, and buckskin in coloring: that is to say, with a tan-colored coat and a black mane and tail. On the morning after he purchased the horse Jordan loaded some of his things into saddlebags, strapping others carefully onto the horse's back behind the saddle. One of the Ojibway people who spoke a little English, and for whom Jordan had done blacksmithing work, offered to go with him as far as the trail to Fort Mackinac. Jordan had decided to follow Trader Stockton's advice and begin his search there. The main army post of the United States government in the Michigan Territory, it was located on an island in the midst of the Straits of Mackinac, the short body of water that connects Lake Huron and Lake Michigan.

Jordan said goodbye to the other Ojibway people he had met and to Trader Stockton and, following his Ojibway guide, who rode a sturdy painted pony, started off toward the Fort Mackinac trail.

After the two men had ridden two hours through thick woods the guide stopped. He got down from his pony and asked Daniel Jordan to do the same. He took up a stick and, crouching on the ground, drew a map in the earth. He showed Jordan where he must fork to the left in order to pick up the main trail to the fort. He told him that once on the main trail he would have two days riding until he reached the Straits of Mackinac.

Jordan gave a good metal knife to his guide for his help and they said goodbye. He then mounted the buckskin and proceeded down the trail by himself. The trail was mostly empty, though he passed an Ojibway family on its way to Sault Sainte Marie and also one of the Canadian men who spent their winters in the woods trading with the Indians for furs.

The night was cool but not unpleasant, and Jordan was comfortable enough as he sat by his campfire, eating some of the dried venison he had traded at the trading post for blacksmithing chores. He slept soundly in the dark night, hardly noticing the cries of an owl near his camp, and at dawn he was awake.

He passed a small detachment of soldiers on the trail that day, and they assured him that he was heading for the Straits of Mackinac. It was not until the sun had begun to drop below the forest trees that Jordan emerged from the woods. He saw ahead the little village of Saint Ignace hugging the shore across from Mackinac Island, on which the fort was located. There was a tavern there, and Jordan went inside and asked how he might get over to the fort.

The tavern keeper, a woman named Mrs. Tallefiere, told him that a ferryman regularly took passengers over to the island, but that he had made his last trip for the day. Daniel Jordan would have to wait until the morning. He asked Mrs. Tallefiere if there was a room available for the night, and she told him that there was. Since he did not have a great deal of money, he asked the innkeeper if there were any blacksmithing jobs he might do in exchange for his keep, but she told him that everything was in good repair. He took out his purse and gave her a couple of coins, and she told him where he could stable the mare.

In the morning Jordan went down to the docks to meet the ferry. There were several others waiting at the dock when he arrived, not only soldiers but also townspeople who lived on the island, running shops and taverns and other businesses that sat along the main street below the fort.

As the ferry pulled away from the docks, Mackinac Island was only a green hump across the water; but once the boat had reached the midway point over from Saint Ignace, Daniel Jordan could begin to make out structures near the shore. As they approached the island's docks the main street of the town came into view, with its whitewashed board buildings lined up in a row.

After leaving the ferry, and asking directions to the fort, Jordan walked along this street, eyeing the shops he passed, wondering if there was anything he might need for his travels. He passed a tavern from which wafted the tempting aromas of hot and freshly-cooked meals, but he knew he must save what coins he had for emergencies, and he walked on toward the fort.

At the end of Main Street the buildings no longer lined the road so closely and, looking away from the water, across a wide open space of grass, Jordan saw Fort Mackinac high on a bluff. Its tall whitewashed walls of strong masonry gleamed in the morning sunlight. Across the grassy space below the fort he noted several wigwams of the sort the Ojibway live in. A number of Ojibway people stood among them, conversing or working at various tasks.

Beyond the grassy space a long ramp led, from left to right, up to the fort. Skirting the edge of the grassy space, Jordan moved toward this ramp, and when he reached it he began to climb. The British had built the fort here so they might keep watch on ships that passed through the Straits of Mackinac. They positioned the fort on the highest place along the shore, where their line of sight would be uninterrupted, and where they would be difficult to attack. After the War of 1812, the Americans forced the British to leave American soil, and the United States government took over the fort.

When Jordan reached the top of the ramp he encountered two sentries in uniforms of red, white and blue, holding rifles at their sides. He explained to them that he had come to the fort to inquire whether anyone had heard news of a lost boy.

"I haven't heard tell of any," one of them said. "What about you, Robert?" He turned to his companion.

Robert stated that he, too, was unaware of any such news.

"Would it be possible for me to enter and speak to the commander of the fort?"

"You want to speak to Captain Daley, you say?"

"If I may."

The two soldiers looked at one another. One cocked his head funnily.

"It's very important," Jordan said, looking humbly into their eyes.

"Who is this boy, anyway?" said the soldier named Robert.

"He's my son, Caleb Jordan."

The soldiers looked at one another again, sharing solemn expressions.

"I suppose that is important," Robert said. "Let him on through."

At that the other soldier stepped aside and Jordan walked through the wide gateway of the fort. "The Captain's office is across the parade grounds and to the left," the one named Robert called after him as he walked away.

Daniel Jordan looked around. Inside the thick masonry walls of the fort were a number of wooden buildings. Some were barracks for the regular soldiers, others were more capacious dwellings for officers. Along one side were stables, a mess hall, and the armory, where the weapons and ammunition were kept. There was also an infirmary, where men who were ill or injured could be treated; a laundry room; a storehouse; and from the particular glow he saw coming from its forge, Jordan noted that the fort possessed its own blacksmith shop.

There were a number of soldiers on the parade ground as Jordan walked towards the commander's office. The soldiers turned out every morning for drills and target practice, and the men had just finished these activities when Jordan arrived at the fort. He asked one of them which of the low wooden buildings nearby was the commander's office and the soldier showed him the way. When he reached the structure, a sentry who stood at the door asked him his business. Jordan told him why he had come and the soldier asked him to wait while he went inside. When he returned, he told him that the commander had agreed to see him and escorted him inside.

The commander of the fort, Captain Daley, greeted Jordan politely and offered him a chair in front of the table which the Captain used as a desk. Jordan told the Captain about how he had become separated from Caleb, how his son had been seen in the company of Singing Loon's family, and how they were said to be traveling north. He told him also of how he had canoed to Sault Sainte Marie with another Ojibway family and then traveled to Mackinac on horseback.

"I'm afraid we haven't heard any news of a lost boy," the Captain said, "though I will be happy to send out word. Perhaps someone else in the fort, or one of the people of the town, have heard something. Where do you plan to go from here?"

Jordan told the Captain that he didn't have a precise plan in mind, but that he intended to continue to search for his son, visiting the summer villages of the Ojibway people in the hope that he might find the family with whom he was traveling.

"You must understand," the Captain went on, "the Ojibway people occupy their summer villages all around the circumference of Lake Superior. It is a distance of many hundreds of miles. You tell me that you have just recently arrived in the Michigan Territory—from Albany, New York? There are many dangers in the woods you will be traveling through. Some of the Ojibway are still hostile. They have not accepted the authority of the United States government. There are difficult fordings, wolves . . ."

"I am aware of the dangers," Jordan replied, "but I must find my son."

"If I understand correctly," the Captain said after a moment, "it has been several weeks since you left Detroit."

"That's correct."

"In that case, let me make a proposal to you. We have a courier who will be leaving for Detroit tomorrow. He will be back in two weeks time. Why don't you stay here until he returns? It's possible that your son has turned up near where you lost contact with one another. Perhaps he has made his way back to Detroit, or to the trading post at Saginaw Bay. It would be a shame if he were waiting for you on the Lower Peninsula, and you were wandering the deep northern woods, subjecting yourself to manifold perils."

Seeing impatience in Jordan's eyes, the Captain continued. "I understand your urgency," he said, "but consider that while you wait here, we can send word around, inquiring after your boy. The American Fur Company has a station here, and there are several fur traders in the town. The traders travel widely, meeting with the Indians to barter for furs, and they hear much news. There are also a number of Ojibway families who have come in to trade their pelts. It's possible that they have learned something of your son. At the very least, one of the Indian families may know where to find the family of Singing Loon."

"My provisions are limited," Jordan told the Captain, "and I don't have much money. How will I live while I am here? I cannot afford to stay at an inn for two weeks."

"Don't trouble yourself with that, my man," said the Captain. "We will find room for you here at the fort. Didn't you say that you are a blacksmith by trade?"

Jordan assented.

"In that case, you can help out in the smithy to earn your keep. Agreed?"

Jordan thought long and hard. He didn't like the idea of a delay, for each passing day during which he did not find Caleb felt like an eternity. But the Captain had said much that was logical. It was true that Caleb could still be near Saginaw, or even back at Detroit. No one knew for certain that he had traveled to the Upper Peninsula with Singing Loon's family. Jordan also considered what the Captain said about the many people at Mackinac who might have heard news of Caleb, fur traders who traveled through the deep forests, and also many Indian families such as those he had seen camped at the base of the fort. Fort Mackinac was the chief place for trading furs in northern Michigan, and once Daniel Jordan left the fort, he would not find other Americans to help him. He raised his eyes to the Captain.

"You say your courier will return here in two weeks?"

"That's correct."

"In that case, you have convinced me. I will wait here until he returns. After that, if we have not heard any news of my son, either from Detroit or from the people of this town, I must continue my search."

"Of course," Captain Daley said.

At that the Captain called out to the soldier who stood at the door of his office. When the soldier entered the Captain asked him to take Daniel Jordan to where he would stay while at the fort. The Captain promised again to put out word about Caleb, and he told Jordan that he would notify him if he heard anything.

The two weeks that Daniel Jordan spent at Fort Mackinac went more quickly than he had suspected they would. There was much work to be done every day, for aside from helping the fort's blacksmith, he also found work among the fur traders and Ojibway families who had come to Mackinac to sell their pelts. These trappers of animals had spent the winter deep in the woods, where there were no blacksmiths to repair metal objects that had given out or broken.

Spring was coming to the Michigan Country, and when Jordan looked out over the town from the fort he saw greening trees, interspersed with the white and pink blossoms of apple and cherry.

He took his meals with the soldiers of the fort in the company mess hall, and after supper the men would sit about a fire and tell stories. One evening one of the men, a sergeant named Osborne, told the story of the capture of Fort Mackinac during the War of 1812. The sergeant was a rugged man, strong of build and rough around the edges. But he was not unfriendly, and his eyes gleamed when he told tales of the battles he had witnessed firsthand.

"Those Redcoats took us by surprise," he started that night, glancing into the faces of the men gathered round. "That's the only reason they were able to take the fort. We didn't even know that war had broken out! Sure, down in Washington town the Congress and the president had declared war on England, on account of the way they kept kidnapping our sailors and making them serve on British ships. But the news hadn't reached us as yet, way up here in the Michigan Country.

"The commander of those British troops, though," Osborne took up again after a pause, "he knew about the war. Sure enough he did. His name was Captain Roberts. He moved his troops down to Saint Joseph Island—that's down a ways from Sault Sainte Marie. That way, he hoped he might catch us off our guard.

"It was July, 1812. Captain Roberts had a couple of artillery men, forty-seven British soldiers, a mess of Canadian fur traders, and about three hundred Indian warriors. The Indians and the British both would have been happy to see the back of us Americans. They must have figured this was there chance to get rid of us . . . clear us out of the Great Lakes once and for all."

"And they just about did, didn't they?" one of the other

soldiers put in.

"Pshaw," the sergeant intoned gruffly, "they just got lucky."

"How many men were defending the fort?" Daniel Jordan asked.

"That's a good question," said Sergeant Osborne, leaning forward and resting an elbow on one of his knees. "If I remember rightly, there were some sixty of us artillerymen. Lieutenant Hanks was in command. We were a good unit, and we had seven stout cannon pieces. The problem was, we never had a chance to fight!"

"Why was that?"

"It was the way they surprised us! It was first thing in the morning, barely break of day. Like I said, we didn't even know we was at war yet, so we weren't on the lookout for an attack.

"That Captain Roberts, the British commander, he was a sly old fox. He landed his men, you see—along with all of his Indian allies—around the back side of the island. They took the civilians what lived over there captive, so as they couldn't warn us. Then they dragged one of their big six-pounders up the ridge and laid a cannon ball right in the middle of the fort. That was their way of saying hello, I suppose. It certainly got our attention, I can tell you that!

"Captain Roberts sent a few of his men here to the fort under the flag of truce. They brought three of the farmers they'd captured along with them, American citizens, and they told Lieutenant Hanks about all the Indian warriors who were fighting alongside the Redcoats. I was there, and I heard the whole thing. The Lieutenant took me aside. He said he feared there'd be a massacre if we put up a fight, what with all those Indian braves champing at the bit to use their tomahawks. So, long story short, he agreed to surrender the fort."

"The government in Washington wasn't too happy about that, from what I heard," one of the soldiers said.

"No, they weren't," the sergeant agreed. "In fact, they put Lieutenant Hanks up on court marshal for cowardice. But I didn't see it that way. Hanks weren't no coward. He just didn't want to see a massacre, especially with the island's civilians being held hostage. Not too long after that, before they could put him on trial, Hanks got himself killed fighting the British down in Detroit. I guess that proved, like I said, he weren't no coward."

"What happened to the fort?" Daniel Jordan asked.

The sergeant turned to face him. "After we surrendered," he said, "Captain Roberts said he'd let us soldiers go free, but only if we promised not to take up arms against the British for the rest of the war. We agreed to the terms, and those Brits just moved right in. They took over all the supplies we'd laid up here in the fort, and also at the trading post."

"The British kept hold of this fort right up to the end of the war, didn't they?" one of the other men asked.

"That they did," said the sergeant. "President Madison sent an American force up here in 1814, with five ships carrying about seven hundred soldiers, but they couldn't take the place back. They landed on the other side of the island, just like Captain Roberts had done, hoping to surprise the British garrison. But this time the Redcoats knew we were coming, and they were ready for us. We didn't get the fort back until the end of the war, when the British agreed to leave the Michigan Territory for good."

As Daniel Jordan lay in bed that night, waiting to go to sleep, he reflected on all the fighting his fellow men seemed to do with one another. He wondered what Caleb's mother, whom he sometimes called "Mother" himself—when he did not call her "Lizbeth"—would say about it, were she alive. The Quaker people, among whom she was raised, did not believe in violence. He then thought of his daughter who had also died in the sickness, as he did almost every night before he went to sleep, and finally his thoughts turned to Caleb. He pondered where his son might be, and he prayed humbly that he be alive and well, and also that he might be among trustworthy people, people of good will and kind hearts.

While Daniel Jordan waited for the courier to return from Detroit he came to learn more about the town of Mackinac, with its row of shops, its tavern, and the patchwork of houses that shared the island with the military fort high on the bluff. There had been a horrible accident in the town not long before, when a shotgun accidentally went off in the trading post of the American Fur Company. One of the Canadians who traveled the deep woods trading furs with the First Peoples was shot in the stomach from a short distance away.

"They called for Dr. Beaumont straight away," Sergeant Osborne recounted to his mess mates one evening after supper, "even though nobody thought that Frenchman had a chance."

"That's for sure," another of the men put in. "Why, he had a hole clean through him!"

Dr. Beaumont was the army doctor at Fort Mackinac. Through quick action, he was able to save the life of the fur trader, a man with the French Canadian name of Saint Martin.

"Yep, it was a near miracle, the way Dr. Beaumont saved that man's life," Sergeant Osborne said. "But there was only one problem," he went on, "and that's that Saint Martin was left with a hole in his belly clean through to the inside of his stomach. Every time he tried to eat, the food would just spill right out of him!"

"But how can a man survive, if he can't keep his food on board?" asked Daniel Jordan, astonished.

"That's what we were all wondering," Osborne said. "But the doctor bandaged up the hole real tight, and that bandage keeps the food from coming out. And listen to this. Once a day the doctor takes that bandage off, so he can study how a man's stomach works. He puts pieces of food in there, like, so he can see what happens to them. It's a scientific experiment! They say that one of these days, Doc Beaumont will be famous the world over—on account of figuring out how the human stomach works."

One day when Jordan was below the fort, down among the fur traders and Ojibway people who were camped there, he met a fur trader by the name of Jacques Lemarche. Jordan told Lemarche why he had come to Mackinac Island, and when he mentioned his missing son, the eyes of Lemarche lit up.

"I have heard about such a boy," Lemarche said. "They say that he is living among the Ojibway people. They say also that he is a brother of the wolves, and that the pathfinders obey his commands . . ."

Jordan was excited to hear of an American boy living among the Ojibway, but he told Jacques Lemarche that he did not believe that his son knew how to command wild animals.

"I am just saying what I have heard," Jacques LeMarche replied. "I did not say that I believe it. After all, men tell many stories. But, you never know . . ."

Lemarche told Jordan that he would soon be leaving Mackinac Island. He was an employee of the American Fur Company who lived in the woods during the winter, visiting Ojibway families at their winter camps and trading for furs. He had come to the Island some days earlier, he told Jordan, to bring his furs into the Company's trading post. In several days' time he would be traveling to Fond du Lac, at the western end of Lake Superior, on Company business.

"If you would like to come with me, you would be welcome. There will be many Ojibway families at Fond du Lac. We can ask if they have heard any news of your son."

Jordan told him that he could not leave Fort Mackinac until the courier from Detroit returned, but that if Jacques were still in Mackinac when the courier arrived, and if the courier bore no news of his son from the south, he would be grateful to be allowed to travel along with him.

That night, as Jordan lay in bed waiting to fall asleep (after he had thought about Caleb's late mother, and his late daughter, and Caleb himself) he thought about his great good fortune in meeting Jacques Lemarche; for the fur traders knew the northern woods as well as Daniel Jordan knew the streets of Albany, New York. He reflected upon Lemarche's kindness in offering to take him along in his travels, and with that thought he fell into a profound slumber.

Chapter 17

The Seeker

Just a few days after Daniel Jordan met Jacques Lemarche, the army courier returned to Mackinac Island from Detroit. Unfortunately, he had brought no information about Caleb Jordan from the south. The captain of the fort summoned Jordan to his office to tell him the news. Jordan thanked him for putting him up at the fort and told him that he would soon be leaving to continue the search for his son. From the fort he went into town and asked after Jacques Lemarche among the fur traders gathered at the trading post. He found the Frenchman playing cards at the tavern with a group of other men who were waiting for their business to be completed in Mackinac. Lemarche told Jordan that he would be leaving for Fond du Lac in a few days' time.

On a clear, bright morning, Daniel Jordan met Lemarche outside the American Fur Company. He had filled his saddlebags with provisions for his journey, and he carried his blacksmithing tools as well. Jacques Lemarche rode a bay gelding which had been provided by the Company.

In the tales which Lemarche had heard about the boy who could speak to wolves, it was said that he lived to the north. The story had become a legend among the Ojibway and, like all legends, one could not be sure if its details were true.

"When I ask where this famous boy lives," Lemarche told Daniel Jordan, "they stretch out their arm and say that the boy lives in the White Direction, the direction of the Old Lady. That is what the Indian people call the north. Some hinted that this boy may actually be a spirit, and not a real boy at all, and that he lives among the Northern Lights . . .

"You can never tell," Lemarche went on after a moment, "for the Indians say many things which I do not completely understand. There is an old Indian trail which will take us directly to Fond du Lac. That is as far as I am going, I am afraid. If we have not found your son when we arrive there, you can continue on your own, along the northern shore of the Lake. If this boy is living in the north, that is where you would be most likely to find him."

Jordan readily agreed to Lemarche's reasoning, for he was a newcomer in the Michigan Country and knew very little about its people or its geography. He knew that Lemarche had spent many years trapping furs in the Michigan woods, and that he knew the Ojibway people and could speak their language. They set out on the trail to Fond du Lac, which in those days was an Ojibway village on the western shores of Lake Superior, where the city of Duluth sits today. The American Fur Company had established a trading post there.

The days were sunny and clear, but the June nights were still cold in the Great Lakes country. Daniel Jordan and Lemarche slept close to the fires they made at their encampments at the end of each day. They tried to camp near meadows, where they would let the horses graze until they had their fill of grass, and when they passed streams they would allow them to drink. They would also fill their own water skins from these watercourses.

It took the two men three weeks to reach Fond du Lac. When they arrived, Lemarche went into the trading post and spoke to the men he knew there. He also went among the Ojibway people in the village that had grown up around the post and asked if anyone knew anything about an American boy living with the First Peoples.

"I am afraid I was not able to learn anything from the trading post," he told Daniel Jordan when he returned to the place where they had made their camp. "They only say that they have heard some rumors from the Indians. A couple of the Ojibway say they have heard about the boy who speaks with wolves, but they don't know where he is. Most of them pointed to the north, but others gestured to the south and to the west. It is very confusing and, like I have told you, I am not always sure that I always understand them perfectly."

"It seems strange to me," Jordan said, "for I cannot see how my son could learn to speak to wolves. He has never even seen one, that I know of. The wolves have all been killed around Albany, New York, where we used to live, although we did hear them howling one night when our stagecoach broke down on the way to Buffalo. As you say, these stories sound like tall tales and legends. But still, the Ojibway do say that an American boy is living among their people. That gives me hope that I may find my son. About the rest, I do not know, and it doesn't much matter. Since most of those who say they have heard about this boy say he is somewhere in the north, I suppose I should continue in that direction."

Jacques Lemarche was scooping some beans from a pot over the fire, and after he had filled his plate he sat on a log that lay on the ground. "You know," he began after tasting his food, "it might be a good thing if I went with you, a little ways at least. You are not so familiar with this country, and you do not yet know the Ojibway people."

"I would not want to inconvenience you."

"It is no trouble," Lemarche said. "I would like to help you find your son, if he can be found. I have fulfilled my mission for the Company, and they will not miss me. We men of the woods, you know, we may not be rich in many things, but we do have our freedom."

The two men stayed around Fond du Lac for another couple of days, so that the horses might strengthen themselves on oats and other good feed that was available at the trading post. During this time Daniel Jordan made blacksmithing repairs for some of the Ojibway families and for the trading post, and he replaced the shoes on several horses. He was paid by the trading post in good American money, which he tucked securely into his purse, and by the Ojibway people with a blanket, two beaver furs, some maple candy, and enough dried pemmican to last for several weeks.

When Jordan and Jacques sat around their fire at night

they talked together about places they had been, things they had seen, and people they had known. Jordan learned that Jacques had been born in Canada, and that it was the fur trade that had brought him to the Great Lakes.

"When I started out," Jacques said one night, as they spoke about their lives, "I was a voyageur."

Jordan asked Jacques what it meant to be a *voyageur*.

"To be a voyageur, well," Jacques began, "means to be a traveler. That is what the word means in your English language, at least. It also means to be hungry, to be cold and, if you are not lucky, to be dumped in the freezing river—or scalped by unfriendly Indians!

"But seriously," Jacques went on with a little laugh, "every spring, we voyageurs would leave our homes in Montreal and paddle the big canoes for the Northwest Fur Trading Company. We would row down the Saint Lawrence River to Lake Erie, and then paddle over to Lake Huron."

Jordan remembered his and Caleb's voyage across Lake Erie in the steamboat *Superior,* and the great distance the ship had traveled. "That sounds like a very long way, especially to paddle a canoe," he said.

"It is," Lemarche replied, "many hundreds of miles. But we were young, and strong, and to tell you the truth, just a little bit crazy. The canoes were loaded with trade goods, things the Indians need like rifles and ammunition, metal cooking pots, and sharp steel axes. We would come to the trading post here at Fond du Lac. That is where our long journeys ended. After we delivered the goods we had brought to the post, we would load up our canoe with the furs that the Indians had collected during the winter. Then we would paddle back to Montreal and deliver the furs to the Company."

"I see," said Daniel Jordan.

"After that," Jacques went on, "the Company would send the furs to France, where they would be made into hats and coats to keep the good people of France warm. Then, with the money the Company made from selling the furs, they would buy trading goods—rifles, pots and pans—and bring them back to Canada. We would load the goods into our canoe and paddle them out to Fond du Lac, where they would be traded to the Indians for more furs. So, you see, it is all one big circle, a big circle made of furs and trading goods and money. And we voyageurs were the ones who kept that circle moving."

"But you no longer paddle the big canoes?" Jordan asked.

"No, I do not," Lemarche replied. "That ended several years ago."

Jordan asked Lemarche why he had stopped paddling the big canoes from Montreal to Fond du Lac.

"We have a saying in the French language," Jacques said. "It goes like this, *'cherchez la femme.'*"

Daniel Jordan did not know the French language, and he asked Jacques to explain.

"What these words mean, my friend, is 'look for the woman.' Have you ever noticed," he went on, smiling a little, "that when a man makes a big change in his life, the reason very often has to do with a female?"

Jordan replied that he had never really thought about the matter before. But he remembered how he had once built his entire world around Caleb's mother, his late wife, and said, "I think I know what you mean."

"In my case," Jacques continued, "there was an Ojibway girl named Running Deer. I met her one year when we arrived with the canoes at Fond du Lac. She had come to the trading post with her family to trade furs. We voyageurs always liked to rest before making the long journey back to Montreal, so we stayed at the post for a couple of weeks. Running Deer's family stayed at the post for a time, also, and she and I got to know one another. You know how these things go," he went on with a little laugh, "and I probably don't need to explain. We just took a liking to one another, I guess you could say. I didn't see her again, though, for another whole year. I went back to Montreal with the other voyageurs, and she went on with her family to their summer village."

"Did you miss her?"

"I missed her terribly," Jacques said. "During that long winter, I thought about her all the time. And I decided that, when we paddled back to Fond du Lac when spring came, I would try to find her. It was a thing of great luck, that when we arrived at the trading post, Running Deer and her family were there again. I learned that she had missed me, too, and we decided to be married. But she did not wish to leave her people and come to Montreal. So I became an *hivernant*."

Here was another French word that Jordan did not know.

"In English you would say a *winterer*," Jacques said, and in response to Jordan's look of puzzlement he explained further. "A winterer is one who stays here in the fur trading country, living in the woods all year long, instead of going back to Montreal during the winter the way the voyageurs do. I lived with Running Deer's family for a while, and I learned a great many things about living in the forests, hunting, fishing, and trapping animals. Later I went to work for the American Fur Company, running their trading post at L'Anse. That's up in the woods, more than two hundred miles from Fort Mackinac. I live there with Running Deer and our children. "

"Is it a good life," Jordan asked after a minute, "trading for furs?"

"It used to be better. There are not so many animals as there once were. There are practically no beavers left in the Michigan territory, and the other animals—otters, raccoons, muskrats, fox—are getting harder to find every year. The problem is, you see, we have taken too many animals from the forests. If you do not leave enough of each species to breed and produce more young, sooner or later they will all be gone. Now the fur traders are moving further to the west, where the animals have not been trapped and hunted so heavily.

"It has been very hard for the Ojibway," Jacques went on after a moment. "They do not have as many furs for trading, so they cannot afford trade goods like guns and ammunition, or cloth for making clothes. Many of the families have borrowed money from the traders, and now they cannot pay them back. I have seen families go hungry, especially in the winter."

"Are all of the Indian families lacking food?" Jordan asked with no little distress in his voice. He felt badly for any Indian family that might not have enough to eat, but he especially worried that Caleb, his own son, might suffer hunger.

"Not all of them, but many," Jacques replied. "If the men are skillful hunters, or if they set up their camps near a lake or river where fishing is good, they may still get by. But the fur trade has seen its better days. To be honest, I do not know how much longer it can last."

When Daniel Jordan and Jacques Lemarche departed Fond du Lac, they followed a trail that ran close to the shores of Lake Superior. At various places along this trail they came to summer villages of the Ojibway people. At each they would stop to inquire whether anyone had heard of an American boy living among them. In some of the villages people had heard tales of such a boy, sometimes saying also that the boy was able to speak to wolves; in other villages no one claimed to know anything about him. In the days before radio, television and, in the back woods, even newspapers, this was how information traveled: in irregular patterns and very uncertainly. When time allowed, Daniel Jordan would make black-smithing repairs, and the Ojibway people would repay him with a place to sleep and delicious meals of fish and venison, which hospitality Jacques Lemarche gladly shared.

One thing that Jordan found troubling was that, as he and Lemarche traveled further northward around the shores of the lake, reports of an American boy living among the Indians became less and less frequent. "If this boy is somewhere in the north," he said to Jacques one night as they prepared to go to sleep, "you would expect to hear more stories about him as you traveled northward, since you'd be getting closer. And yet the further north we travel, the less we hear about an American boy." Another thing that bothered Jordan was that, as he and Lemarche traveled to the north, those Indians who did say they had heard about the boy more often gestured toward the south, or sometimes to the east, when asked about his whereabouts.

"It is like I have told you," Lemarche said, "you can never be sure with the Indians. Maybe this boy they talk about is a spirit, after all. For the Ojibway know of many spirits, and sometimes they speak about them as if they were as real as you or me."

In spite of his doubts, Daniel Jordan continued, throughout the month of July, to work his way along the western shore of Lake Superior with Jacques Lemarche, stopping at Ojibway summer villages along the way, making blacksmith repairs and asking the people they encountered about a boy who could speak to wolves. By the time they reached Thunder Bay, where Jacques Lemarche told Daniel Jordan that he would have to leave him and return to Mackinac, they had ceased to find any Ojibway who had heard tales of the boy they sought.

"I am sorry we have not found your boy," Jacques said to Daniel as they parted by the shores of the lake. "I have two sons of my own, and I know how much you must miss him. I hope that you find him, and may God be with you." Jordan thanked Lemarche for helping him, and then he watched him ride steadily away into the forest.

Daniel Jordan felt discouraged that his journey to the northern shores of Lake Superior, propelled by stories of a boy living among the Ojibway, one who it was sometimes said could speak with wolves, had not been successful. He was not certain what he should now do, except that he knew that he would not give up searching for his son until the day he died, or unless he learned with certainty that his son was no longer among the living.

There was no point in returning to Mackinac by the way he had come, for he and Lemarche had already visited the summer villages on Lake Superior's western shore. Instead Jordan decided to continue to circle the Lake toward the east. He found little information as he moved along the Lake's northern shore, but he found hospitality among the Ojibway in return for the mending of their metal implements. He enjoyed being among them, seeing them at their cooking fires, watching the men fish and the sparkling fish they brought in. Though he felt a certain melancholy as he watched the boys play their games along the sandy shores—for they reminded him of Caleb—their happy shouts made him feel more determined than ever to find his son.

The summer in the Great Lakes country is a sparkling time of bright sun and clear days, but it is also the time when the insects which have waited through the long northern winter for their chance to live in the open burst out in tremendous numbers. Flies, gnats and other small creatures swarm in hordes through the air, enjoying themselves, no doubt, but causing great annoyance and inconvenience for human beings. Among these insects are mosquitoes, whose bites are not only painful and itchy, but who can carry the deadly disease malaria. And it was Daniel Jordan's misfortune, as he sat by his fire one evening near the Lake Superior shore, to be bitten by a creature which harbored the infectious microbe. He thought nothing of it at the time, for the bite was only one among the hundreds he had received that summer. But a couple of weeks later, as he rode or walked along the trails he began to feel, first, just a little off balance and, as the days wore on, increasingly weak and nauseous. Soon the chills came and cold sweats, and when an Ojibway woman felt his forehead at one of the summer villages, he lying straggled against his packs on the ground, she said that he was "on fire" with fever. He became very sick then and could not rise from the bed that was made for him, and Indian women who possessed plant medicine treated him with concoctions made from chokeberry and dogwood and also from gentiana, adding licorice root to sweeten the bitter herb. Jordan remained in that village for three weeks. When he had recovered enough to get up and move about, he repaired the metal tools of the summer village's people in return for the kindness they had shown him when he was ill.

He was not completely cured of malaria, but since he felt well enough to travel, he continued on his way eastward across the northern shore of Lake Superior. He stopped at the summer villages along the way and inquired after his son, but only an occasional Ojibway person had heard the legend of the boy who spoke to wolves, and none had any very good idea where he might be. From time to time he would have another attack of the malaria, which still lived inside his body, and he would feel the weakness, the fever and the chills; but after lying back in his encampments for a day or two he would feel well enough to continue his journey. At the summer villages, when he felt ill, he would ask for the herbs he had been given before, and often he would receive them. He was anxious to get back to Fort Mackinac, for he remembered the doctor who had cured the man with a hole in his stomach, Dr. Beaumont, and he felt that if the doctor could save the life of a man with such a serious injury, he would perhaps be able to rid Daniel Jordan once and for all of malaria.

The summer was nearing its end when Jordan arrived at Sault Sainte Marie, the place he had first come after setting off from Saginaw in the canoe of the Ojibway family he met at Trader Campau's store. He was suffering from a malaria attack when he arrived, with fever, chills and vomiting, and he was very weak. He went into the trading post there and spoke to Trader Stockton, the man who had sold him the horse he still rode. He asked if Stockton had heard any news of his son, or of any American boys living among the Ojibway, but the trader had heard nothing. Stockton could see that Daniel Jordan was very weak and invited him to stay at the post until he recovered. But Jordan declined the offer, for he was determined to reach Fort Mackinac, and Dr. Beaumont, as soon as possible.

Daniel Jordan could barely hold himself upright in his saddle when, two days after leaving Sault Sainte Marie, he reached Saint Ignace. He slept in the stable with his horse, collapsed onto a pile of straw bedding, and in the morning he made his way to the ferry and crossed over to Mackinac Island.

Chapter 18
The Winter Woods

When the ferry arrived at Mackinac Island Daniel Jordan took the reins of his horse, which he had named Molly and which had shared his long journey around Lake Superior, and walked her down the ramp and onto the docks. He led her into the wide street, lined with tradesmen's establishments and shops, and turned toward where, beyond the busy-ness of the town, the American fort sat high on its bluff. He did not mount the mare, for he was too weak from malaria to pull himself into the saddle. It was only through sheer will power that he had made it this far, for he was already very ill when he arrived at Sault Sainte Marie several days earlier. Before he had walked two blocks, his vision began to go hazy and his legs became wobbly.

The next thing Jordan knew he was coming out of a sleep full of confused dreams. He lay on a low cot covered in woolen blankets. It was hard to make out his surroundings, for his fever was very high, his vision blurry, and sweat covered his face and ran into his eyes. But after looking around the room, at its plank walls and spare furnishings, and thinking back to before he fell unconscious on Mackinac Island's main street, he realized that he must be at the fort.

Jordan's supposition was correct; he was at Fort Mackinac, high on the bluff above Lake Huron. After he collapsed on Main Street, several passersby had stopped to help. One of them recognized him from his previous sojourn in the town, and this one said that Jordan had lived at the fort. After talking among themselves, the townspeople decided to take him there, for they knew that the Army had a doctor. Molly, Daniel Jordan's faithful mare, stood by while they gathered up her master, and when they walked off toward the fort she followed without needing to be led by her reins.

When they arrived at the fort the sentries at the gate sent word to Captain Daley. Captain Daley came to see, and when he recognized Jordan he ordered that he be taken to the fort's infirmary. He then went to see Dr. Beaumont, the famous doctor who had saved the life of the man with a hole clear into his stomach.

"I would appreciate it if you could look in on Jordan," Captain Daley said after Dr. Beaumont greeted him. "He's a good man, and he's been through a lot. His son went missing recently, and he's been traveling all over the Upper Peninsula looking for him. It looks like he's picked up a very serious case of malaria."

"He's here at the fort?"

"Yes, he's in the infirmary." Captain Daley hesitated for moment, taking a step or two in front of the desk where Dr. Beaumont was seated. "I would consider it a personal favor if you can give his case your highest attention." Jordan and Captain Daley had become friends when Jordan stayed at the fort in the spring, and Daley had grown fond of him.

"I'll see what I can do," the Doctor said. "We're awaiting a shipment of cinchona bark from Detroit. Until that arrives, I'm afraid we can do little more than try to keep his fever down."

The bark of the cinchona tree, which grows in Peru, was the only known cure for malaria in those days before modern medicine.

"I hope it arrives soon," said the Captain.

"We're expecting it in a few days."

Dr. Beaumont went to see Daniel Jordan immediately after speaking to the Captain. Jordan had begun to vomit, and at times he shivered so violently that the cot nearly collapsed beneath him. Dr. Beaumont called for an orderly, one of the men who helped to look after the patients, and asked him to apply cold compresses, cloths soaked in water, to Jordan's forehead in order to bring down his fever. He also ordered that Daniel Jordan be made to drink water at regular intervals so that he would not become dehydrated. Finally, Dr. Beaumont instructed the orderlies to move Jordan to a small room beside his office. This way he would be able keep a close eye on him while awaiting the shipment of cinchona bark.

Over the coming days millions of plasmodium germs, the microscopic creatures which had entered Daniel Jordan's body through the bite of an infected mosquito, attacked him ferociously. He likely would have died had not Dr. Beaumont spent several sleepless nights at his bedside, sometimes relieved by his orderlies, fighting heroically to keep down Jordan's fever. Fortunately, on the third day after Daniel Jordan's arrival at Fort Mackinac, the cinchona powder arrived. Beaumont began to administer the medicine immediately, and Jordan began to recover.

Recovering from malaria was a long process. The cinchona bark powder slowly but surely killed the plasmodium germs which had taken up residence in Jordan's blood cells, the main focus of their assault. But other plasmodium germs had hidden away in other tissues of Jordan's body; and just as he began to feel a little better, these hidden germs came into his blood stream again and renewed their attack. The cinchona powder was ready at hand, at least, and this second bout of the illness was not as bad as the first. Daniel Jordan was soon moved out of Dr. Beaumont's quarters and to the infirmary with regular soldiers who were not well. As he recovered he took up with these men and came to know their names, why they were laid up in the infirmary, and also something about their lives.

When Jordan was able to get out of bed, he began at first to take brief and slow walks around the fort. It was several weeks before he felt strong enough to go into the town and walk along Main Street. The encampments which the Ojibway people had set up below the fort in the spring, when they had come to trade furs they trapped during the previous winter, were gone. The people who lived in those camps had left months earlier to go to their summer villages on the shores of the Lake.

By the time Daniel Jordan regained his health, the early Great Lakes' autumn had already descended upon Mackinac Island. The great beech and maple trees were decked out in rich tones of ocher and yellow, of wine and scarlet, and many of the tree species were already bare of leaves. And as strength returned to Jordan's body, one thought occupied his mind: to resume the search for Caleb, his son.

The Captain tried to dissuade him:

"Winter on the Upper Peninsula can be a fearsome thing, my friend," the Captain told him one evening as they sat in the Captain's quarters playing checkers together.

"I've seen plenty a tough winter in Albany, Lord knows," Jordan replied.

"Sure," the Captain said, "but Albany's a built-up town, with houses, and stores with provisions, and fodder for your horse. The Ojibway will have broken up their summer villages by now. They'll be moving inland and setting up their winter hunting camps. They break up into small groups and spread out, far and wide. Out there you'll be on your own, following Indian trails through the forests. What's more, some of the Ojibway aren't too happy about white settlers coming into their lands. They might not take too kindly to seeing you tromping through their hunting preserves."

"I'll just have to take my chances. My son's out in those woods somewhere, and I've got to find him."

The Captain realized that he could not talk Daniel Jordan out of his plan. So he gave him the best advice he could, and he ordered his quartermaster, the officer who took care of the fort's supplies, to give Jordan all that might be of use in the winter woods.

After the cranberry harvest, and after great quantities of fish which Singing Loon, Talks Too Much and Caleb captured had been dried and salted by Braided Waters, Grandmother and Morning Star, Caleb's adopted family left the shores of Lake Superior to move to a hunting camp deep in the woods of Michigan's Upper Peninsula. They were invited by one of

Braided Waters's relations to join them at their winter camp, not far from a lake where they could fish, where game was plentiful, and where several streams and rivers, which would soon be solid ice, would serve as roads through the vast forests of the northern woods.

Caleb's wolf was no longer with the family: one day, shortly after Caleb's vision quest, it had disappeared from the summer village and never returned. Caleb was anxious that some harm may have befallen his trusty companion until one afternoon, while hunting not far from the cranberry bogs, he spotted him on a ridgeline. The she-wolf which he had seen with Morning Star the day they visited the cranberry bogs was with him. The wolf began to move toward Caleb, but the she-wolf, standing pat behind him, yipped at him and he stopped. He turned and looked toward the she-wolf, and then back toward Caleb. Finally he raised his muzzle to the sky and began to howl. Caleb howled in return, and they went on that way for several minutes. The she-wolf came to the wolf's side, nuzzled him and yipped some more. The wolf fell silent and stood staring intently at Caleb. Caleb called out to him. "Good-bye, my friend," he said. "I see you have found a mate. May we meet again someday." The she-wolf whined and moved away, the wolf made a few small leaps and then, turning himself, ran after her.

It took the family two weeks, walking along Indian trails, to reach the spot where Braided Waters's relations built their winter camp each year. When they arrived, Braided Waters, Grandmother, and Morning Star began immediately to build the wigwam in which the family would live until spring. They began with poles made from the narrow trunks of tamarack trees, which they sharpened and sunk into the ground. Bending these poles upward and over, and criss-crossing them together like a basket, they make the framework of the lodge. This took them two days, and the men helped with the work of felling the trees and sharpening the pole ends. After the framework was completed, the women covered it all with sheets of tree bark, overlapping them to keep out the wind and the rain. They left an opening through which to enter the lodge, and another at the top where smoke from their fire could escape. They covered these two openings with deer skins so that they could be opened and closed as needed.

Before long the snows came. Caleb joined the men of the family as they went out each day to hunt in the woods. They tracked deer through the snow and hunted them with bow and arrow, and they also set traps for smaller animals like martins and opossum. They could track raccoon to where they hibernated in tree holes; the sleepy animals could be scooped out of their winter beds before they knew what had happened. Caleb joined Singing Loon and Talks Too Much also when they hunted beaver, sliding out on icy streams, breaking up the animals' lodges and killing them as they scurried about trying to escape. The family would sell the furs they collected this way in the spring, when they visited one of the trading posts of the American Fur Company.

Caleb learned a great deal from Singing Loon and Talks Too Much, like how to attract deer with fragrant herbs and how to make a wooden deer whistle, which could imitate the sounds the animal made. He learned how to harness the family's faithful dogs to their toboggan, so that they might haul the heavy deer carcasses back to camp.

After day was done he sat with the others in the lodge near the warm fire. Grandmother told stories and sometimes, when Braided Waters' relations would join them, they would share their stories also. They often played games to pass away the long winter evenings, games with dice made of bone, and also games in which sticks with hatch marks were tossed onto the ground, with points gained according to how the sticks landed.

Sometimes, when it was quiet at the camp and Braided Waters was not too busy, Caleb would speak to her about his father. He told her that he had seen him in his vision quest, and that he felt deep inside that he must be alive.

"What we see in visions and dreams is not always what it seems," Braided Waters responded. She remembered what Trader Campau had said in the spring, how Daniel Jordan's blood-stained cap had been found near the dead body of his Ojibway guide, Standing Bear. She, like Trader Campau, believed that Daniel Jordan had also been killed in the woods between Detroit and Saginaw. "Sometimes those we see in dream and vision are just spirit forms. That doesn't mean they aren't real. But they do not walk the earth as we do."

"Still," Caleb would say, "what if he *is* alive. What if he thinks *I'm* dead. I couldn't bear to think that. We're all we have left, after Mother and Emily died . . ."

Braided Waters was mending one of Morning Star's moccasins. She paused in her work and thought for a moment.

"It is difficult to travel in the winter. But in the spring we can go to Fort Mackinac to trade our furs. Then we can ask the soldiers at the fort if they have any news of your father. Would that make you happy?"

Caleb's face took on a soft glow. "Yes," he said, "yes. Thank you, Mother." Now, as Braided Waters' adopted son, Caleb had begun to refer to her this way.

And so passed the short winter days and long winter nights of the northern woods, hunting, trapping and fishing, and in the evening playing simple games and telling stories. The snows came and then came again and again, and before long the floor of the woods was buried beneath several feet of frozen white.

Daniel Jordan traveled through these same woods, though he was a hundred miles and more away from Singing Loon's winter camp. After leaving Fort Mackinac in October, he had traveled along the lower shore of Lake Superior, hoping some of the Ojibway might still be lingering in their summer villages. When he and Jacques Lemarche had set out in the spring, they had not visited the southern shore, nor explored the Copper Peninsula, for Lemarche had been told that the boy who tamed wolves was living to the north. Unfortunately, it was on the Copper Peninsula that Singing Loon's family had spent the summer, and in deciding to bypass the Lake's southern shore Daniel Jordan had missed an opportunity to find his son. The Ojibways' summer villages had now broken up for the season, but here and there Jordan came across a few Ojibway men who had stayed behind to increase their store of fish from the Lake.

Jordan had begun to learn the Ojibway language, after staying in their villages during the summer, and he was able to ask simple questions to the men he encountered. More precisely, to each group he met he inquired whether they had seen an American boy, his son, living with the family of a man called Singing Loon. Each group responded to this question with quizzical stares or shrugs. But one week after he left the fort he met three Ojibway men on an otherwise deserted beach, scoured by a cold and insistent wind, who said they had seen an American boy at a summer village on the Copper Peninsula. They did not know, however, whether he traveled with the family of a man called Singing Loon. They told him also that the boy was known by the name of Mahengun-wangawi, which they said means "Wolftamer" in the Ojibway language.

Daniel Jordan wished the men had been able to tell him more, but the fact that they had seen the boy called Wolftamer made him more determined than ever to set off into the forests. There was no guarantee that the boy known as Wolftamer was his son. But it was the strongest sign yet that an American boy was living somewhere in the Upper Peninsula.

He chose a trail at random, for he had no idea where to begin to look. From time to time, as he traveled through the deep, snowy woods, he came across a winter camp of one of the Ojibway families. Sometimes they were friendly; at other times they treated him coldly and with suspicion. He offered to make repairs to their metal tools and cooking pots, for he had brought along his blacksmithing tools, as he had done throughout his travels. These tools continued to be his best calling card, for an Ojibway family with a broken pot, or a malfunctioning hunting rifle, was happy to provide hot food and a night or two's lodging to a man who could make these precious items whole again and functional.

As the snows deepened it became harder for the mare, Molly, to make her way along the narrow pathways. It also became increasingly difficult, when Jordan made camp for the night at some meadow, for Molly to paw her way through the snow that she might find a grassy supper. Following an Indian custom, Jordan began to strip bark from trees to use for feed, and Molly resorted to eating the limbs of bushes.

One day, several weeks after Daniel Jordan left the fort at Mackinac, he came to a stream, about thirty feet across. Like the other streams he had encountered, it was completely covered in ice. Through the hard, glassy surface he could see swiftly running water. The ice appeared to be at least two feet thick. He walked along the banks in each direction, to see if he could discover a place where the stream might be narrower, or the water more shallow. But in one direction the land rose high above the stream, with a steep bank down to the watercourse, and in the other the stream grew wider. He realized that the Ojibway who had made the trail on which he traveled had figured out the best place to ford the stream, and that was precisely where he was. He stepped gingerly out on the ice to test its strength. It seemed solid. He came back to the bank, took Molly by her reins, and began to cross.

When Jordan and the mare were a little more than halfway over he began to hear an ominous creaking, and then a cracking sound: the sound of breaking ice. He pulled hard on Molly's reins, in order that they might quickly reach the other bank; but the cracking sound spooked the mare and she pulled back on her reins in a panic. Jordan tugged harder, speaking to her—"Come on girl," he said, "we've got to get off this ice!"—but she just pulled back harder herself, and the cracking sound became louder, and suddenly the ice gave way beneath man and mare both. At first Jordan held tightly to Molly's reins, still trying to guide the horse toward the bank. But the rocks at the bottom of the stream were jagged and slippery and the mare fell over, taking Jordan down into the water with her.

While Molly thrashed in the stream, terrified, Daniel Jordan tried to right himself. The strong current pushed against him and he struggled to come to his feet, groping onto the remaining ice to steady himself. After repeatedly being pulled into the current, he was eventually able to pull himself up and drag himself to the bank of the stream opposite where he and Molly had approached it.

As soon as he made it to the bank he stood and called encouragement to the mare. "Come on, girl!" he hollered, "come over here!" He thought of going back into the stream after her, but he was afraid he would not again be able to escape the current. The mare lurched onto her feet, looking at Jordan with wild eyes and slobber flying from her mouth. She raised up her front legs, trying to get up onto the remaining ice, but as she came crashing down more ice gave way. She was determined to reach Jordan, however, and she battled this way until finally she leapt upon the bank, shivering and throwing water in every direction off her sleek coat.

It was only after Molly was safely on the bank that Jordan felt the icy chill that had overtaken him. The temperature was well below freezing and he was soaked through with cold water. He hopped about, attempting to gain warmth, but it was no good. He soon began to shiver so violently that he felt his bones might break. Finding it difficult to stand, he crawled away from the stream and into the forest. His mind now began to fracture, for he was suffering from hypothermia. When the body becomes too cold, especially after being immersed in icy water, it will cease to function. Lying on the ground, shivering, Jordan thought he saw Caleb coming through the forest. But this was a mirage; hypothermia had made him delirious. He called to his son, but no one answered.

Then everything went dark.

The first thing Jordan saw when he opened his eyes was a blazing fire, its orangey flames reaching into the dark night.

"Where am I?" he stammered out. "Is anyone there?"

After a moment a face appeared before him, but it was hard for Jordan to focus his eyes. He reached out a hand, groping toward the shadowy figure.

"You just rest," the man who crouched before him said gently. The voice sounded familiar; Daniel Jordan was certain he had heard it before. "You've been through one hell of a time." The voice was heavily accented with French, and suddenly Jordan realized that it belonged to Jacques Lemarche, the Canadian fur trader with whom he had traveled around Lake Superior during the summer.

"Jacques," he said, "is that you?"

"Who else?"

"Where am I?"

Jacques laughed gently. "Where do you think you are, my friend? You're in the middle of nowhere, that's where you are. What are you doing wandering around in these woods this time of year? I suppose you're looking for that son of yours . . ."

"Where's Molly?" Jordan asked, straining to look around the small clearing where Jacques Lemarche had made camp for the night.

"She's okay. A lot better than you, that's for sure."

Jacques held out a cup of hot coffee. "Here, drink this. It will make you feel better."

As Jordan accepted the cup and took a small sip, Jacques went on. "That's some mare you have there, my friend. When I found you, lying near that stream where you fell in, she was lying on the ground beside you, keeping you warm. If it hadn't been for that, my friend, I am certain you would no longer be among the living."

Jordan sipped more of his coffee, and his head began to feel clearer. "When did you find me?"

"Just before dark," Lemarche replied. "When did you fall in?"

"It was not long after daybreak. We hadn't been on the trail for very long . . ."

"So, you must have been lying there all day. Yes, you definitely would not have made it without the mare. It is also a lucky thing that I came along. You have to be careful with these streams. Usually they are fine this time of year. But in certain places, if the current underneath is strong, or if there are large rocks that disturb the ice, there are places that can be weak. And with the weight of the mare, and those heavy tools of yours . . ."

Lemarche went off toward the fire and returned with a plate of beans. "After you wake up a little more," he said, "you might want to eat something."

Daniel Jordan, who now sat up, took the plate upon his lap and thanked Jacques.

"You know," Jacques began, "aside from helping you with your little . . . problem, I'm glad I ran into you."

"Why is that?"

"I have recently heard some news of this boy . . . the one they call Wolftamer."

"Where? When?"

"It was far from here, at one of the winter camps I visited. They told me there was an American boy who the Indians call Wolftamer. One of their relations had traveled out to the Mississippi country and had returned just a few days earlier. That man told them that the boy was living in a winter camp west of here."

"Did they say exactly where this camp was?"

"They didn't, I'm afraid. But I have an idea or two. I knew you would be interested, of course, so I went to speak to the man who had traveled from the Mississippi Country and asked him about this camp. He said that it was near a lake, and he spoke of certain streams there and some pine barrens and meadows. I believe I might know the place."

"Can you take me there now?" Jordan's voice was filled with eagerness.

"You don't look like you are in the shape to go anywhere at the moment," Jacques said with his soft laugh. "Besides, I should not want that you get up your hopes. We have heard these stories before . . . of a boy who tames the wolves!"

Daniel Jordan reached out and took Jacques firmly by the hand. "This man you spoke to, did he see the boy?"

"I'm afraid not."

"But you say you know the place?"

"I think I may."

Jordan pressed Lemarche's hand harder. "You've got to help me."

"I have much work to do, you know, visiting my friends in their camps, collecting the furs they are trapping." He looked off, but Jordan continued to stare at him with pleading eyes.

Finally Jacques went on, hesitatingly. "I suppose I could . . . change my plans . . . for you, my friend. Okay, fine," he concluded with an air of finality, "I will travel west with you. We will see if we can find this wolf boy once and for all. Who knows, in this crazy world, it may even be your son."

A tear appeared in Jordan's eye, he felt such relief in knowing that Jacques would guide him to where he might find Caleb.

"It will be just like old times, no?" Jacques said in his cheerful way. "You, me, and good old Molly."

It took Lemarche and Daniel Jordan three weeks to reach the place in the west where Lemarche thought the American boy he had been told of might be living. Along the way they stopped at different winter camps of the Ojibway people. Jacques knew many of the Ojibway families because of the many years he had spent trading furs in the Upper Peninsula. They welcomed him in their camps, gave food to him and Daniel, and allowed them to sleep in their warm lodges.

As they came closer to where Jacques thought the American boy might be living, some of the Ojibway families they met told him that they too had heard of the boy. At one of these camps, one of the men said that he had himself seen an American boy. In fact, he had encountered Singing Loon, Talks Too Much and Caleb while hunting in the woods. Jordan asked the man to describe the boy he had seen, and from the description that was given, it sounded like Caleb.

"We have heard that this boy is known as Mahengun-wan-gawi," Jacques said, using the Ojibway words for "Wolftamer."

"I did not learn his name," the Ojibway man said. "Only dogs traveled with those men, not wolves."

Jacques asked the man if he had learned where the party he met were camped. The Ojibway described a place, two days' travel away, beyond some pine barrens and near a small lake.

"This sounds like the place I had in mind," Jacques told Jordan after they left the Ojibway family and continued on their way.

There was no way to be sure that the American boy the

Ojibway hunter had seen was Caleb, but Daniel Jordan was filled with hope. They did not encounter another Ojibway family for the next two days; they walked alone and made their simple camp by the side of the trail each night. On the third day they passed through the pine barrens, and climbing to the top of one of the sandy mounds, Jacques and Jordan saw, in the distance, a sparkling lake over the tops of the evergreens.

The early winter evening was already falling upon the woods when Jordan and Lemarche approached the clearing in which the family of Braided Waters and Singing Loon made their winter camp. Braided Waters and Grandmother were outdoors, stretching deer hides, from which they had scraped the fur, upon a rack. Molly snorted, and at the sound of the horse Braided Waters turned. She left what she was doing and stepped into the open, facing the two strange men who led horses into her camp. Her eyes rested upon Daniel Jordan, and she was struck by a familiar look about him. Grandmother approached from the drying racks and stood beside her daughter-in-law. Their men had not yet returned from the hunt.

"We are sorry to intrude," Jacques Lemarche said to Grandmother and Braided Waters in the Ojibway language.

"Why do you come?" Braided Waters asked. "We do not yet have any furs to sell."

"We are looking for someone, an American boy. This man"—Jacques gestured toward Jordan—"is the boy's father."

Jordan tipped his beaverskin hat toward Braided Waters. She looked at him again. Again she was struck by something familiar, and now she realized why. This must be the father of Wolftamer, or Mahengun-wangawi, as she and the rest of her family called Caleb! Could it be that he had survived the attack in the forests between Detroit and Saginaw, an attack which left Standing Bear dead and Jordan's hat stained with blood? She approached the two men so that she might examine Daniel Jordan more closely.

He smiled wanly and cast his gaze down.

"There is an American boy who lives with us," she said. "He is out with our men, and they have not yet returned from the hunt. Will you come inside and warm yourselves? My daughter, Morning Star, has cooked some food. You are welcome to share."

She went to the lodge entrance and bade the men enter. After tying their horses' reins to nearby trees they went within. Morning Star was at the lodge fire, cooking in a metal pot which hung over the flames on a sort of spit.

"This is my daughter, Morning Star," said Braided Waters. The men tipped their hats.

"I am glad to meet you," Morning Star said in English, for she had learned much of the Americans' language from Caleb.

"Please sit and rest," Braided Waters said. "You have journeyed far, and you must be weary."

As the men took their places, resting back on some bear skins that been laid about the edge of the wigwam, Grandmother approached Braided Waters and spoke softly.

"We must be careful with these men. What will happen when they see that Mahengun-wangawi is living with us? They will say that we have kidnapped the boy, and they will send the soldiers for us."

Braided Waters thought for a moment. "No, I do not think they will do that. Look at this man. He has kind and humble eyes. And does he not look familiar to you? Can you not see Mahengun-wangawi in his features? He is most assuredly the boy's father. Besides, we did not kidnap Mahengun-wangawi, but only tried to help. Do not fear, Grandmother."

As Braided Waters spoke to Grandmother this way, the sounds of men talking came to the lodge from outdoors. Daniel Jordan rose abruptly from where he sat. Braided Waters left the lodge, and he followed swiftly behind her. After them came Jacques Lemarche, Grandmother, and finally, Morning Star.

Singing Loon, Talks Too Much, and Caleb were entering the clearing. With them was a toboggan, with two of the family's dogs harnessed, upon which rested a freshly killed deer.

The men were boisterously talking among themselves. The hunt had been successful and they were in high spirits. They were glad to be back at the camp, and looking forward to a supper of fresh venison.

When they noticed the little group gathered in front of the lodge, looking in their direction, they ceased their conversation and stood staring back. Who were these two strange men standing with Grandmother, Braided Waters, and Morning Star?

The two strangers gazed upon the returned hunters with equal bewonderment. Daniel Jordan stepped forward from the others, looking upon Caleb. Caleb had been unharnessing the dogs, but now he stood staring at his father, his mouth open with amazement. Everyone was silent for a moment, like an angel had passed over the camp, and then Daniel Jordan stepped rapidly toward his son. Caleb ran to Daniel, shouting "Pa" as he did, and buried himself in his father's powerful embrace.

Braided Waters went to Singing Loon. She explained that the two men had come looking for Mahengun-wangawi, and that Daniel Jordan was the boy's father. Singing Loon was as taciturn as ever.

"It is good that he is here," was all that he said.

There were many stories to tell around the lodge fire that evening. Caleb told of how he had gotten lost in the woods; how he had found the wolf pup; and how he asked Morning Star's family to take him north with them for fear that he would be put in an orphanage and his wolf pup taken away and drowned in a pail. Daniel Jordan then told of how he had awoken in the woods between Detroit and Saginaw with an aching head; of finding the body of Standing Bear, who had been shot by the bounty hunters; and of his long and difficult journeys in search of his son.

"They all said you were dead," Caleb told his father. "But I didn't believe them!"

"I always told you that I'd find you no matter where you are, didn't I?" Jordan replied with a little smile.

There were other stories, too: of life at the summer village; of how the wolf pup grew and one day ran off with the she-wolf; of Caleb's vision quest; and of many other things. There were so many, in fact, that it took several evenings to tell them all, while Daniel Jordan and Jacques Lemarche stayed at the winter camp and rested. Morning Star, who was so clever with languages, helped to translate between English and Ojibway.

After three days Jacques Lemarche left the winter camp to go back to his family. Daniel Jordan and Caleb, however, stayed on for another week.

"Where will you go now?" Braided Waters asked Jordan one evening as they sat by the fire, sampling treats of maple sugar she and her family had made at their sugarbush in the spring.

"They had to hire another blacksmith to work at the Saginaw reservation," Jordan said, "so I don't have a job there anymore. They needed someone to get started right away, and I had to find this lad."

He gestured to Caleb.

"Will you go back to New York?" Talks Too Much asked.

"I don't think so," Jordan replied thoughtfully. "I've made some friends over at Mackinac Island. Maybe I can find work down that way. I haven't asked Caleb how he feels about it, though." He turned to his son. "What do you think? Are you pining for the old home place?"

"I do sometimes miss Thomas," he said, scrunching his face a little. "And sometimes I think about Albany town, how we used to go down to the harbor to watch the ships sail, or how we'd go to the Pastures and watch them bring the cows home." He then looked around the fire at the family which had adopted him while he was lost from his father. "But I kind of like it here, too." His eyes caught those of Morning Star. She smiled, and he blushed. "I mean hunting, and fishing, and stuff like that . . ."

"I see," Daniel Jordan said, a little ironically. "I guess we'll stay on, then. We came out here to make a new life for ourselves, after all. And even if we've had a few stumbles, we may as well keep on with what we started."

He told Braided Waters and Singing Loon that he and Caleb would be leaving the next day. He thanked them for the many kindnesses they had shown his son, and for their hospitality.

After leaving the family of Braided Waters and Singing Loon, Daniel and Caleb Jordan made their way back to Fort Mackinac. Caleb had learned many new skills from Singing Loon and Talks Too Much, and along the way he hunted in the woods, and when they found open water he speared fish. Feasting one night on the meat of a raccoon Caleb had scooped from the tree hole where it was hibernating, Daniel realized how much his son had grown up during the year he lived with the Ojibway people; and he was proud of him. At Mackinac Island Daniel Jordan first found work helping the blacksmith at the fort. More settlers were coming to the town all the time; the town grew; and before long Jordan was able to set up his own smithy on Main Street. Caleb became his apprentice, just like they had always planned, and by the time Daniel Jordan's son was seventeen years old he handled the hammer and tongs almost as ably as his father.

He often thought, while working in the heat of the burning forge, of the times he spent with the Ojibway, and often he thought of Morning Star and wondered how she was doing. One morning in early summer, after he had finished hammering an andiron into shape, he turned to his father who stood nearby tending the fire. "I would like to travel to the shores of Lake Superior—the lake the Ojibway call Kichi'gami—where the clan of Braided Waters makes their summer village."

After thinking for a moment Daniel Jordan asked, "Do you miss your Ojibway family?"

Caleb looked out onto Main Street, where bright sunlight contrasted sharply with the shadows of the blacksmith shop. He seemed to be at a loss for words.

"Maybe it's just one particular person you'd be missing?" Daniel said now, teasing his son, for he had not forgotten how Caleb and Morning Star smiled at one another, and also how he sometimes watched them sit quietly apart and talk together when he stayed at the family's winter camp.

"I've just got to go, that's all."

Without further words, Daniel understood. He helped Caleb to prepare for his journey, and he waved heartily when his son disappeared one morning down Main Street riding Molly, the faithful mare.

It was almost two months before Caleb returned to Mackinac Island, again riding the mare; but this time Morning Star sat behind him. She and Caleb had been married among the Ojibway, at the summer village of Braided Waters' people, and now she had come as Caleb's bride to live with Caleb and his father. She was pretty in the ways that many young women are pretty; but for Caleb, because of the things they had said and done together, her eyes shone like stars, and her smile was brighter than the beaming sun.

Morning Star took her place with the Jordan family as though she had always belonged there. Daniel Jordan came to love her, with her kind ways and helpful spirit, as if she were his own daughter. She not only made the home of Daniel and Caleb Jordan a comfortable dwelling filled with warmth, but was soon sought out by people of the town for her knowledge of healing herbs. In time she became a mother, and Caleb Jordan a father, and over the years to come they would raise a family of three girls and two boys. Sometimes, in the summer, they would travel down the shore of Lake Superior to visit at the summer village of Morning Star's relations.

American settlers continued to pour into the Michigan Country, and by 1837 there were so many that the Michigan Territory became the twenty-sixth state of the United States of America. The fur animals became fewer in number every year, and it became harder and harder for the Ojibway people to survive in their traditional ways. Some moved to the west, where American settlers were still few and game animals plentiful. In Michigan, the Ojibway chiefs had no choice but to sell the remainder of their lands to the United States government; Ojibway families who stayed in the Michigan Country moved to reservations where they learned to farm alongside American settlers. Eventually Singing Loon and Braided Waters came to live on one of these reservations, not far from Fort Mackinac, where they could visit Morning Star and watch their grandchildren grow. Talks Too Much moved west to the Dakota Country, where he found a wife and carried on with the fur trade.

Caleb and Morning Star raised their children and watched them grow, until one by one they found wives and husbands themselves and began life on their own. Daniel Jordan lived to a good, old age, well respected on Mackinac Island as a good blacksmith and a good man, and he died peacefully. Eventually Morning Star and Caleb Jordan grew old also, and sometimes they would sit by the fire at night and remember all the amazing things they had seen and done. There were now big towns in Michigan, many roads and even railway lines, and they would recall how when they were young there was nothing but endless forests, lakes, rivers and streams.

Their children would have children, and those children children as well, and today the descendants of Morning Star and Caleb Jordan still live in the Michigan Country. Each one of them, whether they know it or not, carries a piece of Caleb and Morning Star within, and within each of them still lives, in some way, the ways and stories of their many ancestors, the woods and streams of the northern woods, and the ringing of hammer on anvil.

The End

www.ingramcontent.com/pod-product-compliance
Lightning Source LLC
Chambersburg PA
CBHW031533260326
41914CB00032B/1789/J